PARTIAL ECLIPSE

PARTIAL ECLIPSE

LESLEY GLAISTER

BLOOMSBURY

First Published in 1994 by Hamish Hamilton Ltd

This paperback edition published by Bloomsbury Publishing Plc 1999

Copyright © Lesley Glaister 1994

Acknowledgement is made to the following: Extract from 'Yesterday' (words and music by John Lennon and Paul McCartney) © Copyright 1965 Northern Songs used by permission of Music Sales Limited; 'Santa Claus is Comin' to Town' © 1934 EMI Catalogue Partnership/EMI Feist Catalog Inc. USA, reprinted by kind permission of CPP/Belwin Europe, Surrey, England; lyrics from 'You're a Pink Toothbrush' written by Sheridan/Halfin/Ruvin/Irving and published by Dejamus Limited for the World, reproduced by kind permission; 'Frosty the Snowman' (Nelson/Rollins) reproduced by kind permission of Carlin Music Corp., Iron Bridge House, 3 Bridge Approach, London NW1 8BD; extract from 'The Lovesong of J. Alfred Prufrock' taken from *Collected Poems 1909–1962* by T.S. Eliot, published by Faber and Faber.

The moral right of the author has been asserted

Bloomsbury Publishing Plc, 38 Soho Square, London W1V 5DF

A CIP catalogue is available from the British Library

ISBN 0 7475 4003 9

10 9 8 7 6 5 4 3 2 1

Typeset by Hewer Text Ltd, Edinburgh
Printed in England by Clays Ltd, St Ives plc

In memory of my father

A GROCER'S SHOP

Someone is watching me.

Eyes seen through a slit are never kind eyes. What I would see if I could be bothered to look up would be like a rectangle snipped from a face. An identikit strip – eyebrows, eyes, bridge of nose, glasses perhaps. Eyes seen like this are cold eyes, mean. Take the roundest, bluest, kindest eyes and view them through a slot from inside a cell and they will seem cruel. Be cruel. God, I could do with a smoke.

Slap and the slot closes. And there is the tickle of the key. Reminds me of a letter-flap. Slip slap letters on the mat. Cards at Christmas and parcels. The postman called in the afternoons on the special days before Christmas, laden down with good things: robins, snowmen, chocolate, scent.

No letters for me in here, however. And I have no idea of the time. The last meal was, I think, tea. Grey soup, white bread, grey apple pulp between two pastry squares. A cup of lukewarm tea. Sometimes I think they spit in it. After every meal I vow to starve myself. But there is simply nothing to do and eating – even this colourless crap – *is* something to do.

I call them meals! I dream about proper food: breakfast, lunch, dinner. Hot toast with the butter dripping off in yellow rivulets, chocolate cake, strawberries and clotted cream. Afternoon tea on Sundays after a roast lunch. 'Meal' meant something special. *He*

1

asked me out for a meal, candle-light and whipped cream and silver forks glinting.

Nothing glints in here, nothing glistens or glows. The light is dim. It is never dark and never light, only dim. Perpetually dusk, perpetually the moment before you'd draw the curtains, bank up the fire, flood the room with light.

I think I do deserve it. Or what I did deserves it. I am doubly imprisoned: seven days' solitary for my outburst. It's only fair. I can't complain. I am alive and I am fed and clothed – though this canvas dress I have to wear is hardly flattering. No one to see me though. Just the eyes through the slot. I have a bucket and the air in here is acrid and it is not just my smell. There is an accumulated smell of despair, of desolation.

I have been here before. '*Why*, Jennifer?' the prison shrink says, all sad and disappointed eyes. 'Why can you not behave? You're only punishing yourself.' And I know that, so I turn my eyes away from the silly cow and wait for her to go.

The walls are the same colour as the floor. That is the worst of it. What I would not give for a splash of brightness. But it is all somewhere between grey and beige, a fungal colour, and so is my dress and so is the food and so is my skin in the dimness. Women bite themselves. Bite their arms until they bleed. Self-mutilation, evidence of deep disturbance. Perhaps they simply want to see some colour, the bright luxurious glossy red of blood.

But I could never hurt myself. Strange how I hate violence. Strange I mean that *I* hate violence. I could never bite my arm to see the blood flowering. No, I could not.

I read English at the University of Essex. I didn't finish my degree. I sometimes wish I *had* finished. It would be something to have achieved. I would have been something. Been a Bachelor of Arts as well as, perhaps instead of, what I am.

Mama took me away for Christmas when I was in my second year. To a hotel in Scotland: Pitlochry. We travelled by coach. The wheels shushed along the motorway, through pouring rain, and even at midday it was almost dark, with sharp reflected flakes of light thrown up from the wetness, glittering on the windows.

Mama was dressed up. She wore a soft blue fuzzy hat, doughnut shaped on her soft grey fuzzy hair, and pink lipstick that had spidered into the lines around her mouth. She had her embroidery on her lap. She was making a sampler, embroidered sprigs of herbs surrounding the words *Better is a dinner of herbs where love is, than a stalled ox and* . . . and then a space. She had planned to fill the space on this journey, but the motion of the coach and the cigarette smoke drifting forward from the back seats made her feel sick, so she put her sewing away and closed her eyes instead.

After Bob, my grandfather, had died, eight years before, Mama and I had made samplers. It was the first thing we'd done together. We grew closer for a short time that year, when I was thirteen, drawn by the new television into the same room, drawn by loss into a new need. We sat on the sofa and stitched side by side. Mama's first sampler was a picture of us: a grey-haired woman, a little girl with long pigtails and two bright blue cross-stitch eyes, and Bob – who was a naturist – in pink, silky thread with a lupin growing discreetly in front of him. We all stood in front of a symmetrical red-roofed house; there were roses round the door; the sun was in the sky and little Vs of birds flew by. Underneath it said: *Robert Windsor Maybee 1.12.1897–30.6.71.* My own sampler was chaotic. I have never been any good at fiddly, finicky things. The material Mama gave me started off a crisp pale yellow, though it was grey and limp by the time I'd finished with it. I had stitched a bonfire because the red, orange and yellow silks in Mama's work-box were so beautiful and reminded me of flames. The fire could have been anything. It looked more like a crazy flower, the flames stiff as petals, the material pulled askew where I had dragged the thread too tight across the back, too lazy to cut it off. *Remember, Remember* was all I'd embroidered underneath,

3

instead of the whole bonfire rhyme, because I was fed up with it by then.

'Who'd have thought it?' Mama suddenly said.

I'd been gazing at the dull greenness that had risen into hills. The raindrops jiggled and streaked down the glass.

'What?'

'*Us*. Off for Christmas. And to an hotel.'

'Mmmm.'

'Not stayed in an hotel since . . .' Her memory failed her.

'Did you and Bob? I can't imagine Bob . . .'

'Honeymoon.' She smiled reminiscently.

I laughed at the thought of my grandfather as a honeymooner.

'A *naturist* hotel.'

'But of course.' I closed my eyes against the memory of Bob and the hideous embarrassment of his naked body. 'Were you in love?' I asked.

'Yes. Very much.'

'Was it a naturist wedding?'

'All these questions! You know very well it wasn't.'

And she was right. There had been almost no photographs in our house, but I do remember one, a wedding photo framed in rippled walnut on their bedroom wall. Mama and Bob, young and strange. Bob, handsome but for a certain look, a look that hardened over the years until it became the shape of his head, his whole attitude. And Mama, startlingly girlish with fine bones and eyes, a soft young hand on Bob's arm, a white bird against the black sleeve. Her hands were in her lap now, clutching and fidgeting with her handbag strap. They were broad hands, made coarse and stubby with the years, veins risen like soft blue worms on their backs.

How I crave softness now that all is hard. Here, alone, I touch my own breasts. They are miraculously cool and soft against my hands, the nipples like the blunt noses of docile pets. The pleasure is all in my hands as if they were not my breasts at all.

*   *   *

4

The hotel was what Bob would have called genteel in a tone of voice midway between admiration and scorn. It was built like a castle, set back from the road down a sweeping drive between dark shrubs and trees. The lighting – it was after dark when we arrived, late afternoon on Christmas Eve – was discreet, puddled gold on the thick carpets, drizzling finely from the Christmas tree, a tree all forest green and silver. No lovely tasteless, meaningful tat. No fairy on the top, but a tailored silver bow.

Mama was servile before the servile porter. They were almost competitively deferential and I had to insist that she allow the porter to lug our cases upstairs.

In our room was a Christmas card from the management – sheep lit to a dusky apricot by a low winter sun. It invited us to a festive sherry reception in the lobby at 7 p.m.

Mama raised her shoulders in anticipation. She removed her hat, smoothing down her wispy perm.

'Isn't it lovely, Jenny?' she asked, anxious that I should be pleased, grateful, impressed.

I sat on the edge of my bed, bounced a bit to test the springs. 'Yes,' I agreed. 'Lovely.'

She found the bathroom. 'Look! Little soaps . . . little bubble baths . . . little shower caps!'

'Why not have a bath?' I suggested. 'There's time before seven.'

'Oooh, I couldn't.'

I shrugged. I would not be irritated. This was her attempt, brave attempt, to make things good for Christmas. The truth is, it had never been right at home since Bob died. Seven Christmases where no matter how we arranged the table there was still a gap. And now Auntie May had died, at 106, a brown and shrunken relic of herself, and Christmas with only the two of us was too much to contemplate.

Yes. It is like touching someone else's breasts. I have nothing soft to wear. This garment – strong-dress, shift – is stiff canvas, ugly.

It chafes my armpits. The ends of my fingers are soft and blunt. They clip your nails in here, if you do not bite them yourself, snip and snip them down hard so there is no scratching edge. It feels so childish. We line up, hold out our hands. And along the warder goes with the clippers, clipping so low it snags the cuticles, clipping even nails already bitten to nothing, like mine. With no edge, my finger ends feel blunt and numb as rubbers on the end of pencils. Neat pink stubs.

Possibly it is the loss of control that is worse than the loss of freedom. And the loss of privacy. Oh you might think I'm private enough here, in this grey box. But at any moment the slot can open and the rectangular eyes stare in. It is not a communicative look. It is all one way.

I caught his eye over the sherry. Or he caught mine. Our eyes met, anyway. At first I didn't notice his wife and child. Our eyes met and there was such a warmth flowing from him that I smiled, a real, budding, blooming, flower of a smile. And then Mama spoke and I turned away. But as I listened to Mama I could feel his eyes on me still, feel the warmth across my shoulders, trickling down my back. A waiter circulated with bright things in aspic on a silver tray. Mama was ecstatic at the beauty of the food: pink shrimps like babies' fingers, asparagus tips and tiny fish all glowing under their viscous aspic skin.

'Don't ruin your appetite though,' she warned.

We had yet to be introduced, and the room was full of shy couples and groups and one ostentatiously lone woman, tall and grey-haired in a floor-length kaftan encrusted with strange designs. I looked round for the man. He was deep in conversation with the woman beside him, a beautiful woman, his wife. But when he felt my eyes on him, he turned and once again there was this tangible warmth. Beside him a small snotty girl with a teddy under her arm pulled at his sleeve. 'Da-ad.' He spoke to her distractedly, hardly breaking the look between us that was like some sort of gravitational pull, something irresistible, inevitable.

I studied him. His hair was brown, thinning, pushed back from his face. He had a clipped beard, dark with two badgerish grey streaks. He was old around his eyes, much older than me. The beautiful woman's look broke my own. Her eyes met mine and she smiled quizzically. She had a neck like a stem and hair piled high and soft, blue-black hair, black eyes, a rose-brown skin.

Dinner was called and Mama and I took our places at a small table by the door. The lone woman had an even smaller table beside us.

'Poor thing,' Mama whispered. 'All alone on Christmas Eve. What do you suppose she's got on her frock?'

'No idea,' I said.

The man and his family were across the dining room by the window. The electric light was low, and red candles with holly leaf bases were all lit so that the room was suffused with a wavery waxy light. The man had his back to me and I quenched a flicker of disappointment. He wore a fair-isle sweater and his hair curled over the neck of it, a bit unkempt. He was not as well groomed as his wife. The child had blue patches under her eyes, a tired fractious child who should have been in bed. I caught her voice now and then throughout the meal in little whining snatches.

Mama read the menu. 'Exquisite calligraphy,' she remarked. 'Prawn cocktail, chicken goujons or melon balls. What, do you suppose, is a goujon?'

'Excuse me,' said the lone woman, leaning towards us. 'Excuse me, but might I peruse your menu? After you, of course.'

'Of course,' I said.

'The same old story,' she continued in a voice both husky and loud. 'A woman alone, shoved at a rickety table in a draught. Look!' She wobbled the table to demonstrate its ricketiness so that the glasses slid and the candle tilted perilously.

'Shocking,' Mama agreed.

I got up and handed the woman the menu. 'Ursula,' she said. 'Ursula Glass. How do you do?'

'Well, thanks,' I replied. 'I'm Jenny and this is my grand-mother.'

'Lilian,' Mama added. She was looking curiously at Ursula's kaftan.

'Marine artefacts,' Ursula explained. She rose from her chair, wobbling the table again so that the candle actually tipped and singed the edge of her fan-folded paper napkin. She approached our table and displayed the seashells, the desiccated starfish and sea-horses. I caught a whiff of rotting seaweed. 'Appliqué sau-vage, I call it.'

'*Very* effective.' I could see Mama's thoughts running ahead. She loved a new idea. Once, in a mosaic phase, she had smashed most of her perfectly good china to add their fragments to her teapot stands and lamp bases. 'Why not join *us*,' Mama said. 'There's plenty of room. And you shouldn't be alone, not on Christmas Eve. We'd love you to join us, wouldn't we, Jenny?'

'Yes,' I said. It was nice to see Mama so animated. A waiter reorganized us and Ursula sat down, shifting about until she'd arranged the kaftan so there were no shells sticking into her.

The beautiful woman was sipping something sparkling. She wore a plain black sweater just low enough to show the moulding of her collarbones, a shadowy hollow in between. The man reached across the table and touched her cheek and I looked away.

Every morning, when they have taken away the stinking mattress and blanket, I suck the skin of my inner arm, the whitest tenderest part. I suck until I make a mark – a love-bite. It is hard to do, there, near the crook of my elbow, because the veins are so far beneath the surface. But I suck until there is a small risen oval of skin prickled red with broken capillaries. There is no love involved. This is simply a method of recording the passage of time. Otherwise, with the sameish meals and the utterly sameish pattern, the patternless days, I might lose count, lose my bearings, they might trick me. And that is my fear. The light is always the same, grim grey, as if light itself could be grimy and stale. It is mean.

There are two lozenges on my arm, my calendar. One dull speckled red – today's – the other one a soft purple, edged with maroon. So I lied when I said there was no colour. I have colourful bruises too. One on my shin, a ragged, pleasing bruise, blue and purple, grey where it fades at the edges into the unstained skin. It has the look of a mountain range, far off and clouded. When there are seven love-bites lined up on my arm they should release me into a place where at least there is light, where there are faces, and work to do. Where there is a soothing childish rhythm. Bedtime at eight. Get up at six. Early to bed, early to rise. And I am healthy. Scarcely wealthy. But certainly I am not wise. Else what am I doing in solitary? It is not the first time. Oh what I would not do for a smoke.

I asked to be transferred to the garden. I asked several times. It seemed quite reasonable to me. I'd been behaving. 'I'll make a note of your request,' they said, or, 'I'll take it up with the governor.' But nothing ever happened, never another word. So I played up, didn't I. I caused a rumpus in the cutting room, waving scissors about, shouting, swearing. I wouldn't have done anything with the scissors, wouldn't have dared, had no wish to *hurt*. But they didn't know that. I did get a change of scene. I got banged up with my own sweet self for company. And I did get a change when I emerged, pale as a mushroom from the dimness. I got switched to stitching teddy bears. Soft option you might think, stitching the pieces ready for stuffing, but the wisps of fur fabric get up your nose, you can choke to death on all the bloody softness. At night, when you pick your nose you find it clogged with wisps of fur, brown and golden, sometimes pink or blue. So I did it again. Most unwisely. Chucked a sewing machine at a screw, or tried to, too heavy, bolted to the table, bolted to the floor. So I did my stuff again, wishing I wasn't, heart not even in it as I shouted and fought. And got slammed back in here. Where I stay, for seven days, with my loneliness.

*   *   *

Ursula had never married, she said, but she had walked the length and breadth of France. She had never married but that did not mean she had not known *love*. She told us this in a loud, intimate whisper, between the *Boeuf en croûte* and the seasonal spiced ice-cream. As well as the sherry we had shared a bottle of wine, and it had gone abruptly to Mama's head.

'I loved Bob,' she objected, '*and* married him.'

Ursula swallowed the last of her wine. 'But love that is given in freedom, snatched by the wayside, so to speak,' her long nose was tinged red and the candle-flames danced in the lenses of her spectacles, 'that has the flavour of wild game compared to, say, frozen chicken.'

Mama's lips tightened.

'Bob was no frozen chicken,' I defended, remembering his bony, bruisy shins.

'Oh, my dears, never for a moment did I mean to suggest . . .' she caught hold of one of Mama's hands, and smiled roguishly at me, 'it's this dreadful old tongue of mine. How it does run away with me . . .'

'That's quite all right,' Mama said, withdrawing her hand and tasting the ice-cream which had arrived in front of her. 'Cinnamon,' she remarked, as if that was an end of the matter.

'This is our first Christmas away from home,' I said.

'I always hotel,' Ursula said. 'No family, no shortage of pennies. Best option. Usually strike up with someone.' She looked almost coyly at Mama.

We finished our ice-cream in silence. I looked across at the man, saw him stretch, smooth his hair back from his forehead, his fingers meeting at the back of his neck. A restless man. His wife was wiping the child's nose.

After dinner, we gathered round the Christmas tree in the lounge with coffee and brandy and truffles like miniature Christmas puddings and joined the staff in singing carols. Mama and Ursula were both quite drunk and their voices rose in a bright and warbly unison above the rest.

I felt rather than saw the man enter the room. He approached and sat on the arm of the sofa beside me. There were other empty seats he could have chosen. We were singing 'Good King Wenceslas', and he joined in unaffectedly.

'I'm Tom,' he said, leaning towards me when the carol had finished. 'Funny how few of the words of these bloody things we actually turn out to know.' I smiled, it was true, the collective diction had become very vague towards the end.

I introduced myself and Mama and Ursula before we launched into 'The Twelve Days of Christmas'. During the singing of this I felt a warmth all down my right side. He was not touching me but there was a warmth flowing from him into me. I could not look at him. He leant further towards me as the ten lords leapt.

'My wife is putting our daughter to bed,' he whispered, with brandy-flavoured breath. And then, 'There's a new moon.'

I followed him out of the lounge, aware of Mama's eyes on my back.

'Stuffy in there,' I said.

'Come outside.'

We went out through reception, past the Christmas tree and into the clear cold dark. 'The rain has stopped,' I remarked.

'Look at the stars and the sly moon, see how he smiles at you.'

'She,' I said, 'the moon's a she.'

'Of course.'

I tilted my head back. Pines like black feathers stirred against the sky. The strains of 'Silent Night' drifted out. I shivered.

'I cannot bear it,' he said.

'What?'

'Christmas.' And then he kissed me. I was not ready – though what did I expect? Why else did I follow him out? He kissed me experimentally one, two, three times and when I did not object, took me in his arms, pulled me tight against his soft sweater and kissed me deeply. I had never been kissed by a man with a beard before. It was a warm oaty scrunch against my face, his tongue slipped between my lips and I tasted the brandy.

There is a way of kissing that I do here. I close my thumb against my hand and lick the join until it is slippery as lips. Then I kiss it, smother it with my lips, force my tongue into the gap, taste the saltiness of my own skin.

I learned to kiss with my friend Susan. One day we were walking along in the snow, talking about boys. We stopped to print the delicate snowy hedge tops with kisses. I closed my eyes and pressed my lips into the powdery cold, licked a curl on to my tongue. We walked in a passage at the backs of the houses where the snow was undisturbed. It creaked under the soles of our Wellington boots.

'I'm dreading it,' she said. 'Actually kissing a boy on his actual lips.'

'So am I.'

'We could practise.' She looked at me out of the corner of her eye. Her skin was flushed from the cold, her fair curls stuck out round the edges of her blue woollen hat.

'Together you mean? Us?'

I looked away. I had had a friend called Bronwyn who had gone away, and now Susan was my friend. Bronwyn had talked about sex, maybe even done it, although she was only the same age as me. Her bosoms had been massive, serious things and I had shied away from the sweaty bacon smell. But Susan was light, slight and wholesome. She smelled of the cachous and Parma Violet sweets we liked to suck.

'After all we are thirteen,' she said. 'It won't be all that long till the real thing.'

'No.'

'So shall we? Let's go back to mine.'

Susan's baby brother was sitting in his high chair gnawing a rusk. Her mother was painting a door-frame. 'Mind the paint,' she said. 'Leave your boots in the kitchen.' We pulled each other's boots off and our socks came with them and little worms of grubby snow fell out of the treads. We took some apples up to Susan's bedroom. The stairs were strewn with bright toys. It was a warm messy house, smelling of coffee and wet paint.

'Well, there are two types,' Susan said, closing the door. 'There's the ordinary kiss on the cheek, we needn't bother with that. Then there's the French kiss, the sex one. It's that one I'm worried about.'

'How do you mean?'

'Open or closed mouth? How wet? How long? Are you supposed to hold your breath or breathe at the same time? Where do you put your nose?'

We bit into our apples, considering. 'You haven't got anything?' she asked. 'No germs or anything.'

'No.'

'All right then.' We put our apples down on the bed. She was wearing a pink angora sweater. The little white fibres stood out round her shoulders like a halo.

'Sitting or standing?'

'Standing.' I stood up. I was slightly taller. I put my hands on the light ridges of her shoulder-blades. 'Ready?' I asked. She nodded and we pressed our lips together. It was hard and dry. She stepped back. 'I closed my eyes, did you?' I hadn't and had watched her two closed eyelids merge into one.

'Let's try with open mouths,' I suggested.

So we tried again and this time I tasted the babyish apple taste of the inside of her mouth. I felt the little fish of her own flickering tongue tasting me. I felt a terrible fierce joy at the beating of her heart through the pink angora. We squeezed hard together for a moment and then she pulled away.

'Well I think that was right,' she said, looking down. She brushed some stray angora hairs off her black trousers. 'Let's ask Mum if we can make some popcorn.'

*   *   *

13

Here there is room for memory. There is only memory, imagination and me and the walls of this room. Look at me. Look at my
legs. The hairs on my legs are brown and long. My pubic hair is
lighter brown. It is neat and discreet hair, a curly muff. Under my
arms the hair is the same colour but straighter. I do not like this
hair, it is like the shaggy moss that grows under the arms of trees
in dismal places. Soon as I can I'll shave it off, shave my legs too. I
do not shave my arms although some women do. It is only a light
fluff. If I hold my arm up to the light I see the little hairs standing
up, fine, some long, some short. The hair on my head is brown
and short but it is not real to me now because I cannot see it, only
feel how greasy it is. Oh I must look such a sight! They cut your
finger-nails but not your toe-nails. Mine are yellowish and
curved over the ends of my toes. Underneath them are little
slivers of dirt that smell of cheese. Smell is something you get
more of here. Less to look at, hear, touch, taste – but there is an
entire repertoire of smells, and all my own. I have never learned
them before because on the outside, with the other senses so
bombarded, the important thing is *not* to smell. Not to smell real,
that is. You can smell of some floral squirt, talcum powder, thick,
pink caked soap.

Now I have identified a catalogue of smells. Beautiful. Mine.
The longer I am here, the smellier I am and the richer. There are
the obvious smells of shit and pee. The smells of fear and shame.
But fresh urine has a bright pear drop smell. And shit, if you can
evaluate the smell without prejudice, is not necessarily bad.
Variable, of course, depending on diet. Not so variable here.
But it is a brown smell of animals, leaves, earth. The smell of
decomposition which is part of the cycle of life. I cannot pretend
I would not love to bathe in fragrant bubbles, rub a fat cake of
scented soap between my hands. But I do appreciate what I
have.

Between my legs the smell is complex. I touch myself, of course
I do, for acute sensation. What do they expect me to do in here?
And my fingers smell of the seaside, a weedy smell, salty, frondy.

Under my arms the sweat has dried to ginger, my feet smell of cheese, my skin tastes of fish and salt and yeast. Oh I am so rich in perfume! I am a grocer's shop, a Christmas hamper. I could eat myself for lunch. Oh Christ but I am bored.

Christmas Day. The child carried a new doll, along with her old bear. It was balding and tufts of stuffing leaked from its paws because she chewed its paws and ears. She was not a small child, but she chewed her bear, just like a baby, there in front of everybody. She was the only child in the hotel and everyone made a fuss of her, little pet, little petulant reminder of what Christmas is really about. 'What's Christmas without kiddies?' people kept repeating, all over Christmas, eyes poached with booze, voices sentimentally slurred.

The wife wore a snow-white sweater and tight black trousers. Her teeth and the whites of her eyes were as bright white as the sweater, diamonds glittered from her ear-lobes. She was utterly, boringly, magazine-cover beautiful. The beauty was not inherited by the child, unless she intended to save it for an ugly duckling routine. She was a plain, snotty, toothy child gnawing endlessly on her bear, or if not, whining.

Tom wore a dark red shirt, it looked like silk, and a black waistcoat and jeans. From the pocket of his waistcoat poked the corner of a red handkerchief. He looked preposterously sexy – and he looked at me. When he looked my lips parted involuntarily, just as they had parted at the pressure of his lips, at the movement of his tongue.

We sat around the tree at noon sipping champagne cocktails and awaiting our gifts from Mary Christmas, a sort of seasonal bunny girl in red fish-net tights. The child helped to distribute the gifts, tripping and graceless and flushed with importance. Mama and I got identical manicure sets and Ursula, a powder compact with a mirror in the lid. Today she wore a hand-woven two-piece – hand-woven by herself, from wool collected off barbed wire fences blended with combings from her late ginger tom. In the unusual handicraft stakes, poor Mama had met her match.

There were others too, of course, a hotel full of them, Christmas refugees. There was a pale family beside us, all had beige skin and hair: two similar, if not entirely interchangeable, women; a man and two girls of about twenty. All of them wore glasses. They muttered among themselves like people from another planet and were hardly ever seen to separate. 'Girls your own age,' Mama had said on catching sight of them, but even she could see that they were hopeless.

Mama had been stiff with me that morning. We had exchanged our gifts – a red hand-knit cardigan and a golden fish for my charm-bracelet for me; a book on *découpage* for her – without the customary pretence of surprise or joy. Where had I been? she'd asked. She'd seen me slope off with that dark woman's husband in the middle of the carols – as, by the way, had everyone else – and then what? Then where had I been? She hoped I wasn't sliding off the rails.

'Fresh air,' was all that I would say.

I had lain awake for hours between the stiff white hotel sheets remembering every touch, every kiss, every word.

'*So* attractive,' he had breathed. 'I've never been so utterly, so quickly, so overwhelmingly attracted.'

I had lain awake tingling and trembling with longing. 'Tomorrow,' he had said, the last word before we'd parted. 'Tomorrow,' he had murmured into my mouth and I had swallowed his promise whole.

'I suppose you're an adult,' Mama had said suddenly, long after I had supposed her asleep. 'I suppose I must trust that you know what you're doing. Jenny, tell me it's not what it seems.'

In the darkness I smiled. It was *exactly* what it seemed. I turned over in bed to avoid the question that hovered like a mosquito over my bed. And between the stars, sailing past the smiling moon went Father Christmas with his sack of promises.

But it was not a stocking full of gifts I wished for as I closed my eyes.

Later, when Mama was at last gently snoring, I went into the bathroom to look in the mirror. In the artificial light I was pallid. My hair was brown and ordinary. My eyes were clear but not spectacular. My mouth was small, my nose was straight. 'Overwhelmingly attractive,' I whispered. I pressed my lips to the mirror and left a kiss print in a smudge of cloud.

PEACOCK FEATHERS

Here there is memory, volumes of memory, here where they could put shelves on the walls and fill the shelves with books to feed the minds of the wicked and the bored, they put nothing. Not even colour. Not even variations of light. There are no books but there are the volumes of my memory, organized and classified as comprehensively as any library. Fortunately, I have an orderly mind.

I am not the first of my family to be convicted of a crime, to serve my time. When I was a child, Mama told me about Peggy, our ancestor, who had stolen a peacock and been transported to Australia. That is all that is known about Peggy, that she stole a peacock, and I used to wonder, did she steal it for its beauty or for her dinner? I used to think that was the main thing, the *point* of it. But now I'm not so sure. Perhaps it is only the action that matters, the stealing and not the bird.

That is all that is *known* about Peggy, but not all that is imagined. For I have invented her, grown her life in my head from the seed of a snatch of words sown many years ago.

Peggy stole the peacock for its feathers. She had a baby – Samuel – though she was not married. Her family were reasonable and realistic people and she was not badly treated. There was shame, of course, but it was no rare shame.

Peggy Maybee was the middle child with two brothers either

side. She was not the most beautiful child, or the most hard-working. The family – Mr Maybee was a blacksmith – lived in a low three-roomed cottage at the edge of a small East Anglian market town. There was hardship, but never the threat of starvation. Peggy's favourite occupation as a child had been to watch her father making shoes for horses, watching the magic that changed dull lumps of iron into slivers of gold, sun-shavings. Watching him, his arms and body protected by a creaking leather apron and sleeves, hammering so that the sparks jumped out of the iron and splashed on the ground. She liked to watch the horses and sometimes she helped with a fidgety horse, stroking its neck, inhaling the salty velvet of its skin, calming it with her voice. Her father said that no one could calm a jittery beast like she could. She liked her father best because he looked at her and smiled. Her mother was too tired and grey to notice her properly. But she was kind. There was no cruelty.

When she was twelve, Peggy left home to work as an under-housemaid in a neighbouring village. It was hard and she was unhappy and homesick. For five years she saw her family only four times a year for one or two nights, bringing her pay in shillings wrapped in a handkerchief. A better position became available at the manor nearer home – twelve shillings a year instead of seven and the opportunity to visit her family every Sunday afternoon. It was here that Peggy met Percy, the son of the house. He was a year her junior, a boy who could make her forget herself and her position, make her laugh out loud, and then suddenly shame her for her impertinence. He was arrogant and charming. They had a friendship entirely defined by his power over her, his whim. And it was his whim that decided that when he was seventeen and she eighteen, he would take her for his lover. He had to learn and who better to learn with than Peggy, so available, so unable to resist. No chore the learning of the carnal skill, no chore for either of them.

But after a few months, the sickness and the tiredness came and then the fatness. She fended off the dawning truth until it bundled inside her, until her skirts were held together with loops of string, until her new bulk was remarked upon. Percy left for a tour of Europe before Peggy's mother put her hand upon Peggy's stomach, snatched it away and slapped Peggy's cheek. Mr Maybee went to the manor house and came back with Peggy's belongings and a year's wages – for Lord and Lady Barr were reasonable people and dismayed at Percy's unfortunate indiscretion.

When the baby was born on a sultry August night, Peggy was amazed to find that she loved him, loved this nuisance that had blighted her life. She sniffed the crown of his fluffy head and marvelled at his fingers, at his tiny innocent cock and the bright challenge in his Percy-blue eyes. And when he learned – the genius child – to sit up, to creep on the floor and then to stagger on his sturdy legs, she was unutterably happy. She bore young Lord Percy no ill will. The thought that he could have taken her for a wife was so ridiculous she didn't even entertain it. She was grateful to him for this exceptional child. But her love for Samuel made her want things for him, things that she could never give him. In the nursery where she had lit the fire every morning and sometimes served the younger Barr children their tea, she had marvelled at the toys that scattered the floor: painted wooden dolls with real hair; soldiers with gaudy uniforms; coloured animals, tops and skittles; and a rocking horse painted gold and scarlet with a leather saddle and reins and even an iron bit in its open mouth. This was what she wanted for Samuel. Not the rocking horse – she might as well have wished for the crown jewels – but something *bright*. Her father carved wooden cows and pigs for the boy, her mother sewed him soft dolls as shapeless and bunchy as herself, but they were all dull things. Peggy wanted something bright to reflect in his bright blue eyes.

In the centre of town lived a rich business family, not a drop of aristocratic blood between them, but plenty of money for ostentatious show. Their house was white and lofty and from the upper windows the pale-haired daughters would look down at the people in the streets. And sometimes Peggy would look up and see them, indistinct behind the muslin curtains, and she would feel envious of them for all the things they had. Of all the things they would be able to give their babies. At the back of their house was a large walled garden. It was possible to see into it over a gate which opened on to the river bank at the back. There was a glass house full of orange trees and an intricate garden with hedges clipped into tidy shapes, raked gravel paths, grey and green clumped herbs – and birds. White doves chuntered in a thatch-roofed dovecot and a peacock strutted the paths.

On Samuel's first birthday, Peggy carried him along the river bank. They watched the ducks in the leaf-shadowed water and Samuel uttered his first word – duck – and stretched his fat fingers towards them and Peggy glowed with pride. And then they peered over the gate into the lovely garden. The oranges were as bright in their glass house as little suns, the air was scented with lavender and roses. And then the peacock walked towards them, its tail sweeping the gravel behind it with a shushing sound. It turned its head from side to side as it approached, regarding them coldly with the ebony beads of its eyes. And then suddenly it showed them what it had. It lifted its tail into an enormous, gleaming, iridescent fan and baby Samuel shrieked with delight, stretched out his fat fingers once more. 'Duck,' he cried, 'duck! duck!' And Peggy could not speak. The hundred eyes spread on the trembling plumes caught her own eyes and held them and she could not look away. The air quivered with the beauty, the sheaf of eyes stared, the baby shrieked and wriggled and reached. Then the bird turned, its tail muscles relaxing, its feathers sighing as they folded down, dragging the gravel as it strutted away. Peggy became aware of a gardener watching her. Samuel turned down his bottom lip and began to cry. Peggy carried him home.

If only she could have left it there. If only the hundred eyes on the glistening fan hadn't been so teasing, so bright. If only Samuel hadn't wailed so at the snatching away of all that brightness. But in the night, when Samuel lay sleeping in his crib, a grey doll clutched in his chubby hand, his lashes like little peacock fans themselves on his flushed cheeks, Peggy went creeping out. The cottage was full of sleeping breath washing round the walls like soft waves, stirring the curtains. She walked in the spangled navy blue of the night seeing the moon winking on the river's surface. She walked straight along the river bank to the back of the white house. The gate was fastened but she climbed over it. She was tall and athletic. She was determined. There was no fear in her, no sense that she was doing wrong. Was it the peacock she wanted, or was it just the feathers? She found the bird roosting in a mulberry tree, its head under one wing, its plumes a watery cascade in the moonlight. She grabbed at its feathers but her fingers slipped on the hard cool silkiness and the peacock jerked and its voice was as harsh and shocking as the devil's voice. She grabbed its neck to keep it from escaping and it pecked at her, darting its little beak into the flesh of her arm. She struggled with the huge flapping creature, pinning it against her side with her arm, pulling at the rattling feathers. Some of them scattered on the ground. If only she had let the bird go then, picked up the fallen feathers and run. The peacock pecked her cheek and she felt the blood run down. If only she had run before they caught her – a gardener and some of the other servants caught her by the dress, and flung her on the ground and called the master – if only she had run then she would have been free.

And there would have been no story. I would never have heard of Peggy. For attempting to steal a peacock, Peggy, properly Margaret Maybee, was tried and sentenced to death. She believed that she would die. She sat in a cell contemplating the noose, sobbing for baby Samuel whom she would never see again, who would forget her; remembering his first word, duck, the fans of his lashes on his cheeks, the shimmering of the hundred eyes in the peacock's tail. But Royal Mercy was exercised and the sentence transmuted to one of transportation. Peggy was to sail around the world, to go to a place no one she knew had ever seen or even heard of, a place called Botany Bay. It might as well have been the moon.

If I close my eyes and rub them hard, rub the heels of my hands into my eye-sockets, I can see stars. First I can see what look like stars, gleams and sparkles of light. If I keep my hands against my eyes, tight against so there is no light coming in from outside, I can see the light inside me. It makes firework trails, greenish and white. I see a smoky spiral, a speck of light at the very base. Not so much light as a hole in the darkness like a little tear. I can stare into the pits of my eyes, stare backwards. But it is not *looking*, it is not looking because my eyes are closed so how do I see the vague shapes inside my eyes? What am I seeing with? And when I move my hands away so that the light comes through the lids, the colours are almost dazzling. I see brilliant green and pink, fuzzy light displays, stripes and spirals. I see a keyhole, I see a tree. When I open my eyes the walls are awash with colour, it sloshes like light in a swimming pool making vague images too trembling and nebulous to recognize.

'Your wife is very beautiful,' I said. It had to be said. It was Christmas night and we were dancing. I had spent the day quivering and tense, all my senses yearning towards him, fascinated when he was not there by his wife, even by the child. I had gone out for a walk, after a greasy Christmas lunch, with Mama and Ursula. They still wore their paper cracker crowns above their winter coats and boots. It was mild, the ground was soft with decay; twigs were decorated with drips of melted frost; berries burned red on a holly tree. We even saw a robin hopping on the path, its breast a bright smudge of rust. The sky began to darken early, an orange stain spread in the sky, the sun snuggled down behind the hills.

Mama and Ursula walked bent over, searching for interesting scraps. They had been discussing wall hangings all day, weaving and collage. Mama had invited Ursula to come and stay with us so that they could make something together. Triumphantly, Ursula plucked a handful of withered heather from the ground.

'Texture!' she exclaimed. 'Take orgasm. Used to be a dodgy business for women. There are still those who never have and never will experience a full orgasm.' They had also been discussing sex, or rather Ursula had been discussing it and Mama had been quailing. She looked uneasily at me. I looked up at the black edge of the mountains against the orange sky.

'A matter of education . . . in my day there was simply no understanding that women had anything at all. They had a space, that's all, a space to be filled, a hole to be plugged.'

'Well, yes,' Mama said. 'We have teazles at home in the garden, teazles and honesty. Would they work in?'

'Oh splendidly. But they know all about it these days, don't they, Jennifer? Clitoris. I used to think it was an alpine plant. They grow up with them nowadays, don't they? Clitorises or clitori?'

I didn't reply. I was gazing at the muscular outlines of the hills and thinking about Tom. It would only be sex, I thought, only a fling, only a borrow of someone else's man. But I didn't care. *Then* I didn't care. If only he would take me. I wanted to be taken. I was not a virgin but I had never made love to a man like that. Like what? A *man*.

'Life-enhancing,' Ursula crowed. 'Just look at this lichen.' We stopped to look at a bearded mustard-coloured crust on a rock.

'It's almost too dark to see,' Mama pointed out.

'First thing then.' Ursula took a ferocious-looking knife from her handbag and tried to prise the lichen from the rock.

We danced. His hand on the small of my back. The band played a smulchy medley of Christmas songs. *Frosty the snowman, is a hap-hap-happy man.* There was heat in his hand. I could feel him breathing. I moved my hand on his shoulder and the red silk slid against his skin and I caught my breath. He increased the pressure of his hand on my back, just slightly. His breath was in my hair. Already the scent of his skin was becoming familiar to me. *You'd better be good, you'd better not cry, You'd better be good I'm telling you why.* He kissed me, I swear he kissed me right there in front of his wife, in front of Mama, on the top of my head. *Santa Claus is coming to town.* I looked towards Mama, but her eyes flickered away from me and on to Ursula who was demonstrating something with a paper doily. I looked at the beautiful wife who was studying her fingernails.

That is when I said, 'Your wife is very beautiful.'

'Yes.' He held me away from him a little. 'Tell me . . .' he began but the band had stopped playing. Reluctantly, I let him go.

'Tell you what?'

'Later.' He turned back to his wife. I watched her look up at him, an ironic smile on her face. They danced together next. The band played Beatles songs. *Yesterday, all my troubles seemed so far away.* They were the same height, both at least six inches taller than me. They moved as if they were the same person. The tops of her breasts showed creamily above the front of her green sequined dress. Her legs looked glossy and expensive. He was proud, you could see that, even *I* could see that he was proud of her. I wasn't the only one who watched the elegant couple who danced so well together: the almost inhumanly beautiful woman, the rakish sexy man. The man who had parted my lips with his tongue on Christmas Eve, under a smiling moon.

What is this grey meat? It bears no resemblance to anything I've had before. It is not red meat. It looks like something that has been spun from the worst bits, the gristle, the ears, the testicles, the eyeballs, all pounded to a mush and spun or moulded into this grey stuff, softer than Spam. At least Spam was pink. We had Spam fritters at school, my favourite lunch, rectangles of a bright improbable pink crusted with greasy batter bubbles.

Grey meat and a lettuce leaf, brown round the edges, in bread. A cup of fawn tea and a slab of cake. I would not eat it, this rubbish, this crap, but what else is there to do? If only there was more taste. But my own skin is tastier than this reconstituted meat.

Someone is looking at me again, through the slot. Watching me eat. A rectangle of eyes through a slot. Which one? Jenks, the young one, the one who is way, way out of her depth in here among the dregs. Why is she watching me? All this isolation and yet no privacy.

Fuck off, I would like to say, to yell, but I don't want another day in here. Three love-bites on my arm now like a row of clouds in an orderly sky. So I smile sarcastically through my mouthful of cake. Slap and the slot closes and the smile drops as abruptly from my lips. The cake is dry but not bad. It is sweet. And sweetness is something rare. It is crumbly white cake, shop cake, the sort I used to long for as a child. I longed for the sort of cakes the other girls had: Battenberg, angel cake, curly jam Swiss roll. Eating is something to do. It is not at all bad this cake. The rhythm of my chewing makes a song in my head. Any song. *Frosty the snowman is a hap-hap-happy man*. Soon there will be frost. If I could only work outside . . . that's all I ask. If I could only dig in the soil, watch the birds, the clouds, the free traffic on the roads. If I could work alongside Debbie. She is like something from the real world. The rest of them, good, bad or indifferent, are indistinct. Nobody wants to be a part of this life. It is a dream-time – bad-dream-time. But Debbie has never stopped being part of the real world and when she comes in after work she brings a whiff of it in, the fragrance of fresh air on her hair and clothes.

I wonder if it's dull outside, or bright. Bright, I think. There could be frost sparkling, tickling the edges of the brown leaves with silver. It will be all crispness and sparkle. Sun on ice perhaps, puddles glazed and crazed. I loved to step on frozen puddles when I was a child in my rubber boots, put my weight on the slippy whiteness and see the black muddy bubbles ooze underneath until the ice cracked and the water leaked out.

Sometimes puddles freeze really solid, no water left and you have to chop, chop, chop with the heel of your boot to smash the ice into a sparkling dust. If I close my eyes I can see the glint of sun on ice. But no, no. It will be dark. This meal is supper. Cold meat – ha! So it will be dark or darkening.

What I wouldn't do for a fag.

In number five they will be having supper. Round the table, quietly. We hardly speak in number five. Family concept! Home-making it's called. I have never been a home-maker. Home breaker, that's me. But I mean since I've been banged up I've always gone *out* to work. Doreen is the home-maker. Doreen let her boyfriend batter her child. She stood by while he shook him until his brain was damaged and threw him at the wall. She stood by and never said a word, picked the kid up when he had finished. I can just see her, dim and dull, picking up the floppy child like an old rag doll. But later, when her boyfriend was asleep, she stabbed him not once but forty times. She does not speak much, the silent cow. She *is* like a cow, heavy and slow with big soft stupid eyes. Sometimes I look at her and think it is incredible that she had it in her to do that, to stab someone forty times. Maybe that is it, why she is so slow and blank, that was it, her energy used up. She is our doormat, our stay-at-home, our wife. She cleans the way it has to be done. It is pretend house-work, doll's house housework, not the real thing. There are rules, stupid rules, made to madden. I could not do it. Every day she has to polish the floor three times. *Three* times! The floor is slippery as ice and Doreen, bovine Doreen with her big blinking eyes, is learning to be neurotic about smudges.

We eat quietly in number five because even there in the kitchen, sitting round the table, we cannot talk. Breakfast is brought in and Doreen serves us, as if she's prepared it herself. That is the illusion we are meant to have. There are little vents in the walls and in these vents are listening devices, so we do not talk. Nothing more than 'Pass the sugar,' or 'Lend us a smoke.' Lest we forget, there are piercing hisses periodically as a screw adjusts the volume. So we sit round the table like uneasy children playing house, aware that they are listening. But even that is better than this, the hell of myself all day, all night.

They put irons on the convicts' legs, heavy fetters that prevented them from escaping overboard. Out of the port, far out to sea when there was little danger of anyone diving overboard and swimming for it, they released the convicts' legs and when they walked the decks for exercise and air, one knee – of the leg that had been fettered – would spring up high, giving a most comical walk. Some laughed, but not Peggy.

She was convict number 211 on board the *Cunning Maid*, a ship that took her breath away when she saw it berthed at Greenwich. She had never seen a ship, never seen the sea, only the wide tame river at home, only sometimes a flat sheet of water when the fields flooded with the winter rain. This ship stretched its mast and intricate rigging up against a sky that looked so tight and shiny it might squeak. Small red flags flapped against the blue.

Peggy was chained in a procession of female convicts that dragged and clanked its way along the harbour towards the ship. A crowd had gathered to watch them, tearful relatives – and hecklers shouting obscenities at these twenty degraded women. The rumour that worked its way along the line was that two hundred male convicts were already stowed away below the decks. The ship was gargantuan and yet there could not possibly be room for the hundreds. Peggy could see that. The surface of the water was crumpled grey: rubbish, rats and turds bobbed round the ship. And yet there was silver too, dancing on the far-off ripples. The rigging rattled and clanked in the breeze. There was an oily, fishy stench in the air, and also a tang of salt. The crowd jeered and threw things at the women, eggs and rotten fruit. 'I will never forget you,' a man's voice cried, and the woman in front of Peggy, hit by an apple, jerked angrily round, almost dragging Peggy off her feet.

Peggy kept her face turned away from the crowd, turned up to the bright towering prow of the ship. After weeks in a gloomy cell awaiting this voyage, the ship looked glamorous and golden in the cold winter light. There was almost relief now that the waiting was over, that the voyage was about to begin. She kept her face turned away from the crowd in case she should see a baby boy stretching out his arms. But it was her father's voice that caught in her ear.

'Peggy . . . look here, Peggy,' he shouted, his voice a familiar curl among the tangle of rough shouts, jeers and the seagulls' shrieking. 'My child,' he cried, and she searched the crowd for his face, so loved and familiar, as he jostled his way to the front. As he neared she saw that his face shone with tears and when he stretched out his hand and she managed to touch the tips of his fingers, they too were wet. When their fingertips touched, just a split second's touch which was all they could snatch, there was such a force of love in it that it jolted her like a shock and the tears that were always so ready sprang to her own eyes.

'Sam?' she asked.

'He is thriving,' he said. 'He is well, Peggy. Mother thought the journey too hard for him . . . he is speaking now . . .'

Peggy was dragged along in the procession and the crowd was too thick for him to follow. 'Don't let him forget me,' she shouted. And he shook his head. 'Never,' he replied, his voice jagged and broken. She turned back once more to see him and saw his face in his hands as if he wept, and the cruel sunshine shone prisms on her own wet lashes to remind her of the greed for brightness that had put her here.

The ship was such a thing of beauty. Impossible not to see it as escape, adventure. And once the voyage started Peggy would be sailing towards her future, in a way she would be sailing towards home, for she had been sentenced to seven years. And what was seven years? She was young, not twenty yet. She'd return to Samuel before he was ten. She would write to him often, teaching him about sailing and ships, about Australia, opening his eyes to the wide world. The time would fly and she'd return to him grown up and wise. It was anticipation she felt, as a counterpoint to her wrenching grief, as she stepped aboard the ship and felt the creaking lurch of it under her feet.

To reach the convicts' quarters, the women walked through the boat, glimpsing on their way the interiors of plush cabins, tidy treasure houses of comfort full of gleaming wood and brass. Peggy understood that their quarters would not be of this quality. But still she was not prepared. They had to descend an almost perpendicular ladder, a laborious process for the fetters had to be loosened at the top of the ladder and then refastened at the bottom. The crewman who fastened her fetters slid his hand up her skirt, reached right up between her legs but she held her tongue. Common meat she was now, felt now. In the cells, awaiting transportation, she had become accustomed to treatment of this kind. The soldiers and the crew touched all the women, up their skirts, on their breasts, and only one or two of them struggled.

'Fat cunny here,' the man shouted to his mate. Peggy looked down at him, the crude red-faced man, somebody's husband no doubt, somebody's father. He pulled his hand out and sniffed his fingers and then spat. The spittle stuck on her brown skirt, silvery like cuckoo spit from long grass in the garden. Peggy did not move or say a word. She looked down at the greasy top of the man's head. She was above hate. These brave men who molested chained women were merely vermin. The seven years was no more than an interruption. She would not be broken. Her body was not hers now, not for seven years. They touched her body rudely, they took away her freedom, they took her from her son. Well, she would stay above it. Somewhere inside she could not be touched. They could molest her body, but they could not molest her soul.

In front of her were a row of small crudely erected whitewood cabins. From one of them a baby cried, and that sound, a new baby's la-la-ing cry made her breasts tingle. When she was taken away she had not yet weaned Samuel, treasuring and prolonging the feeling of him at her breast. And at night, as she had lain on the hard floor of her cell, her breasts had ached as she fancied she heard his cries carrying over all the distance between them. And tears had run from her eyes as she had clutched her nipples and felt the beads of sweet milk running uselessly away.

She supposed that these mean cabins were the convicts' quarters and though they were dim and cramped they were all right. She was not prepared. To her left was a wall studded with iron knobs and pitted with holes, to let in light and ventilation for the comfort of the male convicts behind it. But Peggy was innocent. A door was dragged open in this wall, a narrow door, big enough only for one person to stoop and squeeze through at a time. The women were shoved inside. They tumbled and jerked painfully, the chain jarring and tangling around their legs; they were disoriented, half-blinded by the sudden soupy gloom. The muzzles of muskets, that's what the holes were for, they were not designed humanely to let in air and light. Peggy supposed that this was a corridor in which they waited, a passage that led to their quarters. It was not until her eyes grew used to the dimness that Peggy realized that this was it. This was her home for the next several weeks. It was a long berth, right on the curved hull of the lower ship, with double rows of bunk-beds – flat wooden pallets – equipped with rings for chains. The women were put in threes on the bunks, chained tightly by their ankles and then the door was banged and locked and they were left in the dark.

THE SUMMER HOUSE

He led me outside. He *led* me? Strictly speaking, yes. He held my hand and walked before me, but I held on. My will was at least as strong as his. But I wanted him to *take* me, I wanted the illusion that he was taking me. Together we walked up the garden path between the dark muttering shrubs. The cloud was a fusty charcoal blanket hiding the tops of the pines, the hills, hiding the moon. The air was moist and sweet.

He put his arm round my waist and I breathed in the smell of him. 'There is a summer house,' he said.

'I know.' I had noticed the small round, half-glazed structure earlier while out with Mama and Ursula and my first thought had been of Tom. We stopped and held each other. I was pressed hard against his chest, my head against his shoulder and I could hear the steady thump of his heart. Our breath mingled cloudily around us.

'Can we really?' He held me away from him. Escaped light from the hotel windows showed me the shadows on his angular face, made his eyes enormous. 'You are so . . .' he breathed and printed his lips on my forehead.

'What were you going to ask me in there?' My breasts were a soft pressure against him. I felt strangely safe.

'You've already answered,' he said. He took my hand and we walked together out of the light towards the summer house. The door was not locked. He opened it and we stepped inside. The wooden floor creaked under our feet as we kissed in the darkness, deep kisses that made us stumble and lose our balance.

'Wait.' He took a candle and some matches from his pocket.

'You planned this!' I accused, delighted, for hadn't I planned it too? Hadn't the plan started the moment I saw his face?

'Beth gave me this candle,' he held it up for me to see its shiny red surface.

'Beth?'

'My little girl.'

I felt a momentary chill, a rebellion against him for just a second, just the sliver of a second. It was something about the pride in his voice. '*My* little girl.' Something about his smoothness. And the idea that he felt no uneasiness at using his child's present to illuminate our love-making.

He lit the candle and moved it around so that we could see what there was to see. Tiny candle-flames wagged back, like scolding fingers, from all the black panes of glass. There were some folding canvas chairs stacked against the wooden wall and a heap of nets.

'What are they?' I nudged them with my toe.

'Tennis nets. There are some courts.'

He put the candle on the floor. Its little tongue lapped the darkness and made shadows tremble on the rounded walls. It was like a cave, the round summer house, lit warm in the centre. Love-nest, I thought. He seemed so good and practised at this, so smooth, that I nearly turned and walked away. He took off his coat, put it on top of the tennis nets and I allowed him to pull me down.

My chilliness went as soon as he was close again, as soon as he kissed me. I was overwhelmed by him, his badgerish beard against my face, his warmth, the smell and the taste of him. 'I love you,' I gasped and oh God I didn't mean to say it, I didn't even mean it. It jumped from my mouth naked and spontaneous and squatted in front of us on the floor. He hesitated, pulled away a little. I thought he flinched. I opened my mouth as if somehow to try and take it back, but he put a finger on my lips.

'And I love you,' he said. Of course, I didn't believe him but I did start to love him then, grateful for his kindness. I took his finger in my mouth, bit it gently, tasted the tinder of the match. Then we moved together. He touched me in an expert way that made my body sing, my skin scream, silvered paths followed his fingers. It was almost too much to bear. I made him wait, pushed his hands off me, unbuttoned and unzipped him, enjoyed the textures of his body under his clothes, the smell and the taste. I took him in my mouth like a fat plum and sucked until I believed I could taste the sweetness of its juice, until he pulled my head up, groaning. And when he entered me it was a shock. It was so perfect, like two halves jumping together. It was a shock of recognition. And we were still for an exquisite moment, a moment like a crystal drop poised above the tension of its own falling.

And then . . . oh what then? . . . there was a sudden movement, somebody's limb – my arm? his leg? – knocked the candle over on to the net. I didn't see, my eyes were shut, my other senses stuffed with him when suddenly he jerked away and I heard the sizzle of the nets catching.

'Oh Christ!' He leapt up. He stood above me as the flames blossomed and I saw his penis standing like a reed against the sudden orange. And then I scrambled up, and we rushed together, half-naked into the night.

'Dress and go back,' he ordered. 'Don't say a thing.' He was struggling with his belt. 'I'll follow you in, raise the alarm . . . no one will know. Oh Christ . . . my coat. Oh fuck it.' He approached the door as if he was about to go back inside to rescue it from the centre of the nest of flames.

'No!' I grabbed his arm.

He jerked his arm away. 'Sorry . . . but just go, Jenny. Go.'

I hurried back, blinking back tears, struggling through a tangle of emotions; hurt, disappointment, exhilaration. I scuttled back into the healthy light of the hotel lounge where board games were taking place. No music for once, just a mumble and the occasional shake of a dice. Mama, Ursula and the Beige Couple were hunched over a Scrabble board.

'A quiet interlude before charades,' Ursula explained.

'Where on earth have you been?' Mama asked but the veiled look in her eyes told me she didn't really want to know. She patted the sofa beside her. 'Come on, you can help me now you're here. Look, four Ts.'

I sat down, noticing that my cardigan was buttoned up wrong, feeling an uncomfortable wetness against the twisted pull of my tights. Ursula looked at me curiously.

And then Tom came in. He didn't look at me, or anyone, talked to the tops of all the heads. 'I've just been out for a breath of air,' he announced, 'and it seems that that folly thing, that summer house affair, is on fire.'

His wife darted me a look. It was a glittering slice of a look which I did not acknowledge. Everyone left their games and crowded round the window to look. There were shouts outside as the staff began to work with fire extinguishers and buckets. I went to the window too, and saw how beautifully the fire blossomed, a bright chrysanthemum in the dark. And I smiled.

If we had only left it there. If we had left it like that, gloriously: the roar of flames and the thrilling shooting splinter of exploding glass, the burst of orange in the dark. If we had only let the flames be our consummation. But it was not finished. You cannot do that, just stop like that. It is not possible. Our passion remained unconsummated, *my* passion for *him*, and on Boxing Day I stood among the grey ash and cinders of the summer house and I knew that.

Most of the guests had gone to watch the hunt gather: Tom, his wife, the child, the Beige Family. Everyone except Mama, Ursula and myself. Ursula was opposed to hunting and Mama agreed that it was barbaric so they had gone out collecting material for their project instead. I had joined them at first.

They had walked through the hotel grounds down to the river bank and I had followed, stopping at the circle of ash.

'Odd, it going up like that,' Ursula observed and Mama narrowed her eyes at me.

'What?' I said.

'Nothing.' They walked on. I paused in the centre of the ashy circle. I did not care what they thought. I found a thick wad of burnt cloth that might have been his coat, and the metal tag of a zip. I stirred my toe in the wet ash. It had rained in the night, and it was a sticky charred mess which exuded a terrible wet burnt stench. I found a twist of melted glass embedded with ashy flecks and I put it in my pocket. As I stirred the mess with my foot, coating my boot with sticky ash, I discovered, despite the wetness, a smouldering chunk of wooden floor. A tiny ghost of smoke rose from it. I held my hand over it and it seemed an omen. There was heat still, and still heat between Tom and me. I pressed the end of my index finger against the smouldering wood, held it there, teeth gritted to feel the burn.

I say I do nothing – but I do exercise. Once or twice or three times a day I exercise hard. Bob used to make us do what he called the 'daily dozen'. Every morning, before breakfast, entirely naked, Mama and I would stand in front of him and obey. He worked us hard, made us stretch, twist, bend and run on the spot until we were breathless. How I hated it. I hated the nakedness most – Mama would be behind me and he in front so I felt completely exposed – but I hated the exercise too. Not when I was a little child – then I thought it was something everyone did, like cleaning their teeth – but later. Because I began to see how odd he was, not like anyone else I knew and I resented the difference that made me different, made me feel a misfit. But he was a man born ahead of his time, I see that now. What he made us do behind furtively closed curtains is fashionable now. Aerobics. And all that stretching and bending as I grew up made me supple and strong, if not graceful. What do they say? *Feel the burn.* I felt the burn all those years ago in the muscles of my calves and thighs as well as in my cheeks.

I feel foolish exercising in here. And they *do* look, alerted by the noise of the activity but they cannot interfere for it is not self-destructive. Quite the opposite. I stand with my back to the slot and I count in a voice that gets breathier as I wear myself out, work myself hard, order myself, urge myself as Bob used to do – *And one and two and over and down and stretch and twist and one and two and stretch and stretch and stretch and stretch and –* and I do it until the sweat runs down my sides from my armpits and my face is slippery. Oh God what a sight I must be! No comb, no shampoo, no mirror. Without a mirror I am losing my face. And when I am finished, when I am panting and gasping for breath what I want most in the world is a smoke, my lungs cry out for smoke.

I have a headache. All the time a steady, thrumming, low-grade headache. Maybe it's the lack of fresh air, the lack of proper light, the lack of tobacco, something they put in my food. It throbs more when I exercise but I do not care. I have to do it, have to get the blood surging through my veins, get my heart thumping, or I will stagnate.

This morning I thought I had a cold, my throat was dry, I felt light-headed, but the exercise has chased it away. It is good for you, the exercise, in some ways Bob was very wise, I can see that now. The child always had a cold. There was always a yellow candle between her nostril and her lip. A snotty child – some allergy, Tom thought. I wondered why they didn't just tell her to wipe her nose.

'Fancies herself Jane bleeding Fonda,' someone said and the slot slapped shut. It was Barker, the cruel screw with the kind face. There are three that I regularly see: Barker, Grant and Jenks. Grant is hard. Her eyes are green behind her tinted glasses and narrowed as if she has a fag in her mouth. She has the sandpapery voice of a heavy smoker – but I have never seen her smoke. She is straight, unbribable, harsh – but she is fair. You know where you are with Grant. Sometimes I think I have noticed a gleam of something in her eye, almost a look of liking, almost a communication, almost a two-way look.

Jenks is young and unsuitable for this occupation. Not cut out to be a screw, too vulnerable, too eager to be liked. What possessed her? What sadistic careers officer pointed her this way? She ought to be a nurse or a primary school teacher. Little and sick people would respond to her watery kindness but here we are mad and bad and we cannot stomach weakness. She tries to get us to like her. She tried, but she's learning. She has this blonde hair, used to be long, and she wears ear-rings. Correction: she *wore* ear-rings, some silver dolphins one day, swimming against her neck. Until someone took a fancy to one and grabbed it, slit her ear-lobe. Very little blood, that surprised me, but Jenks went green and sank to her knees in a sort of faint. Now she wears her hair very short and her lobes are bare. Lil, who did it, got solitary for seven days. She was in here like me, and what did she think about for 168 hours?

I hardly saw Tom on Boxing Day. His wife hardly left his side, his daughter, never. He didn't glance at me during lunch, but his wife did. She was wearing a bright mohair sweater and although she was still beautiful, she looked tired. I wondered if he might have told her about us. No, no. That she might have guessed.

Mama and Ursula were full of plans. They had carrier bags full of twigs, bulrushes, feathers, bark, lumps of stone and shaggy crusts of lichen. Mama tipped some out in a messy scatter on the bed to show me.

'Sculpture sauvage,' Ursula said striding into our room without knocking. Her grey hair was loose and she had mistletoe wound round her head like a crown. She looked entirely mad.

'Sculpture of what?' I asked.

'A non-representational representation of natural form made with natural . . . er . . . bits and bobs,' Mama said, looking to Ursula for support.

'You could have left everything as it was,' I said, 'lying about representing nature, *being* nature, naturally in its natural environment.'

'The girl's a philistine,' Ursula said and Mama frowned at me. I picked up a rose-hip that had rolled off the bed and on to the floor.

'You're making the bedspread filthy,' I remarked. 'Anyway, we're going home tomorrow. You won't have time.'

'Ursula is coming home with us,' Mama said. 'I've been meaning to ask you if you mind.' Ursula showed me the grey bar of her smile.

'Oh no,' I said. Although I did. I objected to Ursula's hawkish nose, her lumpy hand-spun sweater and the stupid way her long hair trailed down and the pusy-looking berries in her hair.

'I won't get in the way.' Her eyes glittered behind her huge glasses. 'You'll hardly know I'm there.'

'Anyway, I might go off for a few days before term starts,' I said.

'I thought you had masses of work?' Mama looked at me searchingly.

'What colour is this?' Ursula demanded holding up a berry.

'Red,' I said.

'Ah, you see you have to learn to look. Most people would say red, but I would say there is no such thing as *red*. There's vermilion and crimson, scarlet, magenta . . . nature's palette.'

'Where?' Mama said.

'Just away . . . for a break.'

'I thought this *was* a break,' she grumbled. I shrugged. I didn't really know what I was saying or doing. It all depended on Tom. All through lunch I had kept my eyes on the back of his neck where his hair curled over his collar. And his wife had seen me looking, but I didn't care. I pretended to be staring out of the window behind them. If I kept my eyes on him but focused them past him, I could see the edges of the hills against the sky, like the most delicate trace of ink.

'Almost time for the treasure hunt,' Mama said, looking at her watch. 'Wrap up, Jenny, it's chilly.'

'Don't think I'll bother.' I was tired. I wanted, if I could not be with Tom, to be alone.

'But it's the last organized activity,' Mama said. 'It'll be fun. *Do* join in. Show willing.'

'All right then.' I put on my jacket. In the morning we had seen some of the hotel staff preparing for the treasure hunt, hiding scraps of paper in the grounds. 'Coming then?' I asked Mama.

Mama looked at Ursula. 'Are we?' she said.

Irritated, I turned and left the room. 'See you later,' Mama called after me. It aggravated me to see Mama so subservient to Ursula after, what? less than forty-eight hours! And yet, I realized as I descended the stairs, it was the same length of time that I had known Tom, we had spent less time together, hardly spoken at all – and yet I had lost my heart.

Lost my heart! What a cliché, oh I hate them, the love clichés. Head over heels, love of my life, the real thing, love at first sight, falling in love . . . had I really done that? Fallen in love, *in* love, as if love is some sort of treacherous bog, safe enough on the surface but trust your weight to it and you go through into the thick sucking mud and then you are lost. You are at the mercy not only of another person, but of your own dark emotions, the ones you never knew were there, the ones that pull you down.

In here, between these four walls, I suffer these emotions if I am not careful. My organization, my categorization, the careful library system of my memory disintegrates if I drop my guard and emotion leaks in. The walls are empty screens and the images of my memory are projected on to them and I am forced to watch. My eyelids are no protection, the images are inside too.

Is this the idea of solitary confinement? Is this intense reflection supposed to be improving? No. It is for their benefit. Get shot of us for days at a time. It does no other good. It could drive you mad, the four walls flickering with desperate images of self, the self leaking out, the smell and the sound and the sight of self. Sometimes I want to shout and scream, 'Let me out!' and I don't know what I mean. Let me out of this box, or let me out of my sickening self? When it leaks out like that, when images wobble like swimming pool reflections on the walls, when all my self is out filling the room, every corner of it, there is nothing left inside. There is just my own stench and my rubbery pink limbs. The space where my face used to be is the only space.

But be constructive. There is good in me that is the seed of self. There is good in me. But when I examine it, it slips away. Even the good things have a flip side. Every unselfish act is in the end self-interested. If I am kind to someone, generous, understanding, it is because I wish the same from them. Because I have a vague dread of the future and the help I might need.

Oh quite the philosopher! Who is saying that? I see Mama's face on the wall, a wavery image. Yes, it is like light reflected from water. Is it there outside my eyes? I have to blink and scrub my eyes with my fists and then what a swirl of colours there is, such a swirl of flesh and hair and eye-bright dots as if someone had dabbled their hand in the reflection.

Oh let me out.

The ship bucked and heaved and the women were sick. Each had a thin mattress and a blanket scarcely big enough to cover her body. Peggy's two companions were a girl called Hester and a woman who muttered her name, Sarah, through whitened lips. Sarah kept her arms folded round her body as if protecting herself. She had grey hair and fine lines on her face but she was not old, just scribbled with lines of anguish and sour with the smell of pain. Hester was fifteen but looked nearer twelve with her bird-boned body and pointed face.

'What is wrong?' Peggy asked Sarah, but the woman only shook her head and clasped her arms more tightly round herself.

'Is she with child?' Hester whispered to Peggy. Although she was wasted in her limbs and hollow of cheek, Sarah was bulky round her middle and might indeed have been expecting a baby.

'Is it that?' Peggy asked. She lay her hand on Sarah's arm and flinched.

'She is burning,' she whispered to Hester. 'She needs water . . . clean water. She is burning with fever.'

Hester stroked Sarah's brow. 'I will tell the surgeon,' she said. 'When he comes down.'

But the surgeon superintendent, in charge of the prisoners as the captain was in charge of the ship, did not come down. The ship cast off and began its journey from Greenwich to Gravesend with the women still stowed below, three by three on their wooden bunks. Their ration was brought down to them, and in the clamour of voices that surrounded its arrival, the jeering at the crew who delivered it, the cacophony of argument, greed, laughter, Peggy and Hester were unable to signal Sarah's condition. Their rations consisted of salt-beef or mutton and biscuits so hard they snapped the teeth at the roots of the old and poorly nourished and all the convicts learned to suck them soft first and chew very gingerly. They were given also a quart of water each a day which was not enough for anyone – let alone Sarah who burned away steady and quiet as a candle.

'What is it that ails you?' they asked her many times but she only pressed her face against the hull and muttered to herself through her chattering teeth. She took sips of water when they held it to her mouth but no morsel of food passed her lips so that Peggy and Hester, greedy and ashamed, had a little more to eat.

'She was brought to child-bed in her prison cell,' said Rose, a tall, gruff woman with curling hairs on her chin. She peered across the walkway between the two double ranks of bunks. 'The child was a puny thing. It took one look at the cell and at its miserable mother, grizzled and pissed and turned up its toes. And *she* took down in grief could not get it into her head that it was dead. They had to snatch it away, bend her fingers back to get it off her. And now she is took with the child-bed fever.'

'Poor Sarah,' whispered Peggy.

'God take me swiftly to be with my babe,' muttered Sarah, the clearest words she had spoken.

'Save your pity,' Rose said. 'A dirtier trollop never walked the streets.'

Peggy and Hester nursed Sarah as best they could but it was hopeless. No doctor came, nor would until the *Cunning Maid* was out in the open sea. From below the convicts heard the stomping feet and rough cries as the bulk of the crew were boarded at Gravesend and, soon after that, the motion changed. The ship began to buck and sink and lurch and sickness overcame most of the women, but not Hester who was a fisherman's daughter and used to the motion of the sea. Hester held the cup to Peggy's lips as she had held it to Sarah's and sang softly for there was no one to speak to. All around the women lay and groaned in the cold and vomit-stinking gloom. The stench was like a monstrous animal, crouching between them all, pressing its filthy fur into their noses and mouths, robbing them of breath.

Once Peggy woke, and felt that something had changed, that it seemed colder than ever and when she reached out her hand to touch Sarah's arm she discovered why. The fever had burned her away and she was cold and as still as wax.

'They must be told,' she mumbled thickly to Hester.

'Soon,' Hester said, 'only I am saving her rations, and yours that you have not eaten, for days when we will be glad of them.' For every day someone delivered the women's rations without bothering to strain his eyes in the gloomy stench to ascertain which of the women were dead and which merely wished to die.

Peggy screwed up her eyes to focus on Hester's face. She was shocked by the girl's practical callousness but too weak to object. She only edged away from the horrible cold of the waxen body beside her.

'She looks peaceful,' Hester said, and it was true. Sarah's face had smoothed in death and there was even the trace of a smile on her lips.

On the third day of the voyage, the surgeon superintendent descended. He was a sandy-haired man with a gold tooth that glittered oddly in the light that slid like oil through the open hatchway.

'Please, Sir,' Peggy said, though Hester scowled. 'This lady here is dead.'

'Lady!' scoffed Rose.

The man walked along to where they were, held a white handkerchief to his mouth and bent down to look. He lifted Sarah's wrist and dropped it. Peggy smelled lavender on his handkerchief. He sighed. 'Remove the corpse,' he said to the guards behind him. 'Any more gone, or feverish?'

Someone called out that her neighbour was ill, feverish and delirious and the woman was taken off to the sick-bay, never to be seen again.

When Sarah's body had been removed, the surgeon returned. 'Sea-legs,' he announced, letting his eyes travel over the miserable sickly collection of women. 'We'll give them a chance to grow their sea-legs, then we'll have them up on deck. Take a look at them. Sluice their quarters. Home sweet home, then my pretties.' He towered above them hardly visible in the gloom, light powdery round his shoulders.

Whether it was that they had grown sea-legs, or whether the sea had merely calmed, the surgeon was right and they woke much better on the fourth day. They lay in the dim hot stench and began to talk.

'Poor Sarah,' Peggy said. While she had been so seasick the thought of death had not been terrible, it would almost have been a relief. But now she was half recovered, she felt the beginnings of a strength in her limbs again, felt hungry for the extra food Hester had saved, and grateful to her for her sense.

'I think she's better dead,' Hester said.

'Better off dead,' agreed Rose. 'Thieving whore.'

'Well she's in heaven now at least. At peace with her little child,' Peggy defended.

'In heaven! Hell more like. And her poxy little bastard with her.'

Peggy and Hester exchanged glances and fell silent. When they began to talk, they talked in whispers.

'For stealing feathers!' Hester was incredulous when Peggy told her of her crime. 'You stole feathers!' She laughed, then straightened her face mockingly. 'I am a much more serious felon,' she said and told Peggy her story. She had been convicted of stealing some silver plate. She had been tricked into stealing it for someone else, a young man who deceived her into thinking he loved her. Who loved her so much, he saw her tried and convicted and never spoke a word in her defence. A young man who was now free and no doubt charming some other poor fool into committing his crimes.

'I hate him,' Hester said bitterly. 'He betrayed me. I would not have thought of stealing if it hadn't been for his soft words . . . and now here I am and how will my little brothers do without me?' She looked as if she would cry, her small features pinched in the triangle of her face. Peggy put her arm round her bony little shoulders. Despite her own distress and weakness she felt a surge of motherly warmth for Hester, as if the mother part of her had been sleeping and was now awakened. She talked about Sam.

'He's a sturdy lad, my Sam,' she said and as she spoke she closed her eyes and could not see his face. She could enumerate his separate features: his round blue eyes, blue as stolen scraps of sky; his rosy cheeks; his dribbly mobile mouth with the three new teeth in a pearly row; but she could not put them together and *see* him and pain bloomed freshly in her heart.

'How many brothers?' she asked Hester quickly before her own tears fell.

'Four little tots,' Hester said and her voice strengthened and grew proud. 'Abel, Isaac, Dan and Nat. Nat's the baby, like my own baby since Mother has been so hard at work and so worn down.'

In the gloom the two of them discovered that Sam and Nat

were born within a fortnight of each other and they described and boasted about the children's beauty and accomplishments, comparing – as if the two of them were playing round their feet – the slim darkness of one and the fat fairness of the other, almost forgetting their circumstances, wresting a bright moment from the gloom. And then they fell silent each feeling more strongly than ever the distance growing steadily between the babies and themselves.

SCULPTURE SAUVAGE

We gathered in the lobby for the treasure hunt. The sun shone through the windows on to the Christmas tree, making the lights pallid, illuminating the sharp needles scattered on the carpet. I stood behind Tom and his family. The child chewed a teddy bear, I could see the snail trail of her snot on its fur. The beautiful wife held his arm. Her hair was loose around her shoulders, thick dark hair with a kink and I noticed with satisfaction that she had a few grey hairs. I liked the sign of age. It was to my advantage. She might be more beautiful, but weren't men always leaving their wives for younger women?

The Beige Family, noticing that I was alone – since Mama and Ursula were hunting their own treasures – invited me to join them in searching for clues. And at first I did. Each group were handed the first clue in an envelope and after that, clue led to clue. The prize was to be presented to the winning team at the farewell Boxing Day dinner. Beige Father was most definitely the head of this family. He gathered us round, opened the envelope and read in a carrying whisper: '*I rush along but never arrive. Watch out when I'm crossed.*' He read it several times with intonations in different places and they buzzed together with their apologetic voices.

'It's obvious,' I said.

'No it's not,' one of the daughters said to me irritably. I saw that even the irises of her eyes were beige.

47

I shrugged. I was good at riddles because that was the sort of thing Bob had loved, games and crosswords, anything with clues. Just for a second I missed him, felt sad. He would have loved this.

'What then?' Beige Mother said eventually.

'We have to go to the bridge,' I said.

'Shhhh . . .' Beige Father held up his finger and thought – then shook his head. 'Don't get it.'

'The river rushes,' I explained, 'and the bridge crosses it.'

'She's right!' Beige Mother said and they hurried out, watched resentfully by the other players who in their lunch-befuddled state had yet to click. I looked back and caught Tom's eye but he did not smile. It didn't matter. Just the catching of his eye and the warmth I thought I saw there flowing towards me, the longing, caused my heart to lurch.

I followed the family out into the bright afternoon. The sun had partly melted the frost but in the shadows grass blades still stood stiff and furred. The low sun spilled strange shadows, even of the smallest twig, stone, tussock, curled leaf so that the lawns looked pocked and textured. Bare twigs glinted like tangled wires where the sun caught them.

The river roared, rushed muscularly, swelling over boulders, swirling tea brown in deep places, twizzling twigs and leaves and bracken snatched from the hills. We found the little arched bridge and the clue tucked in a gap between two stones, and they all clustered round while Beige Father read it out: 'I weep baskets,' he read. 'I *weep* baskets. I weep *baskets*.' I leant over the stone bridge, swallowing the freshness of the river's breath. There was brilliant moss growing low on the stones, lapped black and wet underneath but so startlingly green above the water's surface that it almost stung my eyes.

'Willow,' I said over my shoulder. I could see they were irritated, and anyway it was too easy, I could imagine Bob's scorn. He'd have liked a proper challenge. I left them and wandered back to the burnt-out summer house. I felt like a criminal drawn irresistibly to the scene of the crime – though there was no crime but carelessness.

My anxiety had turned to sleepiness. I stood in the ash which was quite cold now and drying so that little drifts of it floated up as I stirred my feet. I was so tired and sluggish that I thought I might go back to the hotel and lie down – if Mama and Ursula weren't being creative in our room. I stood in a sort of detached dream with my feet in the ash and I heard a footfall behind me, the munch of a shoe on gravel. I did not need to look round. My shoulders tensed, my face was suddenly hot.

'How're you doing?' Tom asked. 'Found any treasure?'

'Given up.'

'Too hard?'

'Too easy.'

I looked round. He was grinning at me. 'Big head.' His nose was red from the cold and in the clear light I could see the age in his face, the crepey skin under his eyes, the shine of his scalp through his hair at the front. But I did not care.

'What about you?' I asked.

'Oh we're hot on the trail.'

We were silent for a moment. He looked down at the ash and grinned. 'You're wrecking your shoes.'

'Last night . . .' I began.

'Not now.'

'When then? When will I see you?' I had never been so bold.

'Would it really be wise?' he asked. I felt sick.

'Wise?' I forced a smile. 'What's wisdom got to do with it?'

'Well . . .'

'Daddy!' called the child. She trotted down the path towards us, her mittens swinging loose from the sleeves of her coat. 'Daddy! Mummy's looking for you.'

'Coming,' he said. 'Look . . . you can write to me.'

'Not ring?'

'Ring then.'

'*Daddy!*' The child had arrived and was pulling at the sleeve of his sweater. 'Why haven't you got your coat on,' she demanded. 'Mummy made *me*.'

'Yes.' His eyes made such shocking contact with mine that I flinched. His eyes were such a colour – deep tobacco brown – with little amber flecks round pupils which flared when they looked at me, despite the brightness.

'Yes it's chilly, Tom, you *should* wear your coat.' I made myself smile at the child.

'What were you talking about?' she demanded.

'Oh this and that, chit-chat,' Tom said.

'I hope you're not cheating,' she said primly.

'Never.' Tom looked not at her but at me. He took his wallet from his trouser pocket and gave me a card. 'Ring me,' he said and he did not smile but took the child's hand, turned and walked away.

I looked at it. Tom Wise Musician: Gigs, Sessions, Teaching, and his telephone number.

I grinned. 'Wise, eh?' I said to myself. 'What do you play?' I called after him.

'Sax, mainly,' he called back.

'Come on, Daddy.' The little witch pulled him away. I watched them go, dragging yards of grey shadow behind them. I suddenly felt how bitterly cold it was. Tonight there would be a hard frost.

I didn't speak to Tom alone again at Pitlochry. All through the last dinner Mama and Ursula planned their sculpture and their wall hangings and didn't notice how quiet I was, how I only played with my food. Mama drank more wine than ever before.

'I'm getting quite a taste for this,' she confided, refilling her glass. 'Bob wasn't much of a one for it . . .' She giggled. 'Alcohol, I mean!' I could hardly bear it. They were so childish and yet so old. It was disgusting. I felt more grown up than them, grown up and filled with serious love.

To my amazement, the Beige Family had beaten everyone else and won the prize, a case of wine. Beige Father went up to receive the prize and made an entirely uncalled-for speech. He then presented me with a bottle for, he said, 'Getting them off to a flying start.' The wine was Liebfraumilch.

'Young maiden's milk,' Ursula translated.

'Shall we open it?' Mama suggested.

'No, I want to save it,' I said. I could see Tom looking across the room at me, a secret, amused look.

'For what?'

'A special occasion.'

'Isn't this special enough for you?' Mama said. 'Boxing Day?'

'We'll order something else then.' Ursula signalled a waiter. As she raised her arm I noticed the strange jewellery she wore, a bracelet and ear-rings set with pointed yellowish stones that looked like animals' teeth. I opened my mouth and closed it again. I didn't really want to know.

Cauliflower cheese. Cauliflower is the foulest thing when boiled to wet pulp. It has a hellish sulphurous smell. It decays instantly on the tongue. Cauliflower cheese and mashed potato. Is colour forbidden in the kitchen? Perhaps that is another punishment: the forfeiting of the right to eat anything that is not white or grey or brown. I can just see them now in number five. Doreen doling out the sloppy mess, her tongue protruding from her lips with concentration. Then they'll all sit down and tuck in, between fags, odd family, the fat and the sharp and the stupid. And Debbie.

And what when I am out of here? Four love-bites on my arm, three to go. When I am out where will they put me? Not back in the sewing room, or with the teddies, not after my outbursts. So where? Please God not the laundry. I dare not even hope for the garden. If I could work outside in the fresh and the wet; if I could feel the rain and the breeze and even the sun on my skin – though I would not *ask* for sun; if I could work beside Debbie, what more could I possibly want? I would be in heaven. My dream is to kneel on the grass and bury my face in the wet Michaelmas daisies. Those colours: delicate twilight mauve, speckled yellow in the centre . . . It is Michaelmas daisy time of year. I have held on to that. It could be January or June in here and the light and the temperature would be the same – but I have held on to the autumn.

Garden work is a privilege. It is the nearest you get to freedom here, because they cannot control the weather, because the plants grow as if they were free and you can see past the fence and out into the real world where real people are conducting their lives. Garden work is a privilege so I should not even think about it, not even dream.

After the cauliflower cheese there is stewed apple and rice pudding. The apple is sharp. It was not peeled properly. There are rough scraps of skin in it that are almost green. With a stretch of the imagination I could say that they are green. And the cup of tea is not bad. It doesn't have the dishcloth taste it sometimes has. If only it was hotter. That is a luxury I never valued before: a cup of tea, freshly made, hot against my lips. With a fag. Oh God I could kill for a smoke.

When I think I will have to scream because I am so trapped, so helpless, so utterly impotent, I have to calm myself somehow. I exercise and that tires me but still my mind jumps, my fingers twitch for a fag. When I am so sickened by my endless self that I want to vomit, I imagine Peggy and I thank God that at least I am imprisoned on the land, that I am not chained.

On the fourth day the female convicts were taken up on to the deck. Their eyes stung with the sudden garish light. A frisky breeze whipped about the rigging and made smooth bellies of the sails. The decks were crowded. The women emerged last, forming a small group behind the male convicts whose necks craned round for a glimpse of them. Peggy winced at the sight of them, as sorry and villainous-looking a crowd of mortals as she had ever encountered. But then she looked down at her own filthy clothes and felt the roughness of her unkempt hair. Who would not look a villain dressed thus?

The crew and their families, all in their Sunday best, were separated from the convicts by a brass rail. The officers were in naval dress, the guards in red coats, all about was the flashing and sparkling of polished silver and brass. The sea was beaten pewter all around. Peggy's stomach dropped, her mouth gaped at the emptiness stretching away. There was nothing, not a rock, not a ship, not a sight of land, just miles and miles of nothing. Nothing substantial, but water and cloud. And with the whipping fullness of the sails, with the curling wake the ship left behind, Peggy felt the distance growing between herself and Sam.

She was awed by the beauty of the sea. Awed and frightened. It was not pewter all around, not when she really looked. The little ripply waves gave it the look of a beaten pewter mug her mother had, a treasure she'd carried with her from her past, but when she screwed up her eyes, she saw all the colours in the water: the deep, almost black-blue that glittered and paled through every shade of blue until it became green, a thousand greens and grey and brown until it met the silver line of the horizon.

The surgeon superintendent, dressed in his Royal Naval uniform, stood up and read in a flat nasal voice from the Book of Common Prayer. The flat planes of his fleshy face were pink in the sun and his gold tooth winked. The convicts and the crew alike were as silent as they were ever likely to be, although a baby cried. Peggy listened to the creaming noise of the sea, the clink of the rigging, the fat flap of the canvas. There was the continuous clucking of chickens and the occasional squeal of a pig – for there was livestock on board. These sounds formed a backdrop to the pious words of the surgeon as he ceased his reading and began to preach repentance and forgiveness to the miserable wretches before him. They listened with a numb docility caused by hunger, sickness, disorientation – and fear.

He spoke of the organization of life aboard ship for the next hundred days – the estimated duration of the voyage to Botany Bay. The convicts were to labour in the mornings: laundering, holystoning the decks, sluicing and scrubbing their quarters. In the afternoons schools were to be formed, the more able convicts to teach reading and writing to the illiterate. Every day there was to be exercise on board deck – a parade to the tune of a fiddler. All these were privileges, to be earned by docile behaviour. On top of normal rations, each convict was entitled to one half-pint of porter on Saturday evenings at the captain's orders. At this news there was an appreciative rustle. Smoke from the chimney on the galley drifted back over the congregation, a homely kitchen smell, a prodding memory of home, and Peggy's heart was squeezed with a mixture of pain and relief that she had not thought about, or missed, her child, for almost an hour.

When I arrived home for a reading week in February, I felt at once how the atmosphere in the house had changed. For a start, Ursula was still there. She had come to stay for a few days and had never left, or only once to collect all her belongings. And such belongings. They had transformed the house. Everywhere I found unfamiliar objects: a stuffed boxer dog; an elephant's foot umbrella stand; a fish-bone and flower arrangement – and a massive sculpture sauvage that had taken up most of the sitting room. And it wasn't just the things. The intense absorption of Mama and Ursula in each other made me uneasy. It seemed somehow unwholesome. I felt I did not really belong any more, not that Mama did not make me properly welcome.

The sculpture sauvage poked me in the eye when I entered the sitting room. It was a great dangerous branching thing, half a tree by the look of it, dismembered and reassembled, stained with dye and hung with leaves and berries, feathers, ragged tufts of sheep's wool and animal hair, a squirrel's tail and small yellowish skulls.

'It has seasonal potentialities,' Ursula explained, mistaking my silent horror for admiration. My eye watered and I wiped away the tears.

'You see, Jenny, when we go for a walk which is most days – isn't it, dear,' she looked fondly at Ursula, 'we pick up a little something and add it . . .'

'And take things off, of course,' Ursula said. 'To maintain the integrity of the thing.'

'Or if they start to smell,' Mama added. 'It's a bit like a Christmas tree, isn't it, Urse? We could use it at Christmas, couldn't we? Hang it with baubles, string up some lights . . .'

'Stick a fairy on top,' I added.

'Please . . .' Ursula grimaced.

'I'll make some tea then,' Mama said and went into the kitchen.

'Don't you find it a nuisance?' I asked Ursula who had sat down beside me. 'I mean it gets in the way, doesn't it? It poked my eye when I came in.'

'It demands vigilance,' Ursula conceded, 'but that's part of its function – to draw attention to space. You should not take space for granted.'

I could think of no answer to that. We were silent for a moment. I could hear the familiar sound of Mama in the kitchen, the sound of my childhood.

'How long are you staying?' Ursula asked.

'That's what I was going to ask *you*.'

'Ah . . . you don't know yet,' Ursula said. 'Lilian was waiting to see you face to face, so to speak, to give you the news.'

Mama came in with a tray of tea and in her hurry, snagged her cardigan on a twig.

'Vigilance, Lilian,' Ursula reminded, getting up to unsnag her. And something stirred in me, an uncomfortable memory. What was this like? I had the muffled tantalization of a *déjà vu*.

'Here we are,' Mama said. 'Yes, Jenny, I do have some news. Good news I hope you'll think. Ursula has moved in. For good.'

'For good?' I accepted a cup of tea. The same old cups and saucers. Everything so familiar and yet odd.

'Yes. It seems the most sensible course,' Ursula said, 'since we hit it off so well. Financially and otherwise. Lilian doesn't need this great big place.'

'There's me,' I pointed out, in a small voice.

55

'But hardly, dear,' Mama said. 'You're hardly here.'

'You've flown the nest.' Ursula sounded decisive.

'No I haven't,' I said. 'I'm at university but I need somewhere to come home to. I haven't left. Not properly.'

Ursula and Mama exchanged glances that told me they'd anticipated this very conversation. I sipped my tea, good old familiar tea made in a pot with a chipped spout, kept warm beneath an old crocheted cosy, and as I sipped I tried to swallow the lump that was growing in my throat.

'It's still my *home*,' I said.

'Oh nobody's denying that, dear.' Ursula grated her cup across her saucer to stop it dripping on her lap.

'I *should* have consulted you,' Mama said, 'before we decided.' She smiled at me, a pleading smile that demanded a return.

Ursula looked at her sharply. 'Not that it would have made *much* difference. I mean you're hardly likely to object, are you, Jenny?'

I shrugged. 'S'pose not.'

'And it is your home,' Mama said. 'You'll always be welcome, you know that.'

'Eternally,' said Ursula with a little too much emphasis.

'OK.' I had finished my tea. 'I'll go upstairs and unpack. Do a bit of reading.'

'Good idea.' Mama was relieved. 'You look a bit pale, dear, doesn't she, Urse? Needs a good rest. We'll feed her up.'

I squeezed out between the chairs and the branches and took my bag upstairs. The walls of the stairs and landing were hung with knobbly weavings in turd-like shades – but at least my room had been left untouched. It was a square room with a square window overlooking the garden. This was my familiar view. The garden was February-bare. The pond Bob had made out of my childish attempt to dig to Australia glinted in the afternoon sun with a white winterish wink. My bedspread was the same old worn pink candle-wick, my trinket box still stood on my dressing table. I wound it and lifted the lid and watched the ballerina pirouette to the jingly sound of the *Nutcracker Suite*. Inside was my charm-bracelet, a hideous thing hung with golden wish-bones and hearts and fish. Valuable, Bob had always sworn. Twenty-two carat. It was not yet complete. I had been promised a charm every birthday and Christmas until I was twenty-one – so there were two more spaces. It weighed a ton already. One of the charms was a little clasped book. I flipped open the catch and a concertina of scenes of Paris spilled out. The photographs looked dated now, tinted in surreal shades.

I unpacked the few books and clothes I'd brought with me. I planned to write my T. S. Eliot essay this week. I lay down on the bed and opened the *Collected Poems*. I had used Tom's card as a bookmark so that every time I opened the book I was reminded of him and every reminder was like a squeeze of my heart. I planned to ring him later, that was the sweet secret I sucked on, that moderated my reaction to Ursula's presence in the house. For now Tom and I were lovers, regular lovers, once, twice a week, whenever we could snatch the time. I knew we looked absurd together. He was over thirty years my senior and already I had been taken for his daughter. I always saw the lines of age on his face. I did not kid myself. I saw the way that his chest and belly were slack and I did not care. I noticed the swollen blue veins behind his knees and these imperfections made him perfect in my eyes. I loved him because of them. I loved him for having those thirty years on me. I saw them like a bag of silver, thirty pieces, like thirty pieces of wisdom. Tom Wise – perfect name. Thomas William Wise.

I was hardly jealous of his wife. In fact I almost pitied her. 'She is *too* bloody beautiful,' he said one night. We'd made love and were wound stickily, lazily together. 'Too bloody beautiful to live up to. Too bloody perfect. Never loses her cool, not for a moment, not once in eight years.' He told me that the child was his but not hers. His first wife had taken their two-year-old son and left him holding the baby. He had had a fling, just a fling, *meaningless*, and she had found out and gone. Just like that. 'So unreasonable,' he complained, and I agreed, so impetuous when children were concerned, so irresponsible. Moira had been one of his students, a promising flute player. She'd been so lovely, so helpful and understanding that it seemed the most natural thing in the world that she should move in and help with the baby. And one thing led to another, as they do, and when his divorce had come through they had married. 'She's wonderful with Beth,' Tom said. '*Wonderful*. But there's nothing left between Moira and me. No passion. Sometimes I think it was a mistake. A rebound thing.' He screwed his face up into a lovable rueful look.

On the train I had been reading *The Lovesong of J. Alfred Prufrock: I grow old, I grow old*. Tom never worried about being old. Well, he wasn't old, just older. *I shall wear the bottoms of my trousers rolled*. No, it's not true that he didn't worry about his age. I saw the way he pulled his belly in when he passed a mirror and the potions he used to stimulate his follicles. He never told me his age. I found it on his passport. He was fifty-two, I was twenty. It was an overwhelming gap.

He had been showering when I looked at his passport. It was our first night together in a hotel at Heathrow, the night before he flew away to record the backing for some American singer. I had had to engineer the situation . . . force the moment to its crisis. He would have left it. Though he *was* in love with me. His feelings when he saw me again had been as strong as my own. But he would have left it because he was honourable. He had betrayed his first wife and had promised himself that he would never betray Moira. That's what he told me, forgetting, apparently, the summer house episode. He would have given up all that was promised between us if I had not insisted. He thought it unfair to implicate me in his complex life, he said. But I would not have it. He was my first love and I would not let him go, not for something as nebulous as honour. And she was too perfect, too reasonable, not once in eight years had she lost her temper. It made him want to scream. It made him want to hit her. He needed *me*.

So I pleaded with him to see me, just once, although once was not all I had in mind. I knew that once we met he would be unable to resist me – and I was right. He took me out for a meal in an Italian restaurant. The tablecloths were snowy white, in the candle-light our faces were soft, our glasses of wine glowed like rubies. He fed me sweet whipped cream from the tip of a silver spoon. Under the table his knees pressed my knees until I thought I would faint. When we parted I said I wanted to spend a night with him, just one night to finish what we'd started. I don't know how I was so bold, it makes my face hot to remember. But he was not hard to persuade. He suggested the night before he flew to the States. It was an easy trick to play on Moira, flying one day later than she thought – hardly a trick at all. We drank red wine in bed that first night, splashing it, making deep blackberry stains on the starchy sheets. We lay naked in lamplight for a long time after we'd made love, just examining each other. The hair on his chest was turning grey and I kissed it, kissed his nipples until they rose in little peaks and he laughed and pushed me off. He complained about Moira's tiresome perfection, he bit my shoulder and then he went into the shower.

While he was showering, I buried my face in his pillow to enjoy the smell of him and I noticed all the hairs that he had shed on the white cotton. I picked them off and put them together. Quite a little bouquet of them and I put them in my purse to keep with my twist of melted glass. While the water still hissed down, I looked at his passport and discovered his age. I looked at the out-of-date photograph. It showed a darker-haired man with a firmer jaw, wearing a scarf round his neck, a scarf that I had never seen and would never see and I felt a spurt of jealousy, for nothing in particular, for all the overwhelming sea of his past: of lovers, friends, travels, clothes, meals, illnesses, triumphs, dejections. He had been thirty-two when I was born, already a grown man, already a husband . . . The passport told me that his birthday was in August and that the child, Bethany Beulah Wise, was on his passport but that his wife was not.

When he came out of the shower, dripping wet, a towel around his waist, he said he was hungry, so we rang room-service and ordered mushroom omelettes and then we lay in each other's arms until morning. He slept and I watched him, his face loose, his breath deep and throaty. I touched his penis while he slept and felt it twitch, then he turned over and I pressed my face against his back, between his shoulder-blades and breathed in his smell which was the right smell, the smell I wanted to spend all the nights of my life breathing.

I must try not to experience emotion. Emotion is motivation. Same root, see? Emotion drives one to action: to flee, to pursue, to make love, to fight. But here there is nothing to do. No contact which will allow me to expend emotion. So I try to separate memory and imagination from emotion. Rage in a blank walled box and you will know frustration. I do not rage. I exercise. That is good for the body, and perhaps, the soul. *And one and two and over and down and* . . . I bend and twist. I jump and jump, run up and down on the spot. They look. Who? *And stretch and stretch and stretch and stretch*. Before I look up and catch the eye of Jenks.

'Hello!' I say, as if she is a neighbour dropping in for coffee. She hesitates before she shuts the slot and I hear the twisting of the lock. She won't last long. She probably has applications in everywhere for teacher training or nursing. There is no joy in trying to be nice to us. She is nervous. She brought in my last tray, and Barker stood on guard by the door – as if I'm likely to fly at Jenks and sink my teeth into her white neck. I noticed how trembly nervous she was, how the nails are bitten down on her long pink fingers.

I keep saying four walls, but of course that is not true for one of the walls, the most fascinating, has a door. The walls are brick painted pale grey and the paint is pitted as if women have butted and scraped at it. There is a small partial graffito in one corner. FCUK it says, and the beginning of another letter. I have pondered for hours on how this was achieved. Some woman must have had a sharp implement concealed about her person. Impossible? I would say so. I wonder how the message would have finished. FCUK FOF perhaps, or FCUK EM? Some hope, in here.

The light is sunk in the ceiling. No flex to dangle from, no bulb to smash and slice the skin.

And the heavy metal door is painted dark grey – a classy colour under different circumstances. It too is chipped and pitted and then there is the flap like a mouth in the door that opens and snaps shut over the peering eyes. There is a little lock at the bottom, round and silver. I do not hate the eyes of the screws, or the screws themselves. We are all in this together. Christ! I would not do their job for the world. I would rather be banged up in here. Is that really true? An interesting question.

Only three more days and I'll be out again. I'll have a smoke and see daylight and see Debbie. I'll wash, lather under my arms and between my legs, shampoo my hair. I'll wear my own clothes and I'll work. What kind of work, I'll have to wait and see. I should not even think about the garden. If I let myself hope for that I could not face the disappointment. But I am longing to work. I would even love to be back with the teddy bears, coughing up stray fluff from the fur fabric with my morning fag. I used to hate it, the monotony, the high buzz of the sewing machines, the sharp needle stabbing in and in and in, drawing the thread through. Usually the bears were grey or brown, high-class bears for high-class children. What would their mummies say if they knew who had made them? The sewn up skins were piled by the door, eyeless, flat empty teddy skins. Sometimes the bears are pink or blue, and once we did pandas. Oh the excitement of black and white! I used to hate that monotony but now I would kill for it. Of course I would not kill, but I would give anything – if I had anything to give – for the monotony of work and paid work too.

I bet they put me in the laundry. Well even that, even the bleach, the starch, the steam and the reddened hands, the dermatitis, the gaping pores and the lank hair of the laundry workers would be better than this. Better than nothing.

If I had money now, if there were things to buy, what would I choose? Pink soap: luxury, lathery soap with an artificial smell. Tobacco of course. It's killing me, not smoking. The cruelty. They could send in a roll-up with supper. Instead of supper. Perhaps I should simply ask. Ingratiate myself with Jenks. My lungs yearn for the hot sting of smoke, the buzz, the slope down into relaxation as the smoke rolls out. I didn't smoke before, not outside where it is real. I will not when I am released. But here it doesn't count: smoke, swear, lie, it doesn't count. It is not the real world.

It is *not* the real world. Life in here is like a game, a compulsory game. So although I would say I'm a non-smoker, in here I do and that is not a contradiction. If I could have anything now, what would it be? Not a million pounds, not world peace, not even, at this moment, my liberty. It is too difficult to be free. No, I would have a bottle of wine – something rough and red – and some tobacco and papers. And a chair to sit on. And a book to read. *And Tom.*

Oh just see how I torture myself!

Sometimes I think I can hear breathing. I hold my own breath and, no, it is not me. It is an even breathing, calm as a sleeping child's. At first I was afraid. Thinking of ghosts, the ghost of some poor woman, – the graffiti women perhaps – who managed to smuggle a weapon in with which to harm herself. Or the ghost of a woman who passed away in despair. Or perhaps I am simply mad, hearing breath like hearing voices. It was said by some that I *was* mad, by those who could not comprehend that I was simply bad. Now I am not afraid of the sleepy breathing rhythm, rather it comforts me. And I am not all bad.

THE CUNNING MAID

Peggy was not a bad person, only greedy for a bit of brightness for her son – who was, after all, the son of a lord.

The *Cunning Maid* rocked her way across the ocean. Now that Sarah was gone, it was just Peggy and Hester chained to the bunk a good part of the time. And although Sarah had vanished as completely as if she had never been there – indeed her name was hardly spoken again – Peggy left room for her, not liking entirely to eclipse her space. Peggy's motherliness, all that love with such a distant and receding object, spilled over on to Hester. Guttersnipe she called her affectionately, holding the small hand in her own, marvelling at the branched bones under the roughened skin. Hester was a fisherman's daughter, and not as delicate by half as she looked but both she and Peggy enjoyed the pretence.

It was a poor kind of life, no poorer could they imagine as the hours passed in the dim womanish stink below deck. For they could not imagine isolation. The plans of the surgeon superintendent hardly came to fruition. No schools were set up, for between some of the male convicts and some of the crew, there was trouble. Rose's husband was among the men – together they had been convicted of fraud. They were not permitted to speak to each other, but somehow, he managed to communicate to her an idea of what was happening. The brother of one of the convicts was among the crew and rival factions were growing, trouble was rumbling and threatening, because convicts and crew to-

63

gether were aligning themselves against the command of the *Cunning Maid*. The scent of danger leaked out to the captain and so most of the convicts were kept stowed for hours on end in the dark of the hull till, when they did emerge, they did so with blinking eyes like moles who cannot stand the light.

And in the gloom that grew steamy as the ship rolled farther south, as the sun heated the fabric of the ship so that even far below deck the timber was hot against their skin and spots of melted pitch dropped and burned them, even in that gloom, friendship grew between Peggy and Hester like a shimmering bubble, a glistening fabulous thing. They talked for hours, learning the details of each other's lives, reliving memories together until sometimes they became confused in the sleepy heat. Was it the baby Hester who had tumbled down a well one day and been hauled out unharmed, or was it Peggy?

Hester would put her finger on the dart-shaped scar on Peggy's cheek and Peggy would tell her the peacock story. Hester, who had never seen a peacock, only half believed that such a creature existed and even for Peggy, the memory of the hundred iridescent eyes rising tauntingly from the back of a bird began to seem fantastical.

The convicts spent some time on deck too, exercising and working. They marched round every morning, while a male convict, a young fellow with hair the colour of cinders, played the fiddle. The music helped to lift their feet but the sun pressed down on them, hot flat hands smothering. They gasped at its foreign strength. Hard to believe they were in southern seas, in foreign climes, when all around them were the same voices. The same faces. Only the light changed, the character of the sun, and the colours.

Much against the surgeon's will, as the sneering edge in his voice made clear, the captain had insisted that the Saturday night ration of porter for every prisoner was still to be dispensed. He might have thought it a way of keeping the peace, a generosity that might sweeten the tempers of those that simmered in the depths of the ship, but if he thought that then he was a fool. In order to include an element of exercise in the ritual, the fiddler played and each prisoner had to dance through a door into the room, prance round the room, receive and swallow their porter and dance out again. There was much occasion for abuse. People were tripped up as they danced, or if not tripped ridiculed. Many of the women would rather have gone without the drink than have to dance past a row of rowdy crewmen who laughed at their breasts jumping against their dresses and passed loud lewd comments that angered the male prisoners on the females' behalf. It was a ritual that only served to increase the ill-feeling and unease.

Back in the female quarters after the drink there was much mirth. Women sang songs and taught each other new ones. They swapped bawdy stories, talked lewdly of the men they had known till Peggy was shocked and tempted to stop Hester's ears. Rose joked about her husband's member, claiming she needed a spy-glass to find it and had to take his word for it that it ever got inside her at all – she couldn't feel a thing. And it got to many of them comparing the size of men they had known, laughing at their silly pride in the stiff or drooping rod of flesh. One woman, who had been the keeper of a country inn, silenced everyone with her story of a traveller she had spent a night with whose member was as big as a half-grown marrow and always hard, so he had to wear a long coat to conceal it. 'Nearly too big to get in,' she said, 'thought I was like to come in half.' And many of the women moaned and wriggled at the thought, for they were frustrated, the ones who were accustomed to a regular lover, and even for those who were not, the conversation tickled their fancy.

One day, the motion changed. Peggy woke to quiet and stillness. She could not imagine what had happened. She had become so used to the rolling that the stillness made her dizzy. Hester who had spent half her childhood on fishing boats knew at once. 'We are becalmed,' she said. When they were taken up on to deck they saw that the sails had dropped and the sky was white and stagnant. The sun burned like a fever and the sea was a sullen and greasy expanse of yellow and grey. There was an ill-at-ease feeling, the temperature rose without a breeze and the convicts and the crew alike muttered darkly among themselves.

Peggy and Hester were set to work scrubbing the deck, first with flat stones and sand and then with buckets of sea water. Their dresses steamed wet about their knees as they knelt and scrubbed. It was painful work, painful for their joints stiffened by habitual confinement, painful where the sun burned down on their uncovered heads and arms, painful where the sand rubbed sores between their fingers which the salt water stung. The sun swelled in the sky above them, like the pupil of a huge, enraged eye. Together but alone, perhaps they might have borne these hardships, encouraging each other, reminding each other that this was not for ever, this hell was part of a passage to something else and, in the end, part of the journey back home. But behind them stood two of the crew, greater villains in Peggy's eyes than any of the convicts. For who would skivvy on a convict ship but men with no choice? These were simply villains who had escaped capture – so far. They were crude wretches. Peggy had lost count of the number of hands up her skirt, fingers pinching, pushing in, breasts crushed in rough hands. She had left her shame in England. It angered her more on Hester's behalf when one of them stuck his fat filthy fingers up her skirt. Because of Hester's child-body and innocence, it made tears jump to Peggy's eyes when they did that.

Hester laughed at Peggy. 'I've grown up among fisher-folk,' she reminded her. 'I'm no stranger to the ways of men.' And indeed Hester was a most eager and lascivious listener to the Saturday night stories that grew more fantastic by the week.

'But not all men,' Peggy said, 'not always. It is not like that when there is *love*.' She was anxious that Hester should not believe all men to be such foul wretches. 'If you love a man and he loves you, it is heaven.'

'I am sure.' Hester arched her eyebrows, bleached white by the sun. She was half serious, half mocking. She made it plain that though Peggy was the one who *knew* love, who had had a child, she saw her as the innocent one. Peggy had told her dreamily, many times, about the tenderness between herself and Percy, how they had learned about love together, laughing and gasping at the sweetness of their union, and Hester had nodded, envious and sceptical.

'I would not go back on it,' Peggy said. 'Despite everything, I would not undo a thing.'

'Not the peacock feathers?' Hester asked.

Peggy smiled. 'No. I would have been defter, quicker. I would not have been captured.' And it was true, it was only the capture she regretted, not the impulse that had driven her to her crime, for Sam *deserved* those feathers and the bird was unbearably impudent, strutting in the fine garden, taunting baby Sam with what he could not have.

Sometimes she closed her eyes in the strange white salt heat of the middle ocean, closed her ears against the sounds of the sea and the ship and the swearing and tried to conjure her home. Cool green, lush grass, shadow and damp. The feel of a green leaf between her fingers . . . the taste of an apple: the exquisite scrunch through the skin and the bright juice on her tongue; blackberries glowing on September brambles; frost ferns on puddles; the terrible melting beauty of a snowflake. She groaned to remember the taken for granted things. And the main thing: the skin of her baby, the milky silk of it, those cheeks red as apples themselves. Sometimes she couldn't believe Sam was real, that any of it was real – the coolness or the kindness. It was as if the sun was burning the old life out of her skull. Or as if her life had begun on this ship and the rest was just a dream.

As they scrubbed the deck the sun beat in waves on their heads, the sweat dripped from their foreheads and ran down their aching arms. Behind them stood two of the crew, two of the wretchedest devils – Peggy thought – ever to draw breath. They jeered at Peggy and Hester, they prodded their backsides with their toes, prodded hard, pushing them forward on the wet deck, until Hester's arms gave way and she tipped forward, banging her head and grazing her cheek. Peggy looked round at the two men who towered above them, laughing now, as Hester struggled to pull herself up. The heat and the hurt fused in Peggy's heart and a redness suffused her body, rose behind her eyes: a scarlet well of anger.

Which is a luxury I cannot afford. Anger. Hate. No, they cost too much. Anger. Hate. All those needles in the soul, all that searing. Oh, you need energy for hate, energy to spare. It eats you up. Hate can eat the soul from within you leaving a smiling shell. Love, too. If there is nowhere to direct it, no one to receive it, or if it is thrown back in your face, it can eat you too, with more sweet pain. Hate and love are made of longing. And I will not long. I will try not to long for tobacco or freedom or for the kiss of a man. Certainly I will not long for a man.

The time is going. That is the good thing about time, that it is reliable. It passes. It will pass and I will be out of here. Strange, almost alarming, to think that I *will* be out of here, out of the swaddling of my own imagination in a place of real voices and faces. I will work in the laundry – that is it. That is what I am bound to have to do and I will do it with good grace. My fingers will swell and wither with the water and the bleach and the starch and my hair will hang in rats' tails. But I will smile.

There is no one else to love so I will love myself. It is either that or hate and I cannot hate myself. Love of self is not pride. I am not proud of what I have done, not proud of myself. My self. Self. Where is my self? What is it? Perhaps I do not have one.

Sometimes I look at my hands. My palms are square, my little fingers crooked. My future is scribbled there, my past and my personality in the fine mesh of lines, in the unique swirls on my finger ends.

*   *   *

My hands on his skin. His weight on top of me, almost squashing, a wonderful weightiness, a pinning down. My hands in his hair, soft as a child's hair. My hands on the hot skin of his neck, the first knobs of his spine. Knotty tension in the shoulder muscles which my hands can squeeze away. I am good at that, he says. A patch of hair between his shoulder blades, coarse as dogs' hair. Softness further down, a little fatness round the middle but good. I like that, I like his middle age. I am pinned down by his weight and the weight of his years. The flat of his spine, a small plateau and then the division of his buttocks, two furry hills and the dark valley where my fingers reach. My hands did love him. Every printed finger pad fed on him.

I look at them, the pink whorls and scrolls, the criss-crosses, the stars, the triangles, the little scar on my fingertip. How fantastically detailed I am!

'Jenny, it's ready.' I woke fuzzily from a dream that shrank back through the doorway into the darkness of the dreaming place before I could recognize it. My mouth was dry. I had slept crumpled on the crumpled candlewick. My hair was wild about my face, stuck glueily in the corners of my mouth. I could not think for a second when it was, why I was here. A bit of dream leaked out round the light edges of the dark door. There was a girl I used to know, Bronwyn, a girl who disappeared. In the dream she was sitting among a row of dusty dolls on a shelf and she grinned at me and winked.

'Jenny!' Mama called again, her old voice making its familiar journey up the stairs so that I woke as a child. And then as I rubbed my eyes and picked the hair out of my mouth I saw Tom's card on the bed, his name and the telephone number I loved for its rhythm 242 4262. I heard Ursula's voice, not the words, just the spiky edge of it, bossing Mama by the sound of it, and I remembered how it always used to be Bob's undertone I heard, his complaint.

I got up and pulled my fingers through my tangled hair. After we'd eaten I would telephone Tom. I'd go out to the telephone box to do it. I did not want Mama to know. She'd given me significant looks whenever the subject of the beautiful woman, or the summer house fire had come up – but she had never asked me what had happened.

Mama doled out platefuls of toad-in-the-hole and fried potatoes.

'Notice anything different?' Mama said, leaning forward as I took my first mouthful.

I tasted and considered. The sausages were like something knitted. 'What?' I asked.

'Soya protein,' Ursula said. 'We've gone vegetarian.'

'It's quite nice,' I said.

'Just an experiment,' Mama said. 'Bob *toyed* with the idea.'

'Good idea,' I said.

Ursula ate with her mouth open and made a dreadful squelchy noise. I kept my eyes averted, but my ears became fascinated and would not stop listening. She chewed regularly, six times each mouthful and then a clicking gulp as she swallowed before the next.

'It wasn't a conscious decision,' Mama said, after an uncomfortable pause in which I believe even she became embarrassed by the noise of Ursula's mastication.

'What wasn't?'

'Going vegetarian. I mean we didn't discuss it . . . over the weeks we found we were buying less meat . . . becoming quite experimental. And then we thought, well why not go the whole hog.' She laughed. 'Oh dear, the whole hog!' She looked at Ursula who didn't see the joke, who looked irritably at Mama.

'Can one make, I wonder,' she asked querulously, 'an *un*conscious decision?'

'Pardon?' Mama said, the smile falling from her face.

'You said it wasn't a conscious decision. I was just wondering if it's possible to make an *un*conscious decision.'

'Well, I don't know . . .' Mama looked crestfallen and I re-

70

experienced the feeling of *déjà vu* I'd had earlier. And then recognized it. It was Ursula's presence in the house, and the effect she was having on Mama. She was acting on Mama as Bob had, making her nervous, subtly oppressing her, bullying her kindly into shape.

'It's a common enough figure of speech,' I defended. 'And in any case, of course you can.'

'Can what, Jenny dear?' Mama asked.

'Make an unconscious decision.'

'Nonsense,' Ursula snapped.

'You can wake up one morning decided about something without formally working it out.'

'Oh, I'm not denying that,' Ursula said. 'What about the cake, Lil? You can *come* to a decision by a back-door, so to speak, *sub*conscious route, but not make it. *Make* implies deliberate action, don't you think?'

'You and your brains,' Mama said fondly, looking from one of us to the other. 'You've lost me.'

'It's still been made,' I insisted.

'*Come* to, that's quite a different matter.' Ursula smiled and put down her fork with a sharp clink that signalled that the subject was closed, and that hers was the final word. 'What about the cake, Lil?' She looked at me, 'Your grandmother tells me it's your favourite. She made it this morning.'

Mama opened a tin and took out a marble cake. She cut the first slice for me. It was a deep, sweet-smelling cake, loose and crumbly, swirled pink and yellow and brown inside.

'Thank you,' I smiled at Mama. 'I haven't had this for years. Remember you used to make it for my birthday? I used to think the inside was like maps of foreign countries.'

'I remember! You used to say you were eating Africa, Australia! Stopped making it when Bob died. We went mad on shop cakes then, didn't we, Jenny? Shop cakes and television and hairdressers!' She laughed and then checked herself. 'Poor Bob.' She looked down at her hands.

'A man of principle by the sound of it,' Ursula said.

'Certainly that,' I agreed.

We were eating at the table in the kitchen. After Bob had died, Mama and I had taken to eating in front of the television, our food on special TV trays with spindly legs in front of us. But with the sculpture in the sitting room that was hardly practical. I realized that I had not seen the television among the branches.

'It's in Lilian's room,' Ursula said.

'What?'

'The television.'

'How . . .'

'Lilian was saying that after your grandfather's death you were "mad on it".'

'Ursula's very intuitive,' Mama explained. 'Aren't you, dear? Almost psychic I should say.'

Ursula looked at me coolly. There were cake crumbs stuck in the soft hairs round her mouth. *I don't like you* I thought, loud and clear, hoping that she *could* read my mind.

'It's in Lilian's room, as I said.' Ursula gave me the chilliest of smiles. 'Do feel free to come in if you like, and watch.'

Who was *she* to invite *me* into Mama's bedroom? 'I've got work to do,' I said stiffly. 'Books to read, an essay to write. No time for television. I'm quite out of the habit.'

'Glad to hear it,' Ursula said. 'A modern curse, don't you think?' But I ignored her.

'I thought we might go shopping,' I said to Mama. 'Just look round, window shopping really. Have lunch somewhere nice.'

'That would be lovely!' Mama said. 'We haven't done that for ages. What about it, Urse?'

'Oh I'm sure I'm not included in Jenny's scheme,' said Ursula, with accurate spite.

'If you want,' I grudged.

'Oh *no*, I wouldn't *dream* of intruding. Coffee?' She looked at Mama, who rose and began fiddling with a great chromium contraption.

'I'm sorry, Urse. I still can't get the hang . . .'

'Bella,' Ursula explained. 'My espresso machine . . . a little temperamental but she makes the most exquisite brew.'

'Not for me,' I said. I could take no more of Ursula at that moment and my finger was itching to dial Tom's number. I rubbed the end of it where there was a slight tenderness still, a soft raised ridge of scar. 'Leave the washing-up,' I said, 'I'll do it later.'

I was angry. Angry not so much with Ursula as with Mama. After Bob's death it had taken her years to relax, to escape from the cramping effect of Bob's foibles, to realize that his foibles had died with him. She'd been free to cut her hair, wear nylon next to her skin if she so desired, to watch TV, to have the old heating system ripped out of the house and a modern gas boiler installed. And now in the face of her freedom she had allowed Ursula to latch on, Ursula who had an uncannily Bob-like quality, of obliquely criticizing, of making her self-conscious and uncomfortable. Only I thought it was worse because I did not even like Ursula. I did not like the way she looked or the way she spoke or the things she said, and I did not like all the awful stuff that she had brought with her, all the revoltingly homespun hangings, the dead desiccated and stuffed things. I had discovered a mock dental surgery peopled with stuffed newts in a glass box in the bathroom which made me feel quite nauseous as I cleaned my teeth.

But in my room, with the door closed behind me, and all my things untouched, I let my anger and irritation go. I looked in the mirror at the face Tom loved. I traced the edges of my lips with my fingertip. When he was not with me, I could hardly believe he was real. I picked up his card and put it in the pocket of my jeans. Not that I needed it. His number was tattooed for ever in my memory.

I shouted good-bye and banged out of the house. It was a dark, raw February evening, the air like dog's breath on my face. I walked along the familiar street, so recently *my* street. Now it was not. That house was no longer my home. I couldn't take it for granted any more, not with Ursula ensconced. I felt displaced. I also felt an exciting sense of impending freedom, as if the string that held me to my childhood was unravelling.

I looked through the windows of the houses. In almost every one a television flickered. They all looked so cosy behind their glass, their half-drawn curtains, all the families. By one window stood a woman holding a small baby up against her shoulder, patting its back. She looked out as if she was waiting for someone, her husband or her lover. I could hear the baby wailing. I could almost feel it in my arms. I allowed myself a day-dream. I allowed myself to be that woman behind glass, that baby to be Tom's baby, Tom to be in his car hurrying home to me with wine and flowers and a nightful of kisses.

I reached the telephone box and dialled Tom's number. I knew he knew I'd be phoning so he should pick up the phone upstairs. He had a studio upstairs, a separate flat really, he said, but if he was not there his wife might answer from downstairs. 'No problem,' he said when I mooted this possibility. 'People are always ringing, men, women. Just say you'll ring back.' It was not the wife that answered the phone on this occasion though, it was the child.

'Hello,' she said. 'Who are you?'

'Is your daddy . . .' I began and then Tom picked up the extension upstairs.

'I think it's that lady from Christmas,' the child said.

'Put the receiver down, Lamb-chop,' Tom said.

'Daddy . . .'

'Put it down.'

'But, Daddy . . . Mummy said . . .'

'Now!' The receiver was slammed forcibly down. I heard Tom sigh.

'She's unnervingly good at voices that girl,' he said. And then, 'Jenny darling. How are you? Are you home? Safe journey?'

I smiled into the phone and relaxed at the sound of his voice. I enjoyed the way his voice changed when he talked to me, the way he became so lover-like.

'Fine. Only it's murder here. This friend has moved in with my grandmother. Ursula, do you remember?'

'The sea-horse woman! She's moved in! I don't know. This older generation, so precipitous!'

I laughed. 'Too right. And I don't feel at all at home now. They practically gave me my marching orders.'

'No.'

'Yes. And you should see the place, full of branches and stuffed dogs.'

'Oh, Jenny . . . how am I going to do without you for a week?'

'Maybe you won't have to,' I said. 'I can't bear this. Couldn't we meet? I want you, Tom.' I flushed, standing in the dimly lit phone box, reading the graffiti: DONNA IS A SHAG-BAG. UP THE TOWN. GAZ LUVS MAZ FOR EVER, feeling shameless.

'And I want *you*,' he murmured. But he did not know what I meant. I didn't just want to make love to him, I meant I wanted all of him, every day, for ever and ever.

'Can't I see you?' I insisted.

He hesitated. 'Well, actually Moira's taking Beth to her mother's for a few days. It's half-term.'

'So we could meet? Why didn't you say before?' A little bubble of excitement rose and popped against my ribs.

'I was trying to resist suggesting it, but I suppose you could come here.'

'To your *house*?' I had never considered the possibility. I had been content to be entirely illicit, an inhabiter of borrowed flats and hotel rooms.

'My studio is separate,' he said, 'self-contained. I often have people staying up there. Colleagues, friends, if I don't want to burden Moira. Or if the house is full.'

'But what if someone sees me?'

'No one would think anything. You are a musician, aren't you? What is it that you play? The trombone?'

I giggled. 'No, no, the trumpet. And the cello.'

'Well then, I look forward to playing with you.' My knees were weakening with desire for him. I could imagine the smile on his face, the way he was cradling my voice in his hand. 'Come on Wednesday. You can stay till Saturday morning – Moira's not due back till Sunday, but just to be on the safe side . . .'

'Oh, Tom.' I felt I had been given a slice of heaven, this was beyond my greediest imaginings. I had been hoping for a tumbled afternoon on a hotel bed. Or even just a drink with him – and I was being offered four whole days of Tom. The longest, the most, I had ever had.

'It'll be terribly boring for you,' he said.

'Don't be silly!'

'And what about your work?'

'Oh stuff that.'

'I don't want you messing up your degree.'

'I won't.'

'I warn you, you won't get much peace when you're here.'

'I think I can deal with that.'

Once he'd gone, I stood and listened to the silence in the phone, the rustling and shushing of all the space between us. Then I put the receiver down and left the little capsule of grimy light. I didn't go straight home. I was too restless, and couldn't bear an evening of Ursula.

I walked along the main road and looked into the windows of shops. The newsagent was open. I went in and bought a bar of chocolate. I looked at the greeting cards, racks and racks of hearts and flowers – it was nearly Valentine's Day. I had no intention of sending one to Tom, they were all so dreadfully corny. Would he think me ridiculous? I picked the cards up one after another. Really, most of them were quite revolting. But he needn't know it was me. He might wonder. I realized that it was on Valentine's Day that I would be seeing him. It would be fun if my card got there first. Though he wouldn't know. I would never admit it was from me. And what about his wife? I didn't care. A

Valentine's card was nothing. If she couldn't cope with a Valentine's card, well . . . I decided to choose the most tasteless, the most utterly fatuous card in the shop so that he would know it was a joke.

I was torn between a padded pink heart which doubled as a cherub's bottom, and a shiny red cellophane heart-shaped window through which could be seen two chipmunk-type creatures, kissing. I opened the cellophane heart card and read the verse: *Oh my darling, when I sleep, I dream that you are mine. The sky is blue, the bells ring out. Please be my Valentine.* I liked the extra pleading note of this one, and the irrelevant sky. I had a stamp in my purse, so I borrowed the newsagent's pen and addressed the envelope, putting nothing inside the card except a question mark. No clue at all.

I posted the card and then walked farther along the High Street, grinning to myself at the thought of his face when he received it. I walked past a cemetery and a mausoleum, towering black against the sky. This had been empty once, one of my lonely haunts – for I had been a strange and solitary child. It had been the haunt of tramps, odd, frightening, temporary people, but now it was a community centre. Posters outside advertised a barn dance, a jumble sale, a toddler group. I wandered round the playground beside it, there was no one else about. I remembered it as it used to be: an old splintery roundabout that shrieked like a donkey if you tried to push it round, empty dangling swing chains and between them the hollows worn by years of swinging children's heels. Now it had been updated. There was a complex log structure with slides and rope ladders. It had nothing to do with me. I wasn't a child. I had no right. Once I regarded the old playground as my own, a deserted place grown round with briars. I had been such an odd child. I turned and walked away.

I tried not to think about Tom as I walked, quickening my pace to get back into the light. I tried to think about work. I had to write an essay on Prufrock. I tried to imagine the fussy self-conscious man, worrying about his etiolated limbs, his bald spot, his fear of being a fool. I imagined the covert, sideways way he looked at women, salivating over the sight of bare arms in lamplight. But I could not keep my mind from Tom, from comparisons with Tom, who had very little self-consciousness about his body. I thought not, then, at least. I imagined what it would be like to make love to Prufrock and shuddered at the thought of the cold crabs of his hands scuttling on my skin. Poor Prufrock and his struggle for expression. Striding through the February dark I knew that he was right. '*It is impossible to say just what I mean.*' His exasperation was justified. Words are clumsy and approximate expressions of feeling. The only way I could express my love, my passion, for Tom was through my body, through the tender profound play of our bodies together. That language. No words held quite that meaning.

And then I stopped, thinking of the words on the stupid Valentine. My face flushed. For of course there would be a clue on the envelope: the Ipswich postmark. I was appalled by my stupidity, humiliation washed over me in hot waves. Such a bloody stupid childish card. And I did not want him to see me as a child. What if he didn't get the joke? I didn't know him well enough . . . he didn't know *me* well enough to know that it was meant as a joke. My ears rang with embarrassment. And the bells, what was it? *The bells ring out.* Oh God, did it mean wedding bells? Would he think I meant wedding bells? Cringing, I hurried back to the post-box but, of course, there was no further collection till morning. I would have to leave the card – potential devastator of my affair – in the box until morning and then beg the postman to let me have it back. I kicked the letter-box before I stalked back home.

I put my head round the sitting room door. Mama was balancing on a ladder threading some vertebrae on to a twig.

'Sheep's,' Ursula explained.

'I'm going straight up,' I said. 'Night.'

'Oh won't you help?' Mama looked beseechingly at me. Her grey hair stood up around her head and her glasses – one lens of which was cracked – had slipped to the end of her nose. 'Jenny's quite artistic,' she said, turning to Ursula.

'No I'm not,' I said. 'Good night.' I went upstairs thinking that Mama looked quite mad, crooked and unkempt. Ursula was not good for her. She was changing Mama, changing the character of the house even. It had been comfortable and dull before her arrival, now it was odd and uncomfortable. Mama was seventy-seven, too old to be changing, too old certainly to be balancing on a ladder mucking about with old bones.

LOVE-BITES

Another night gone. I suck at my arm. The first love-bite has faded to greenish. Inner arms are not good for love-bites. The veins are too deeply buried in the dense white flesh. Necks are best, of course, the curve where the neck meets the shoulder. Tom used to bite me there and leave marks. He sucked my nipples so hard one night that there were dark speckles around them. How I loved him to leave marks on me to treasure in his absence. In the times between our meeting, when I could hardly believe that he was true, it proved our passion.

He didn't let me do it to him, of course. A married man.

Last night I dreamed that I was on a ship, a prison ship, but not like Peggy's. It was a modern cruise liner with a blue pool that didn't move. It was still though the sea all around was rough and grey and the wind blew frills of yellow froth into my face and seagulls wheeled and screamed and brushed the deck with their wing-tips. I was not frightened of the gulls, or of the sea that raged until the waves loomed like crags above the ship. I was not frightened because the pool was undisturbed and I knew that, whatever happened, I could immerse myself in there and I would be safe.

I woke relaxed. I have become accustomed to tension and the relaxation was a peculiar sensation, a feeling of something missing, like the sudden silence when a refrigerator switches off. My limbs were soft, utterly comfortable on the thin mattress under the rough blanket. I am relaxed still. If I close my eyes I can see the stillness of the blue pool, a round pool, deep so that the blue grows deeper the harder I look. This is an escape. How rigid my shoulders have been, my elbows and my knees. The constant gnawing at my temples has vanished.

Time is passing. The earth is turning, the sun flashing its light impartially over mountain, city, ocean, cloud. I am so tiny. It does not matter whether I am here or elsewhere. It does not matter what I have done. Not in the scheme of things. Surely it does not matter? Only I would love to see the sun today, or the rain. Even fog. I would like to breathe outside air. I would like to see a smile. Will I ever make love again? No, I cannot imagine ever letting anyone that close. The tension returns. Can I hear breathing? Sometimes I feel there is someone with me. If I listen hard it disappears, but there is breathing, regular sleepy breathing like the breath of a lover late at night. Once I was afraid. Now I do not mind the sound. It is almost a comfort.

Breakfast arrives with Grant. Sometimes I cannot react when someone comes. I get so used to myself. Grant's sandpapery voice rasps. She is all rough and flaky, dandruff on her shoulders, flecks on her glasses, rough skin on her hands. She does not wince at the stench from my bucket. Not polite but stoical. I almost like her. 'Lovely day,' she remarks and I detect no sarcasm. Out there it probably is. A lovely autumn day: brightness, berries, cobwebs in the hedges. A dewy cobweb, that's what I would love to see. Just that, sparkling gossamer stretched between the twigs of a thorn hedge. A temporary wonder. A spontaneity.

Brown jam on bread, lukewarm tea. It makes me want to weep. But I must try not to feel. It is useless in here to feel. Don't experience emotion. Memory yes, but memory divorced from emotion. Once I studied Wordsworth. Emotion recollected in tranquillity, was a way that he described his poetry. But I cannot do that, therefore I am not, can never be, a poet although that is what I've always wanted to be. I cannot recollect emotion *without* emotion. Perhaps I lack a faculty, some sort of safety-valve. Emotion is emotion, recollected or not. I think the re-collected emotion can be more powerful than that of the moment because it is overlaid with desires, wishes, discontents. And memory plays tricks. My own memory is cruel, it rubs salt in the sore places with its bony fingers. Memory is dangerous but imagination is safe. Peggy is safer than me. She is allowed to feel but I . . . I must not. Must not. Weep? For what? For a fag, proper hot tea, a cobweb in a hedge. What crap. Outside people have these things, much more, and still they are not happy. Was I ever truly happy? People walk past cobwebs, past dim mauve flowers in dewy gardens, past frosted puddles and swaying trees . . . past berries glowing crimson in the hedges and they do not look. Oh they may look but they do not *see*. And I was the same, don't get me wrong. And after a week outside – as much as a week? – I too would take it all for granted again. All the bloody beauty, the comfort of hot tea, the luxury of a book and a fire and a window to gaze from. The unbelievable luxury of love. To think that I, this grimy woman in a rough dress, hair so greasy it lies in rats' tails on my skull, once had a lover who kissed every inch of my body, left the marks of his mouth on my neck and breasts. I cannot bear it. I must not think of that, must not feel. Just must not. It will not be for ever.

I am so lonely I could die.

I set my alarm clock and woke early to its fierce buzz. It interrupted my dreams like a hornet and when I woke enough to switch it off it took me a moment to remember why I had wanted to wake. Then I felt the hot flush of shame again, thinking of the stupid red cellophane heart and the inane verse. I dressed quickly in the clothes I'd dropped on the floor and crept to the bathroom. The spare room – Ursula's room – was next to the bathroom, so I was stealthy. But when I came out, I noticed that her door was not shut, not quite and that her curtains were open admitting a strip of street-light. I peered in. Ursula was not there and the room had an air of emptiness. For a hopeful moment I thought that Ursula had packed her bags and left in the night, but when I got downstairs, there she was in the kitchen brushing her long grey hair. She was bending over brushing it from the roots to the tips. It was impressive hair and her brush crackled through it. Loose hairs drifted to the floor.

'Early bird,' she observed through the hairpins in her teeth. I noticed her brush was backed with seashells and clogged with iron hairs.

'I thought I'd have an early walk,' I said.

'Quite a one for the great outdoors, aren't we?' She gathered her hair and twisted it into a grey snake which she coiled and secured to her head with her pins. 'I'm making tea for Lilian. You?'

I shook my head. 'See you later,' I said. I banged the door behind me and ran, the cold air rasping my lungs. There was a hard frost that twinkled orange on car windscreens under the streetlamps. It was quiet but for the moaning of a milk-float and a car starting here and there, choking on the cold. Exhaust fumes huddled coldly in the gutter. I arrived at the letter-box, just in time, just before the post-office van. The postman got out, ignored me, unlocked the box and began filling his sack.

'Could I have my letter back?' I asked.

He looked up. 'Sorry, darling. Against regs.'

'No one will know.'

He regarded me for a moment and just for a moment, in the half-light, I thought he looked like Tom, about the same age, same height, same build, but his voice was not Tom's, nor his attitude. 'Put it this way, Miss. How do I know that's your letter? That's the property of the Royal Mail once it's through that slot.' He tapped the letter-box emphatically and went back to filling his sack. I could not see the card, or I would have snatched it and run.

'Please,' I said.

'That's more than my job's worth,' he said. 'Now you run

along home.' He swung the sack into the back of his van, slammed shut the door and with a swift officiou the van and drove away. I stood by the empty moment, shrouded in his exhaust fumes, watch the corner and disappear. I felt sick from runn cold morning with the sleep still in my eyes an was angry with the stupid, petty man, so mean of power. But the card was gone. There was no do.

I feel my face as if I am discovering myself for nose feels huge to my fingers, a doughy lump ri though it is not really a big nose, small if anything, and straight. A good feature. But I cannot see it now and it has taken on a different identity. It is ugly. My eyeballs slide under their lids. My eyelashes tickle. I can pull them out, one by one, little black frowns on my hands. My ears are strange, fleshy, succulent leaves. Tom used to bite the lobes, nip quite viciously with his teeth and the pain thrilled through me like electricity.

Not that I like pain. It was just the intensity of the experience, every fibre of me engaged with every fibre of him. That man. Once I bit his beard, bit his chin, but the crunchy hairs caught in my teeth as I pulled away and he shouted. He was really angry with me. 'You don't know how it feels,' he said, stroking his beard tenderly. I apologized and he made love to me too roughly then, pulling my head back by my hair so that my throat was arched, and biting me on the neck, not love-bites but real hard bites, until I screamed at him to stop.

He sat up, trembling. I was frightened, but I knelt and held him from behind. I could hear his heart skittering in his chest.

'Sorry,' he said. 'It's just too strong.'

'I know,' I said. I stroked his chest, his upper arms, his back. I thought I knew what he meant.

When was this? Where? The memories flicker on the walls and there is confusion. I should get the order right. Sometimes I suspect that my memory is mutating, stealthily, each time a detail different, until there is no truth left.

Another time . . . was it before or after? Oh God it is all dissolving. It was a motel. Was it? In London, a snatched meeting. We hardly spoke but clung to each other on the bed, clawed off each other's clothes. It was a desperate, passionate fuck. We clung to each other as if we clung on to life itself and the petals of my mind fell away. I was scattered on the bed. I lost my centre, whatever it is that holds me together. It was like a taste of eternity that moment. I was edgeless, formless and still. And I supposed he felt the same. But suddenly he jumped up.

'*Which* bank did you say you used?' he said, pulling on his trousers and I knew then that while I had lain in scattered ecstasy glimpsing eternity he had been back in the world thinking in minutes and pounds. I snapped back like elastic into my tight skin.

'Why?' I said.

'Just wondered. Fascinated by you.' He pulled in his stomach and did up his zip. 'Every detail.' He bent to kiss me but I dodged his lips.

'What's up?' He put his head on one side, spoke patiently to me as if I was a tiresome child.

'Do you *have* to rush off like this? *Quite* so eagerly.'

He buttoned his shirt. 'You knew I only had an hour.'

'Is Moira expecting you?'

'I'm picking Beth up from a party.'

'Happy families.' I got up from the bed and went into the bathroom. I scrubbed myself with a soapy flannel, trying to rid myself of him, of the stickiness and the smell of sex. Sometimes I was loath to wash, wore that smell like a secret perfume inside my clothes, but now I was angry, wanted him off me and out of me.

'You did *know*,' he said coldly when I emerged. He had his leather jacket on and looked like someone I didn't know. 'I did say. You know the rules.'

I didn't answer, pulled up my pants and tights, fumbled with the fastening on my bra. 'Let me help.' He reached out to hook it for me but I was angry. *So* angry.

'Leave me alone. Why don't you just piss off. You don't want to be late, do you?'

'No,' he said, 'you're right. I'd better go.' He wouldn't play, he wouldn't get angry. If only he had shouted at me, shaken me back into playing by *his* rules. 'I'll phone,' he said and left, just like that. No kiss. A cold click of the door and he was gone.

Anger. It sings in my ears, it fizzes in my veins. He left me there like something hired, like the room itself.

It was the manner in which the scoundrel pushed Hester that enraged Peggy beyond all endurance. A red wrath had risen within her as Hester struggled up from the deck, so that the glinting surface of the sea was dull red, water seen through red glass. Peggy knelt and waited for the man's filthy foot on her own backside, pressing insistently, almost as if it would penetrate her, pushing hard until she too fell forward, banging her forehead on the deck, gritty with the scrubbing sand. She leapt up and turned on the men whose laughing sunburnt faces were like the faces of gargoyles on a church wall and she flew at them. Her nails were sharp and her hands roughened with hard work – and she had the advantage of surprise. She kicked one man in the balls so that he doubled over with a cry of stupefied pain, and grabbed the hair of the other one, twisted his ears, pushed her fingers in his eyes. And when he fought back, when he had her arm twisted up behind her so that she was part frozen with the pain, she bit hard at whatever she could reach, forced her head back to reach the top of his arm, dug her teeth into the coarse stuff of his shirt, ground them together in a paroxysm of pain until she felt the flesh give through the cloth and tasted his blood. She let go and spat disgustedly. He flung her to the deck by the feet of Hester.

The second man had recovered himself. 'Hell-cat,' he said, stepping towards Peggy menacingly. 'You'll pay for this, you scar-faced bitch.' Peggy's hand went to her cheek where the mark of the peacock's beak was risen and inflamed.

The other man said not a word. His face was bleeding, the scurvied skin broken easily by Peggy's furious nails. He clutched at his arm where the dark blood spread. He peered round as if to see who had seen the fight, and Peggy realized with a species of triumph that he was humiliated by the attack. Such a man to be brought low by a female convict. Such a *man*.

Peggy and Hester were shoved below into the oven-hot stench of misery and chained to their bunk. Tears leaked from Peggy's eyes, but there was confusion in the tears. She was not sorry for her anger and the rank taste of the man's blood in her mouth gave her a sickening feeling of pride. Energy pulsed in her temples, and her arm, twisted behind her almost to the point of fracture, ached. She could not lie comfortably and yet she could not move, the heat was too oppressive. Hester's hand stroked her hair back from her brow.

'I'm sorry I did not fight,' she said. 'You were so quick to attack. I was not prepared. You hell-cat.' She laughed miserably.

'Do you think I will be punished?' Peggy asked her.

'Not if there is any justice . . .' Hester began.

'But there is no justice,' Peggy said. They were silent and then Hester began to sing, in a parched, whispery voice:

> Close your eyes and make a wish
> Wish for gold, wish for a dish
> Of buttered porridge
> And salty fish.
> Wish for more,
> Wish for wine,
> Wish for a handsome Valentine.

She sang her nonsense until the energetic rage in Peggy died and for a few moments she drifted off to sleep.

*   *   *

Tom was waiting outside the ticket barriers at the tube station. I had been anxious that he would not be; anxious that his wife would not have gone away after all; anxious that the card had wrecked everything. He had not sent one to me and that taught me that, of course, it is *not* the thing to do. Not in his circles, which were overlapping with, becoming, mine. He wore a brown leather jacket I had not seen before, that creaked newness, and corduroy trousers and my heart lurched at the sight of him and his brown, brown eyes.

'Sweetheart!' He hugged me close to him, kissed the top of my head. The leather of his jacket squeaked against me. I pulled back and smiled at him, trying to guess what he was feeling. I could read no tension, no criticism, no sign of red cellophane hearts or wedding bells in his eyes.

'Lunch,' he said. 'Are you hungry? You look famished, little one. I should feed you up.'

'I am a *bit* hungry,' I said, although this was not true. I was full up with love and anxiety.

'We could go to the pub,' he suggested, 'or there's a good wine-bar. Or we could go straight home and I could cook for you. Open a bottle of wine.'

I smiled.

'Home then?'

'Yes.'

'Do you mind walking? Moira's taken her car.'

We went out into the street. It was drizzling. Tom did not put his arm round me and I didn't reach for him although I longed to, thinking, this is his home patch. If anyone were to see us . . . but longing for someone to see us all the same, for the first crack to appear in his old life, a crack for me to worm into.

It was a long walk from the underground. An elevated motor-way roared over the road and the air was wet and heavy with its fumes. It was bleak, grey and cold. We cut between squat blocks of flats where washing hung hopelessly on the balconies and rubbish squelched under our feet. I marvelled that Tom was so at home in this squalid world. He didn't look around him, didn't say much. He is hurrying, I thought, afraid to be seen.

We walked along a canal tow-path, past a red and green painted barge, its name in curly golden letters: *Hunky-Dory*. All its curtains were drawn and warm light glowed through. I smelled bacon frying. I wished I could be in there with Tom, that that could be our home, *Hunky-Dory*, warm, compact, too small for anyone else ever to enter. The surface of the water was freckled with the rain that fell more steadily now, trickled down my neck, flattening and soaking my hair which, earlier, I had dried so carefully. I wanted to see Tom's home, yet I could not prevent my feet from slowing down. I was afraid, not of how I would see him, but of how he would see me in the place where he was used to seeing his beautiful wife.

We turned into a street of terraced houses, three-storeyed, with wide bay windows.

'Shitty area,' he said, looking at the smashed television set in a front garden, 'but we like it.' I tried not to rankle at the 'we'.

'Nice to be near the canal.'

'Yes it is. Here we are.' He stopped outside a house halfway up the road. The woodwork was painted red and there were bay trees in pots on either side of the front door. He found his keys and we stepped inside.

The house smelled of him. The hall was painted dark green, bicycles leant against the wall. I saw myself reflected in a huge mirror, my hair wet, my nose red. There was a photo of Moira stuck in the edge of the frame looking sleek and beautiful, of course, stuck there as if in mockery of my reflection.

I followed Tom through into the kitchen, a big quarry-tiled space. Everything, all the cupboards, the tables and chairs were old tastefully battered pine and the walls were stuck with post-cards and childish drawings. A mobile made of egg-boxes and milk-bottle tops hung from the ceiling.

I stood frozen, though it was very warm in the kitchen, warm and messy with washing-up piled next to the sink, and several days' newspapers on the floor and the table. A cat wound round my ankles.

'That's Sid,' Tom said. 'Do you mind cats?'

I bent down to stroke the tabby creature. Tom moved about taking things from the refrigerator, filling a pan, opening a bottle of wine. It was odd to see him so at home. Everywhere else we had been had been strange to both of us, each hotel room a new territory. We had been equal. They had been ours and we had discovered them together. Now I saw the way he did things, efficient, hardly looking. He was obviously used to cooking. The shelves were full of dusty jars labelled in flamboyant silver writing: basil, camomile, garam masala, thyme.

'Take your coat off then!' He laughed to see me standing so uselessly, still clutching my bag. He came and stood behind me, unbuttoned my coat and slipped it off. He turned me round to kiss him. 'All right?' he asked. 'You've frozen up.'

'It just . . . feels odd . . . being here. Doesn't it to you? Having *me* here.'

He moved away and shrugged. He tipped pasta into the saucepan of water that was boiling now. He reached for a bottle of olive oil. 'Why don't you pour us some wine?' he said. I poured out the wine and took a long swallow. It was red wine from Spain, very rough like hessian on my tongue. I moved the child's teddy bear off a chair to sit down and the cat immediately leapt on to my lap, curled round and began purring and kneading my lap with his paws. An unfaithful cat.

'Push him off,' Tom said.

'I don't mind.' I took another sip of wine. I watched Tom slice tomatoes for a salad, and grind black pepper on to them. I watched his hands, the long fingers that were learning me so well, and felt, despite my awkwardness, suddenly happy. This was a new phase. I was in his home. He was my love. The love of my life, I thought, as the wine crept through my veins, as I warmed and expanded.

'Here we are.' He put the salad on the table, swallowed a mouthful of wine and reached over and touched me on the lips. I caught his finger between my teeth and caressed it with my tongue. He groaned and the pupils flared in his bright brown eyes.

After we had eaten I followed him upstairs. I went into the bathroom. I looked at his wife's expensive things: French perfume, creams in frosted pots, Pears soap, a real sponge, a loofah, thick towels in dark colours, forest-green and navy. A giant cheese-plant grew against the window, its split leaves dusty. There was a pile of books and papers next to the toilet and toy ducks in the bath that had a ring round it. It was all so perfect, so fashionably grubby. I realized I didn't know anything about taste. This *was* tasteful. I could see that, the casual richness, the sophisticated patina of dust and grime. I looked at myself in the mirror: jeans, a Shetland wool sweater, a young face, flushed from the wine, messy hair. His wife's pink dressing-gown hung on the back of the door, slippery, silky. I smelled it and it was pungent with the smell of woman, intimate and perfumed. It made me feel raw, a child blundering in an adults' world. I was embarrassed to leave the bathroom and let him see me. I brushed my hair with a brush that was lying by the bath, a real bristle brush tangled with long black hairs. I picked up her perfume – Chanel no. 5 – and sprayed some down the neck of my jumper, between my breasts. Stupid thing to do. It was the wine that made me do it, and made me also, on impulse, take off my clothes. I looked in the long mirror at my body. It looked better naked, a shadowy muted reflection in the dusty glass. There was a hand-mirror and I held it up, to see for the first time in my life, my naked back. I was pleased by the way my hips curved, and the way my hair, drying fluffily now, hung down to my shoulders.

'Hurry up,' Tom called through the door. 'What are you doing in there?'

I jumped. I had lost track of time altogether among all the

fascinating things. I could have stayed there for hours. Now I was startled by my nakedness. I couldn't present myself to him like this, like a gift, not even wrapped. I was quite drunk. I reached for, and then discarded, my plain cotton pants that were so childish.

'Coming.' I left my clothes on the floor and put on his wife's dressing-gown. The silk clung intimately to my skin, warm as breath. I tied the belt loosely round my waist. I felt sensuous, far from childish. Not like my self at all. I opened the door. He was standing outside, waiting.

'Sweetheart,' he breathed and just looked. I thought he paled, I thought for a moment he would turn away. I felt stupid. I had done the wrong thing. Of course it was wrong in his wife's house to use his wife's things. But then I was using her husband wasn't I? So what did perfume, a dressing-gown matter? He pulled me towards him and slid his hands down my back and over my buttocks. He propelled me into the first room, a bedroom, and pushed me on to the bed.

'I thought we were going upstairs,' I tried to object, but his mouth was on mine. I had not thought we would actually make love on their bed. I thought we'd go upstairs to his studio. It wasn't me he made love to. It didn't feel like me. I'm sure his hands travelled over me differently, expecting different planes, different responses, but with the wine inside me and with him so passionate, I could not resist. He pressed his face between my breasts and inhaled, gasping, muttering, 'Beautiful, beautiful,' almost angrily, coming quickly, leaving me high and stranded. He rolled away. He hadn't even undressed properly. I wanted to cry. I lay with the silk dressing-gown open on the crumpled bed. He sat up with his back to me.

'Sorry,' he said. 'Such a rush.' He hesitated. 'Look, Jenny. Perhaps you should go.'

'No!' I was surprised by the strength of my voice. 'I thought we'd go upstairs,' I said. 'I didn't want to come in here.' I covered myself and looked around the room. It was almost dark although it was only early afternoon, brown velvet curtains were half-drawn against the February rain. It was a messy room, a tangle of his things and her things and of the child's toys strewn all over the floor. The floor-boards were bare but for little coloured rugs. It had the kind of scruffy good taste I thought I would never grasp. Then, with a little shock, I saw my card with its stupid cellophane heart on the mantelpiece over a cast-iron fireplace. It stood beside another one, the right sort of Valentine card, a Picasso reproduction.

'We *should* have gone upstairs,' he said dully. 'Look, Jenny, I don't know what I was thinking of when I invited you here. It's my fault. It's all my fault.'

'But I *am* here.' I reached out for him. I held his stiff body with my face pressed against his back until he softened.

'I've surpassed myself,' he said.

'What do you mean?'

'I'm sorry. Seeing you like that in Moira's . . .' He looked round at me out of the corner of his eye and looked away as if it hurt him to see me there. Me and not *her*.

I got off the bed feeling suddenly chilled. 'I'll get dressed,' I said. I turned my face away from him because it was contorting with the effort of not crying, but he stood up and turned me round as a hot tear ran down my cheek.

'Don't,' he said. He wiped the tear away with his finger. 'Don't cry. Go upstairs and get into bed and I'll bring us up some tea. Please.'

'OK.' My head was starting to throb. I never drank at lunchtime, hardly ever, only with Tom. I picked up my clothes from the bathroom floor, took off the dressing-gown and hung it up for her to wear when she got back, to slip into, unaware of me. I wrapped myself in a towel. I heard him go downstairs, heard him talking to the cat, making a telephone call. I went back into the bedroom to look at the cards. There was mine with its curly question mark under the stupid rhyme and beside it the Picasso card, also signed with a question mark, more stylish than mine. Was it from him to her or her to him? I wonder if he thought mine was from her. But surely not? And who did she think it was from in that case? I felt a rush of relief. Whatever anyone thought, I had not made a fool of myself.

A GOOSE-FLESH DISCIPLINE

Peggy stood before a wonderful tree. It was like no other tree in the forest. She walked round it admiring its even shape, its rounded bole, its smooth copper bark. The leaves shimmered blue and purple and green. Every branch was laden with extravagant shining fruit, each one unique. Baby Sam was there, sitting in the long waving grass, pulling at Peggy's skirt and pointing up at the tree, his blue eyes like two cups turned up to the sky, brimming with desire. Peggy stretched up and reached a fruit for him, tugged it free from its stalk. She took a bite but found her mouth full of feathers. It was a bird she held and she dropped it with a cry. The tree was full of birds, not fruit, but fat and shining birds that all began to shriek and squeal and sway the tree with their beating wings. Peggy woke with feathers sticking to her tongue, reaching out for Sam lost somewhere in the waving grass, but clutching a big hand, a man's hand. The face that bent over her was a kind one. She did not know where she was. For a second she thought she had woken from a terrible dream, then found she had woken into a terrible reality.

'Peggy,' Hester was saying.

'Margaret Maybee?' the soldier asked.

'The same,' said she, brushing the sleep-feathers from her lips, watching her dream disintegrate into bright specks of dust dancing in the light from the open hatchway; feeling a cold hand clutch her heart. Against the light stood a guard with a

95

fixed bayonet, nothing but a black shape in the sudden gold. The soldier who bent over her was an officer, a gentleman, but it was no gentlemanly mission he was on. She noticed the fineness of his nose and his delicate girlish lips and she remembered, for one beat of her heart, Percy and the way he had loved her, the bliss of his fine pampered skin against her own.

'Margaret Maybee,' the man repeated. He stood up. 'You are a prisoner aboard the *Cunning Maid*, at the pleasure of King George. Your first duty to God and the king is that of obedience. Your behaviour brings shame on your sex and on the other convicts aboard this ship. You have been accused of making a savage and unprovoked attack upon a member of the crew. How do you speak to this?'

'She never!' cried Hester. 'It was never unprovoked – he kicked . . .'

'Allow the prisoner to speak.'

'I was defending my honour and that of my friend,' Peggy muttered.

'Be that as it may,' the officer said. 'There must be order and discipline aboard ship. Order among the convict class.' He looked not unkindly at Peggy. 'This matter must be seen to be dealt with – at the captain and the surgeon superintendent's orders – or disorder and anarchy will breed.'

'I am to be punished?' Peggy said. '*Am* I to be punished for the behaviour of that foul wretch, of all the foul wretches aboard this ship?'

The soldier sighed. 'You are to be punished for your gross and unfeminine behaviour. For my own part, I do not doubt that there are members of the crew who are as bad.'

'Worse, far worse,' interjected Hester.

'And they will be punished also.'

'What manner of punishment?' Hester demanded. 'And what manner of punishment will you suffer my friend?'

Peggy looked down at her mattress and the patchy stains upon it that showed up in the unaccustomed light. All around other women listened. Fear and fascination caught their tongues and the only sounds from them were the creaking of pallets as they shifted their position the better to see Peggy's face.

'The crew's punishment is no concern of yours,' the soldier said. 'You, Margaret, will receive a female punishment. Ducking. A goose-flesh discipline. It will do you no lasting harm. It will set the necessary example.' His eyes travelled over the rows of women's faces, the old and the young, the innocent, the misled and the truly villainous. 'And let it be understood,' he said to the company in general, 'that this is a mild punishment in comparison with some that will be exacted at the first sign of any further insubordination.'

Peggy was left chained to her bed while the other convicts were led up and out on to the deck. Hester kissed her before she was taken away and Rose touched her arm. 'Bugger them all,' she said.

The guards stood round with their weapons and the surgeon superintendent was preaching nasally when Peggy herself was brought up, blinking, into the daylight. The same handsome officer held her arm, almost courteously, almost as if about to invite her to dance. The beauty of the ship struck her in an incongruous wave of awe. The brass bulkhead rail glinted in the sun, the scrubbed deck was a tender white, soft as the flesh of a new-peeled almond. The ship swayed gently and the shadows of the masts and rigging passed with pendulum regularity over the deck and over the faces of the gathered women. There was a pause in which the farmyard sounds of chickens and pigs could be heard and then the surgeon superintendent turned towards Peggy.

'Margaret Maybee,' he said gravely. 'All you women here today take heed. This wretch has betrayed the beneficent trust of His Majesty who granted her his Royal Mercy, gave her as a gift, her own life. She has betrayed the king and betrayed herself before God as a traitor to her own sex: violent and disobedient. All you women take heed of this punishment and pray to God that the devil will be washed from this wretch's soul and that she be brought to her senses.' As the surgeon continued, Peggy could hear preparations being made behind her, but she could not turn and look. She was held now by both arms. The officer on her left was rougher than the other and gripped her arm as tightly as if she was likely to flee, as if there was anywhere to flee. She watched the faces of the women watching the preparations but she could not bear to look at Hester whose face streamed tears, whose fingers reached imploringly forward.

At a word from the surgeon, Peggy was suddenly turned and thrust into a box like an upright coffin. She was pushed in face first and the door slammed shut behind her. It was a narrow box, her arms were jammed to her sides, her shoulders almost crushed, her face pressed against smooth dark wood. It was not dark inside. It was a lidless box and there was just enough room for Peggy to crane her neck back and see the bottom of a bucket suspended above her. And as she understood the nature of her punishment, the bucket tipped. The water crashed heavily on her head like something solid and then, trapped by the tightness of her shoulders in the box, it swam round her face. She screwed up her eyes and her mouth but she could not pinch her nose. She could not move with her arms pinned to her sides. The water found its way down slowly and she was nearly breathless by the time she could gulp air again. A shout of outrage jumped from her throat, incoherent and natural as an animal's cry. Her head was swimming, water forced its way up her nose and trickled down the back of her throat. Her legs felt weak as if she must lie down. She heard the rope creaking with the weight of another bucket. 'Stop!' she cried.

'Hearken to the wretch begging for mercy,' said the muffled voice of the surgeon, and she pressed her lips together. She would *not* cry out again. She would not give that man the satisfaction. She bit her lip. 'Oh God in heaven help me,' she muttered. She tried to fill her lungs with air, to be prepared this time for the heavy slam of water, the surging in her ears, the drowning wait for the water to clear her face. She opened her eyes as the water cleared them and watched through salt-stung lids the beads of water running down the wood, and sucked air in as the water cleared her nostrils and mouth. She licked her lips and tasted the brine. She could not fill her lungs enough, the box squeezed her chest as if it was tightening and her heart boomed against the wood as if it would burst inside her. She fell into a strange state, only half conscious but suspended by the wood, tickled on her legs and body by the water which rose with every smothering tip of the bucket.

Once she could not wait for the water to clear her nose and she breathed in water and coughed and choked and retched and she thought she heard Hester cry out, or perhaps it was the cry of a gull. She began to shiver. The water was up to her waist. Her dress was wet and itchy against her skin. She lost control and urinated, feeling the heat of it, a burning between her legs before it flowed out to meet the cold water. No lasting damage, she reminded herself to quell her growing fear.

The water ran from her ears in warm trickles and her teeth chattered as the cold water alternately smashed her head, deafened and blinded and suffocated her, and crept down her body – and gradually up. The water reached her shoulders. She knew that one or two more buckets would be all. Then they would let her out or else she would breathe in water and then she would be dead. She hardly cared. If it was not for the dim memory of a child somewhere in another world, she would have let her head sink into the water. Another bucket emptied and this time ran down only to her chin so there was a tickling edge of it just below her lower lip, almost like the tickle of a feather, a tender sensation. Her neck ached with the effort of keeping it craned up and for relief of the pain she had to let her head tip forward so that her mouth and nose were immersed for as long as she could hold her breath. Then she had to force up her neck which felt like a frail flower stem supporting the weight of a stone. She waited for the creak of the bucket that would be the last thing – but there was none. Only the sound of the surgeon's voice, only a rustle in her ears as the water ran out. She could have let herself go. The coldness and the crampedness of wood and water had taken away her legs and her arms. She was only a head and an unwilling will to live. A shaft of sun shimmered on the water's surface only inches from her eyes and when she closed them against the dazzle she saw an explosion of stars.

At some time, it might have been minutes later, it might have been hours, the box was opened and Peggy fell out in a rush of water as if she had been born, weak and mewling, on to the ship's deck. Her clothes were wet around her body as weeds and she had to look at her limbs to see that they were there. Half insensible she was dragged below while the surgeon's voice preached on. Words were spoken to her but they did not penetrate the cold. She was shoved, in her wet clothes, with her blanket on to the bunk.

'Oh, Peggy,' Hester said when she came. 'Why did you not cry out for mercy? If you had cried out they would have stopped! I thought that you would die.' Her voice was thick with tears. She dried Peggy's hair with her own blanket and with her hands she rubbed life back into Peggy's hands and feet. 'You should have begged for mercy to show that you repented.'

'But I do not repent,' said Peggy through chattering teeth.

'You proud bitch,' Hester said. 'I would have squealed like a calf at the first bucket. Look how your fingers are wrinkled.' She held up Peggy's hand.

'It hurts,' Peggy said. The salt had stung the abrasions on her hands and the raw places between her fingers where the skin was broken. Now that she was warming the pain of this began. She shivered violently.

'Poor Peggy,' Hester said. 'Let me warm you.' She lay close to Peggy, covered them both with the blankets and held her tight. Hester's warmth reached Peggy through her wet dress, dampened Hester's dress so that they steamed together in the dim heat. They fell quiet, listening to the voices of the other convicts, all bedded now for the night. The voices were subdued, two women sang, some quarrelled, but they kept their voices low.

'There are other punishments,' Hester said, later.

'Mmmm?' Peggy had grown sleepy now, her shivering had stopped and she was calm.

'Thin water gruel. Starvation. He threatened us with all manner of delights for further "insubordination".'

'Ha!'

'Irons and handcuffs. Or separation. There is a cell where you can be locked alone. "Loneliness is an excellent physic for the felon mind." ' She held her nose and parroted the surgeon's voice and to her own surprise, for she thought all the laughter had been washed out of her, Peggy laughed.

'Am I a felon then?' she asked.

'Oh yes,' said Hester, stroking her hair. 'The most terrible felon that ever drew breath.'

And over and up and over and down and strain and strain and strain and strain. I exercise so hard that my lungs feel fit to explode, that my muscles burn. I will be fit, that is something I can do for myself. That is a form of control. Also, when I exercise I wear myself out, dredge up a feeling of tiredness, almost like tiredness in the real world when all I want to do is lie down. And here I can do that, I can lie down and wrap myself in the blanket of my thoughts – that is when my thoughts run smooth. In here I am going grey. Not my hair as far as I know, but my skin and my mind. I have to do things, physical things to prove to myself that I exist. I have to take an inventory of my parts: two legs with feet; two arms, one mottled with the marks of my mouth; two twitching hands; one scar: a belly, breasts and a face that I can only feel, that is grown mysterious. Walking down a crowded street, would I recognize myself?

I can stand on my head. It lends a new perspective, sends the blood pulsing to my brain. The balance is curious, my legs sway like heavy branches. The top of my head is crushed by the weight of the hard floor. I swing my legs down. There is no carpet, of course. If there *was* a carpet, life would be quite different. I could sprawl. I could stand on my head or my shoulders for hours at a time. It would not hurt if I let myself drop.

I could crack my head on this hard floor if I wished. Did they not think of that, the people who embedded the light bulb so that there could be no harm?

I knew a man who lived by himself in a church. He was a sort of tramp. He lived alone in some style, shaving with a silver blade, dining on Stilton and the very best pork sausages. He spent his lonely hours building something out of wood. When I wandered in, escaped from school, seeking solitude myself, he became my friend. He was a dangerous friend. His teeth were sharp and his eyes had no human spark. He would not tell me what he was building. It was gigantic. It looked like the beginnings of a ship, I thought, a skeletal hull. I strained my eyes to make sense of it but it was not a ship, it was a pair of wings. He told me that when he'd finished the wings, he would fly away. He showed me the parachute silk he would stretch across the framework. It seems a comical idea now, this madman flapping across the sky with all that creaking splintery wood. But part of me believed him. I can see now that it was absurd, that it would be impossible – but I mourn for the part of me that thought it *was*.

He *did* disappear, but he did not fly. And when he disappeared, so did my friend, Bronwyn. She vanished, became just a space where a person was. And somehow it was my fault. She was an awful girl. At the time I hardly thought she was real. And then she wasn't.

I must not think about this. Sometimes I dream about Bronwyn who was so desperate for a friend, who would not let go, and I remember how cruel I was. How much I despised her need. And then I think of Tom and deep inside, I shiver.

It is funny how memory makes chains and snares. How one memory will loop another. There is something I had forgotten for years and years. When I was very small, perhaps only four or five, Bob took me to see a conjurer. I loved Bob. He was my grandfather but I thought he was my dad. It was a cold day and I wore woolly mittens with red strings threaded through the sleeves of my duffle-coat. There was slush on the pavement that went over the tops of my shoes and melted on my socks between the straps. If I try I can still feel the tightness of Bob's hand holding mine. He was so big and solid in his camel-coloured coat and trilby hat, he made me feel safe. My feet were cold and the collar of my velvet party dress made my neck itch but I was happy. That memory is like a scrap of butterfly wing, a precious fragment so fragile I am afraid to touch it lest it disintegrate. I felt excited and I felt loved.

The conjurer was a towering man with a shiny top hat and a moustache like curly liquorice. We sat near the front and I thought I could see cracks in his orange skin, as if he was not quite real. The show was too short. I was transported by his magic and I believed every single thing. I screamed out loud when he sawed the glittering lady in half and separated her so that her legs waved from one box and her hand from another. He produced flags from round the world, bouquets of flowers, sweets to throw into the audience, doves and a trembling white rabbit. Then the lady was there again, all in one piece and even smiling. She was so beautiful she made me want to grow up fast, to be a lady in a sequined leotard and high heels with my hair piled a foot above my head. But at the end of the show he made her disappear. He put her in a tall red and yellow box and shut the door. He tapped it with his magic wand, three smart taps, said, 'Abracadabra!' and when he opened the box she was gone. Just gone. There was just the empty inside of the box. And then the curtain came down and everyone clapped and cheered but I could not move. When we got home Bob laughed and told Mama that I'd looked like a cod-fish with my mouth hanging open. I would not clap and I would not move. I wanted to see her come back. I would not move until the theatre was empty and the bright light came on and a lady with a broom started to sweep between the seats. Bob bought me some chips to cheer me up but it was a long time before I forgot that woman who could be cut in half and mended; who could completely vanish.

We ate and drank and made love. So many bottles of wine, so many mornings and afternoons and midnights in that bed upstairs with the sloping ceiling and the pearly shell mobile clinking above us, that it is all merged into one long fuzzy sensation.

'It's never been like this,' he said. I'm sure he said that. His beard was full of the smell of me, and his hair. We were drenched with each other, saturated with our smells. No other lovers had ever experienced such intensity, ever. Of that I was convinced.

After the first day I hardly moved from his room. It rained every day and the wind lashed rain and sometimes sleet against the sloping skylight. I didn't get dressed for four days. Tom went downstairs to cook, out to the off-licence, out to buy take-away meals and bring them back to bed. He made telephone calls and went out to work once, and I just slept. I was gorged and sated, my thinking mind a blur.

Once he sat cross-legged on the bed and played his saxophone. The notes curled round the room like smoke, insistent, sinuous sounds that made me feel drugged with love. I was bloated by it, watching the ballooning of his cheeks, the firm pressure of his fingers on the keys, the dreaminess of his eyes, the movement of his ribs, and I saw, as he played – I never told him I noticed this, I don't know if he knew – I saw his penis stiffen as the music filled the room, as every throaty, sexy wail of that saxophone insinuated every crevice of the room, of the bed, of me.

Afterwards he lay the saxophone down and rolled a joint. I watched his fingers that were so deft with whatever he did, singeing the greenish dope and crumbling it in the tobacco. I had never smoked before – not even tobacco – but there was no question that it was the right thing to do and I lay back, inhaling the cool smoke, watching its blue and snaky windings on the ceiling following the saxophone's traces. Tom lay his hand on my belly, just the flat of his hand. There was no attempt at stimulation, no movement but the heat of his hand was like gold flooding me. I gasped at the sensation. 'Relax, sweetie,' he said and I thought that he knew what he was doing, that he knew me better than I knew myself. It made me love him so much I almost wanted to die.

He had mentioned a party he was supposed to be going to, and suggested that I come. I wanted to go, to be seen there with him, but then the lines between the days became blurred, the attic filled with fog as if the atmosphere we created with our naked bodies was tangible, was a yellow fog beast that wound round and clogged the spaces until I thought we would drown in the smoke and condensation, the expiration of our love.

And I did not care. After days of wine and smoke I saw from far away our other lives, as if the characters that peopled them were tiny mannikins. Mama and Ursula were faint bothersome scratches on my mind; Moira and the child were less. He hardly spoke of them. Perhaps he phoned them. I don't know. I thought that there was nothing, could not have been anything like this between Moira and himself. Hadn't he implied as much? His life with her had been convenient, expedient. But she was too beautiful, flawed by her perfection. She was a good little doll, a nursemaid. I wished that she would disappear. But she was only temporary. Because the real thing was what *we* had, Tom and I. Love, the genuine thing.

So we let the party go. 'We don't need it,' he said. 'Can you imagine getting up and dressed? Could you bear all that small-talk? It's such a waste of fucking time.'

'Is that fucking *time* or *fucking* time?' I asked and he bit the lobes of my ears and the next time we surfaced it was too late. And he was right. The idea of getting up and going out, preparing a face to meet the faces I would meet seemed preposterous.

Only afterwards did the doubts creep in. On the train. I felt raw, my face, my body, rubbed raw and sore, my stomach aching from the wine, my lungs smarting from the smoke. On the train the doubts crept into all the chinks in me that he had left. He didn't want to be seen with me, that's why he didn't take me to the party, that's why he drugged me and wore me out. He didn't want me at the party where Moira's friends would see me, compare me unfavourably, run back to her with tales. Because she was the wife and what was I?

Oh yes, I saw it all differently on the train as it bumped away from Liverpool Street. I stared out at rainy Chelmsford. He had kept me prisoner in the attic, naked in that fug, full of wine and dope. He had fed me and fucked me. Oh, I had been a willing prisoner but he was a clever jailer, kept the knowledge from me.

Before I'd left, I'd bathed using Moira's scented oils, scrubbed my back with her loofah, rubbed my heels with her pumice stone. Hidden behind the curtain in the bathroom I'd found an old rubber cap, discoloured and perished; a bottle of Hair-Gro lotion – a treatment for hair loss – and a tube of haemorrhoid ointment, all sticky and dusty. Then I had gone upstairs to collect my things to find the room transformed. He'd stripped the bed and opened the window and the cold, sour breath of London had chased away our sexy smoky fug. The mattress was ugly and stained and I saw that it had all gone, whatever it was that we had had and that he was cleaning up for Moira. Soon the sheets would be churning in the washing machine, the wine bottles and take-away wrappers would be in the dustbin and there would be no sign that I'd been there, no trace. Tonight he would hold cool Moira in his arms and say that he had missed her. He might even make love to her, if he had the stamina, and her orgasm, if she had one, would be quiet, a polite gasp and then they would sleep, neat and complete with the child safely tucked up in a neighbouring room. A proper family. Funny that I felt most jealous of the child.

My mother disappeared so completely that I did not know she existed until I was thirteen. Mama gave me a letter on my thirteenth birthday. It was the letter my mother had written me on the day she left me with her parents to bring me up as their own. I read the letter sitting alone on a swing in my secret playground all grown round with briars. I think it shocked me out of myself, out of my old self but not into a proper new one. It was like being born at thirteen. I had no time to grow into my face. She, Jacqueline, my mother, wrote to me from Australia after that. She sent me a photograph of herself, her bearded husband and her clutch of golden daughters, each one prettier than me. I could see that I had been many times replaced.

I wrote back once or twice. I didn't go to Australia although I could have done. She worried me for a year or two and then I made her disappear again. As I made Bronwyn disappear. No, that is foolish. No one has that power.

Oh, nothing is natural in here. The air is dull, no breeze, no draught even, no pollen, no little flies. It tastes of fusty blankets, dries my throat and lungs. I long for dew or rain or snow, for the tug of the wind in my hair. I long, even, to shiver. I sweat when I exercise and it makes me thirsty. From a doorstep, I'd like to steal a pint of milk in a bottle beaded with cold. I'd like to peel the foil top off and gulp it down, achingly cold, smooth and white, fill myself up with the cold white of it. I want a fag. I want a joint. I want a swallow of coarse red wine. Do you hear me? Or a cup of tea would do. Or the opening of a window. I long for something to happen. *Anything*. Things are happening out there and I do not know. The world could end and I would be the last to know.

CROSSING THE LINE

Night fell suddenly in the southern seas. The sun paused for a moment, big, hot, tensed and then sank like a stone and the stars punctured the navy-blue sky. If you knew the secret, you could steer your way by the patterned stars, the tiny ones, the huge ones, big and fuzzy as teazles.

Peggy hardly ever saw the darkness of the sea-sky. The convicts were stowed away by nightfall. They fed on saltbeef or mutton, biscuit and a lump of currant pudding. They drank their ration of cloudy lukewarm water, of porter if it was a Saturday, and they were battened down till morning, till the sun burst raw and dripping with salt-light from the east. Then, if they were lucky, they were brought up for exercise or work.

Peggy lay with her head in Hester's lap. There was something amiss on the ship, nothing clear enough to be put into words, not among the women. Peggy's ducking had not had the desired effect, rather it had increased unrest among the convicts and the temperature was rising among the men. Factions were developing with convicts and crew rounding on their own. Never had the captain, it was said, had such an unruly ship. Almost daily they were treated to the terrible sound of the knotted leather cat biting into the flesh of some poor wretch or other. But the mutterings and rumours of uprising and mutiny did not cease. Among the convicts, and between the convicts and crew there was a secret language of twitches and nods. The rest of the crew was wary, the officers alert, the guards bristled weapons. The convicts spent more time below, but in the heat they might have died if they had been kept down all day, so unhealthy and thick was the atmosphere.

A new rumour had spread among the convicts this day, strange words rustling like a breeze through corn. *Partial eclipse* were the words whispered from one woman to another. *A partial eclipse of the moon.*

'He means to quell the mutiny through prayer,' jeered Rose in the dimness. 'But we are crossing the line tonight.'

'The line?'

'The line . . . the girdle round the centre of the world. There should be a festival on board, and celebration. But not tonight. Tonight there will be preaching in its place. That is the *captain's* thought.' She chuckled.

'Hush!' said a voice from a higher bunk.

'Mutiny?' said Peggy.

'Don't fret. Just follow. The less you know, the better for you.' Rose put her finger to her lips and winked.

The convicts were led up on the deck. They gasped in the air which seemed hardly cooler than in the oven-heat below. It was strange to be on deck in the near darkness. It was oddly quiet. The decks were packed with figures, the male convicts ranked and heavily guarded. Above them, on the poop stood the captain and his officers and the surgeon superintendent. It seemed almost as if the ship itself slept and the activity aboard was its own dream. The surface of the sea was dark and still as polished ebony. On the distant northern horizon there was a storm. The thunder was no more than the faintest grumble. Lightning flickered like minute hairs. The moon had risen, huge, rusty and distorted and the lunar dawn was a warm streak on the eastern horizon, while in the west, the last traces of a golden sunset died.

The surgeon superintendent began to speak and all faces swivelled towards him, all the faces of convict and crew alike, hard and villainous as some of them might be, were softened by the moon's red light. The man's gold tooth was a moving point of light as he spoke: 'I wish all you gathered on this ship tonight, to witness a certain spectacle that is to take place very shortly. I believe this spectacle will produce a strong and salutary effect upon the hearts and minds of this villainous congregation. I do not believe there is a soul aboard this ship who is past redemption. The heavenly phenomenon you are to witness will be a partial eclipse of the moon.' He paused and sniffed. 'Dwell, pray, as you watch the shadow creeping over the moon's face, on the evil and corrupt paths you have chosen to follow. Picture the moon as the image of your own soul and the shadow besmirching it, the darkness of sin. Attend how presently the shadow will pass and the moon will once again shine clear and splendid. And then rejoice, all you sinners, in the passing of sin and the shining pure light of blameless soul. The Lord has provided this spectacle for your improvement. Thank the Lord in prayer.'

There were sighs from among the congregation of emotion, of irritation and a shuffling that signalled unrest. Uneasily Peggy clutched Hester's hand. The faces turned away from the surgeon superintendent and rested on the face of the moon that shrank and hardened and grew more pallid as she rose. The ship was increasingly flooded with a cold silver light that picked out the features of the convicts, that glinted on the blades of bayonets, that cast precise shadows at their feet. The sails were lit to an eery white, flickering with reflections of the distant storm.

There was a gasp as the edge of the moon, frail now as a round white wafer, was touched by shadow. 'It is only the shadow of the earth,' said someone. 'It is the blackness of sin,' answered another. For a moment the silence was profound, as hundreds of eyes looked upwards to see the silver overlapped by darkness, as if smudged by a fingerprint. The moon's reflection flowed in the water with a sparkling wake of greenish silver.

Peggy dragged her eyes from the spectacle to observe the upturned faces of the crowd. But they were not all upturned and she saw that all was not well. There was beauty – the sea so still as if blessed by the moon, the jibs floating gossamer-soft, the sky sequined with a million stars – while the moon sailed above, painted out at one edge as if she was a cheese, nibbled by mice. It made Peggy yearn for Sam, thinking of the stories and songs about the moon he would be learning so far away. *The man in the moon came down too soon and asked his way to Norwich, he went by the south and burnt his mouth with eating cold pease porridge.* Was there an eclipse in England? Was it even night-time there? And her thoughts wandered and jumped and her mind rebelled against the beauty and the surgeon's pious senti-ments. She saw, alert suddenly and chilled as if by an icy finger down her spine, a subtle exchange of messages between the male convicts and one faction of the crew, no more than a narrowing of the eyes here, a hand tugging an ear-lobe there, and her fear was laced with exhilaration.

The shadow passed softly away from the moon, and suddenly as if it had waited its moment, the thunder became more insistent, pounding like distant fists on the skin of a vast drum, and a chilly breeze sprang up.

'Storm approaching,' announced the surgeon superintendent. 'With your permission, Captain, we'll get them all below.'

Something had slipped in me in those days with Tom and I could not get myself back in focus. I could not face my university friends for whom I had constructed an elaborate persona. For them I was bright and breezy. I hid my conscientiousness behind a casual façade. Never did a stroke of work – or so it seemed. And yet the As flowed in. In line for a first, I was, but nice with it. I enjoyed the envy I aroused. I was popular. I worked at that, as hard as I worked at my books. I studied the ways of popular girls. They were fun, they were sincere, they were not too beautiful nor were they plain. They had style. They showed you their vulner-ability but they did not wear it like a badge. They swapped it for yours. I studied and mimicked until I almost believed in myself.

Only in the morning when I rose silently and, wrapped in my dressing-gown, opened my books and wrote my essays, only in that half-light did I see through myself to the quaking creature inside. After Bob died and we got a television, Mama and I used to watch 'Dr Who'. We loved it, loved the monsters, the battles, the Tardis. I remember the Daleks, fat, officious, bustling things. '*I will exterminate. I will exterminate.*' I was fascinated by what was inside. Something soft and formless. Something you could stamp on and torture. Or you could love and pet. Without their shells they had no power.

I knew my friends would be waiting for me to reappear. I had told my best friend, Jaz, about this romantic figure, this older married man, the musician, and I knew she would be dying for the next instalment. But I could not face her. I don't know why. My shell had gone, my face. I quivered as I sat on the train travelling back home from London. I could not meet the eyes of anyone, not the small child who stared at me with flat blue curious eyes, not the ticket inspector's. I could not let anyone look into my eyes which were empty. Tom had rubbed away my personality as if it had been nothing but a flaking skin with his caresses, his kisses, the friction of his body against mine. My self, my fragile skin-self was left on his sheets, dissolving now in his washing machine. It was left on his wife's loofah, on her dressing-gown, in her hairbrush, on her towels, in the dust on the cheese-plant, in the ring around the bath. And what was this thing that was left? Like a hermit crab between shells I was entirely vulnerable. I quailed at the touch even of eyes.

So I had to go home. Even though Ursula was there I still had my room. I had a place in which to reconstruct Jennifer. I did not tell them I was coming back, I did not feel the need. I walked from the station, avoiding all eyes, my legs precarious and jelly-soft. I carried with me the scent of Moira, her perfume, her shampoo. They were something that I was. I walked home and it was a long way to our street, a long straight road of houses and bungalows set back from the road behind hedges and gardens.

The sun that had struggled out from between the clouds lit them all impartially, the smart and the shabby. Ours was shabby, I had never noticed before *how* shabby, with paint peeling from the window-frames and dusty glass.

I stood by the front door for a long time. I didn't know whether to ring the bell or walk straight in. I did not know if it was really my home any more. The brass letter-flap was tarnished. Bob used to polish it. *Bright as a new pin*, was the sort of thing he used to say. Suddenly I ached for him because he, out of all the people I had ever known, he was the only one I trusted. Eventually I lifted my hand to ring the bell. It looked odd. I could not believe it was my hand travelling up, so heavy on the end of my arm, my fingers with all those lines, nails bitten down to the soft quick. I pressed my finger on the bell but nothing happened. So I opened the door and walked in. I went into the kitchen. No one was there, but a half-eaten cauliflower cheese stood on the table together with an empty bottle labelled Peapod Wine. I thought they had gone out collecting twigs and dead mice. I had a drink of water from the tap. I stood by the back-door looking at the scratches on the frame. A record of my growth. I stood with my back against the door-frame and closed my eyes and I almost made Bob be there, resting a book on the crown of my head for a straight line and then measuring with Mama's tape-measure. '*Like a beanstalk*,' he used to say, every time, even if I had hardly grown at all, and then he would gravely record the height and the date. And there they still were, the stripes of my growth that stopped when I was thirteen, when he had died.

I drank some more water and then I went upstairs. I was relieved that they weren't there, that I did not have to talk. But when I got to the top of the stairs I heard the murmur of the television from Mama's room. The door was not quite closed. I hesitated. It would be better to be alone, to shut myself away. I nearly went straight into my room but I thought I should announce my presence. I went to the doorway of Mama's room,

I opened my mouth to say hello. And then I turned to ice. In bed were Mama and Ursula. They did not see me at once, they were engrossed in the television. They were sitting naked in bed watching 'Little House on the Prairie'. Mama held a glass of wine. Ursula's arm was round Mama's shoulders and her hand cupped one of Mama's pendulous breasts. Ursula's hair, the colour of an army blanket, was loose, cascading over her shoulders and chest, tangling round Mama's arm.

I stood for a moment waiting for them to see me, wishing I could shrink away, backtrack through time out of here because I didn't want to know this about Mama. It was so absurd I didn't know what to do. And then a noise jumped out of me, a sort of laugh. Mama turned and saw me. She reddened, snatched the bed-clothes up to her chin and whimpered miserably. But Ursula was cool.

'Jennifer,' she said. 'This is a surprise.'

We were all silent, all of us looking fervently at the television screen as if it might rescue us from this excruciating moment.

'Well now you know,' Ursula said, at last.

'Know?' I echoed.

'Our . . . well our status, so to speak.'

'I . . .' I said. 'I . . . ' I could not make anything come out, no thought, no speech.

'Our, how shall I put it? Coupledom.'

Mama had shrunk as far below the covers as possible, she blurred into the grey of Ursula's hair.

I went into my room and closed the door. I looked in the mirror at myself and saw my cod-fish mouth hanging open, I swam in that glass as if in an aquarium. The muscles in my face had stuck. My sinuses began to ache. I opened my trinket box but the ballerina failed to twizzle, there was no music, the clockwork had wound down. I sat on my bed. I reeked of Moira and leaked Tom from between my legs and my world seemed to be falling around me like flakes of ash. Tomorrow morning I should be back at university giving a seminar paper. On what I did not know. That *I* was nowhere to be seen. I looked out of the window at my familiar view. The right trees were there, some of them just igniting with the first green sparks of spring. There was the lawn, the hedge, the pond, the fence. I kicked off my shoes and got into bed with all the rest of my clothes on. I pulled the pink candlewick over my face and fell, immediately, asleep.

When I woke up, Mama was standing by my bed with a cup of tea. She had put the light on. She looked so normal that for a moment I was flicked back through the years. I was a child in bed and she was my Mama.

'Tea, Jenny,' she said. She looked just the same in her tweed skirt and green hand-knit cardigan. She sat on the edge of my bed. I sat up and took the tea. There was an oatmeal biscuit in the saucer. Her hands struggled with each other in her lap.

I dipped the biscuit in the tea and lifted it up but the soggy edge fell in.

'I'm sorry,' Mama said.

I sipped the tea. There were crumbs floating in it now.

'Sorry that you had to find out like that.'

'I tried to ring the doorbell,' I said, 'but it doesn't work.'

'But you don't have to ring the doorbell,' she said. 'Not you.'

Mama was sexless in her clothes. Her hair and her face were crumpled. Her chest, buttoned inside her cardigan, was bulky and undefined. Once, when she was young, she had been a naturist, she and Bob together. I tried not to remember her breast and the casual way Ursula had cupped it in her hand.

'We were going to tell you. It was just a question of *how*.'

'Are you a lesbian then?'

'A lesbian!' She was shocked. 'Oh no, I'm not *that*.'

'What then?'

'Well . . .' But she could not answer me. She put her hand on my arm and I let her. I looked at the old bones showing yellow through the patchy old skin, the swollen veins. Mama's hands had brought me up, held me, cleaned me, fed me, soothed me, slapped me once or twice. Now they touched Ursula's naked

115

skin, gave pleasure to that old woman. I could not bear to think about it. I looked at my own hand holding the cup, at the smooth skin and the tiny blonde hairs on the back, the flat veins just showing, the bitten nails. I thought how that hand had touched Tom.

'I wish I could explain,' Mama said, 'but Urse . . .'

'No need,' I said.

But she gave a little fretting sound. 'I will explain,' she promised. 'One day. It's not what you think. Not quite.'

I snorted. Tom, I thought, Tom, Tom. It is not all over. Tom is still there. And the warmth of the tea spread right through me until I could feel my edges again. I could not understand my former desolation. Tom was my lover still. What was the matter with me?

Once Mama had gone, sighing and creaking uneasily downstairs to join Ursula in the kitchen, I picked up my books. But I could not concentrate, it was as if they were in a foreign language. I knew I could not do it any more. I slid my hands over my body. The idea of eviscerating those poems seemed absurd. What was it for? The skin-self to whom that had mattered had been shed. Now my new skin was all for Tom, for Tom and love, and I knew that I would have him. I would take him away from Moira and have him for myself, because this was real love and nothing could be more important than that.

I think about Debbie. I don't fantasize about her, that would seem a liberty. But she is on my mind. She is an apple person, flesh crisp and rosy, clear eyes, teeth white and small as a child's. She is older than me, thirty-three, a grown-up woman but there is a freshness about her.

I hardly know her. She would be amazed that she is so often on my mind. She doesn't talk much, she holds herself apart. Apart but not aloof. No one dislikes her which is astonishing. People leave her alone, not in an unfriendly way. It is a sort of respect. She is the only person here who doesn't smoke. Maybe that accounts for her clearness. She smells of the outside, of rain on warm earth. She is the only person in here who seems entirely real. She is like a coloured figure in a black and white film.

She did a terrible thing, terrible. I do not want to name it, I cannot associate the thing she did with *her*. Temporary madness because *she* is not bad. I can see it all, her resentment building up, becoming rage, until one day she snapped. There is only so much a body, a mind, can bear. I can almost hear the snap like the snap of a branch underfoot or the crack of ice releasing a flood, a torrent to sweep away the senses, but only for a while. Once the force is spent that is an end of it, the black spell, the dizzy, terrifying liberation of dream-actions. Only real. And then back to reality to see what she had done. Uncomplicated. It is over now, all she has to do is pay with a few years of her life. Not so bad. She has nearly paid. She'll be out on parole soon. Unlike me, she behaves, keeps her nose clean. But me, I am different. There was no snap. It just goes on. They tried to prove me mad but I think that I am simply bad. If I would behave *I* could get parole. Jailed for life, I've done nearly a stretch. Instead I misbehave, end up banged up, maddened by the four grey walls and the grey food. Where at least I am alone. Sometimes I almost prefer it, my own company. And sometimes I don't. I don't know what I want.

The thought of freedom terrifies me.

What do I want from Debbie? She does notice me, smiles, talks a bit, nothing personal. Would I like to be her lover? There is a lot of it in here, pseudo-marriages, couples bedding silently, fingers, tongues sliding, smothered gasps. And break-ups, of course, jealousies, fights. The screws all know but they don't interfere. As long as it is discreet. I have never been tempted. In eight years I have not. No one has attracted me. I don't want anyone that close.

Lightning crackled on the surface of the sea. The officers shouted orders to the crew to start moving the convicts below but there was only sluggish obedience. And then there came a terrible wail,

117

a wail that curdled the blood, caused cries of fear and excitement from among the convicts.

'I order this company to break up,' bellowed the captain. 'Guards, your weapons. Crew . . .' But the eery cry resounded, louder than at first. Peggy and Hester clutched at each other in the same movement. There was the sound of fiddle music, not brisk, not the jumpy jig rhythm of the exercise music. This was a dragging plaintive tune. The captain and the surgeon drew close and bent their heads in uneasy discussion. The guards moved closer to the convicts, the moonlight made silver slices of their blades and nail-heads of their buttons.

There was a further wail and there arose from below the side of the ship, as if emerging from the ocean itself, a ghastly figure, thick dolphin-skinned, dried seaweed on its head in a great mad tangled wig. It rose with its mouth open in a round black O in the blueness of its face. It rattled with shells and desiccated birds' wings. In one hand it held the long shell through which it blew the plangent cry and in the other it held aloft an iron trident.

'Neptune!' was the cry of the convicts and crew. 'We have crossed the line.' And a cheering followed, a great noise of movement and voices, a great confusion.

At a signal from the captain, a musket was fired into the air, as if at the moon, and in the shock of silence that followed it, the surgeon spoke. 'Yes. We have crossed the line. Be thankful to the Lord for bringing us safely this far. And thankful to our captain for allowing you the sight of the moon's eclipse and the rising of Neptune from the ocean . . .'

'That's none of the captain's doing,' cried Rose, and a guard struck her on the cheek.

'And now we go below . . .' the surgeon insisted, but a clamour had arisen again, a scuffle among the male convicts, loud voices, the crew's voices, jeering at the surgeon. Neptune stood aloft. The storm had swept across the sea towards the *Cunning Maid* and lightning flickered on the prongs of his trident, seemed to stream from it, his thick bluish skin glimmered. Peggy was transfixed. Water ran from him, monster man, and the black holes of his eyes seemed fixed on Peggy. The hot night sucked the breath from her, the slight weight of Hester still hanging on her arm threatened to pull her down.

All around the ship was in turmoil now. Neptune was forgotten by the crowd. The guard next to Hester fell suddenly and his blood ran thick and black on the frosty deck. Thunder pounded, fists on ear-drums and the fabric of the ship quaked with every crashing musket shot. The sea grew rough, waves boiling above the ship's sides, this great ship that seemed a little thing now, a frail vessel of madness on the vast and churning sea. The thin thready sound of the fiddle continued, audible in snatches when the thunder paused. The lightning flickered and flashed. Sheets of white fire flapping, illuminating the struggling bodies on the deck. The fight seemed almost silent, swallowed as it was by the thunder's almost continuous roaring curtain of sound. A mass of silver faces and limbs, black shadows, sudden plunges into absolute black for the clouds had swiftly swaddled the moon and stars, hiding the hideous doings on the deck.

In the fitful illumination the lightning afforded, Peggy alone kept her eyes on Neptune. The monster's eyes were hidden by the thick fronds of weed that streamed from his head. If she had had the breath to scream she would have screamed. She knew that the end had come for this ship and she felt that she would swoon, but the invisible gaze of Neptune held her and she could not fall. Her heart bundled within her, vibrating the ship like the thunder itself. Neptune seemed to tower above the ship now, glimmering blue, the lightning streaking from his trident, green and blue and purple, sizzling the surface of the sea. The sails flashed translucent white, flickered and faded and flashed again. The mouth of Neptune had changed from an O into a black crescent moon and he shook his trident and split the sky so the lightning jagged from directly above.

Hailstones, big as drumming fists, pelted the deck, bouncing

119

higher than the heads of the struggling mass. The ship steamed with the hot, wet fury.

Neptune never let his gaze leave Peggy. Peggy let go of Hester who was shouting to Rose, raising her fist, who seemed a fury herself, almost joyful in the chaos. But for Peggy it was like a dream. The almost silent slaughter and the cottony fiddle notes tangling with the shadows beneath the ear-splitting percussion of the thunder. It was not real. But it was terrifying and exhilarating. The eyes of Neptune were upon her, the fish-God, the dripping one, the one who held himself above and yet seemed to orchestrate the shameful mutinous night. She walked, sliding on the wet and bloody deck towards him, and he came to her and took her as she knew he would, pressing her body against the fishy stench of his dolphin's skin, opening her and entering her as the lightning entered her eyes and she screamed at the sensation, a silent scream beneath the thunder. When he let her go she looked down and thought in the crazy light that his penis was pronged like the trident that he still held aloft. And when he had let her go she was not even sure that it had happened. There was nothing to show but a fishy trickle on the inside of her thighs. As he released her she saw the blackness of the north, as if the sky vomited soot on to sheets of lightning. Peggy felt fists of hail on her head, bouncing up to her jawbone. As she stood wonderingly on the edge of chaos, Neptune looked at her once more with his invisible eyes, held his trident high, raised the shell to his lips and blew a call that sliced through the thunder. And as it did, a fork of lightning struck the mast and it fell to the seething deck in flames.

I dreamed of the swimming pool again. The sea around the ship was rough but the water in the pool on the deck was blue, peppermint blue, mouthwash blue, antiseptic. This time it was unpleasant. There was a strong chlorine smell rising from the surface. The pool was very deep. From this dream I remembered the last one, remembered liking, feeling comforted by the deep still water among the waves. It was as deep and still – but it was not empty. In the depths, where the blue darkened almost to black, there was something. Too far down for me to have any idea of its identity – but there was something. My eyes ached and watered with the blueness and the effort of seeing through it. And then my focus shifted and I saw my own reflection. There was my peering face, the flesh on my cheeks pulled down by the angle, dark lines engraved from my nose to the corners of my mouth. I saw an old person peering into the depths to identify, with a gathering dread, the submerged thing.

I did not wake relaxed this time. I woke to the familiar tight thrum of a headache, a stiff knottiness in my neck skewed by this cruel mattress.

Another day. Barker came in for my bucket. She is a true bitch. I do not like to use that word to insult a woman but there is simply no other word for her. Also, I think she is a sadist. She complains about the smell from my bucket as if her own shit smells of roses. Once she came in with a fag between her lips, a roll-up, and she sucked on it looking at me with her cruel eyes, squinted against the long fern of smoke that she exhaled. She has the wrong face, a grandmotherly face. She could be advertising wholemeal bread or butter. Something wholesome. But she is far from wholesome. She tells me lies. She also has an uncanny knowledge of what will hurt, of where to aim her darts. No, not uncanny, she is perceptive that's all, nothing *uncanny* about it. She has eyes like gimlets that bore into me, eyes that are incongruous between her speckled doughy cheeks and fluffy grey hair.

'Hicks is up for parole,' she said this morning as she gave me my breakfast. Tea that was actually stone cold with a flecked skin of tannin on top and grey porridge like wallpaper paste. I am sure she spits in the food. Sometimes I am sure I can see tiny frogspawn spit bubbles. I have no more control over what I eat than an animal in the zoo.

I didn't answer. I didn't give her the satisfaction of my distress.

Hicks is Debbie. Of course, I would not be distressed if it was true. I would be happy for Debbie. She is a good person who should not be here, in this bad place where most of us are bad. I don't believe Barker. Why should it happen just like that, so suddenly while I'm locked up? She can't just go, not that quickly. I *would* be pleased for her, I really would. But I'd like to see her first. She can't just vanish.

I will leave here. That thought makes me shrink. I used to keep snails when I was a child. I liked to race them on glass, watching from underneath their glutinous progress. I like their eyes, the little balls on tiny stalks, waving. If you prod an eye with your finger, or with a blade of grass, it retracts, shrinks right down, the stalk softly collapsing on itself until it is nothing but a neat nub, and then sometimes the whole beast contracts, condensing inside its shell. Once it is stowed inside it seals its exit, glues itself down so that you have to prise it off with your finger-nail to look inside. That is what the thought of freedom makes me want to do. But if there was a friend waiting . . . If Debbie would be my friend . . .

After three days I'll be out of solitary. Three days. Seventy-two hours – maybe seventy-six. Which is less than 5,000 minutes, which is 300,000 seconds. And a second is over just like that. And that. And that. That's three seconds less. The time is diminishing. I do like that about time – the reliability of its passing. I'm doing time. A good expression. Apt. Although sometimes it feels more like time is doing me.

I rang Tom later that night and told him of my decision. I wrote his name with my finger in the condensation on the glass inside the phone box while I waited for him to answer.

'I'm not going back to university,' I said. 'I'm coming to live in London. To be near you.' I drew a heart round his name. He tried to dissuade me, naturally, taking the role of the older, more responsible man.

'Think of your future,' he said. I believe he actually said that, but I could hear the happiness in his voice. I knew that he did want me. He didn't try too hard to dissuade me. After all, he wasn't *that* responsible.

'Is *she* back?' I asked.

'Yes,' he said, and I could hear, very faintly, a woman's voice singing. I don't know if it was Moira, it could have been a record but it could have been her, there, near him and happy enough to sing. I looked at Tom's name and saw how the heart dribbled drips all down it. I wiped it off with my sleeve.

'Look, I can't talk now,' he said. 'Don't for Christ's sake do anything hasty. Go back and I'll ring you tomorrow.'

'No. I'm not going back. I'm coming to London. *I'll* ring *you*.'

I put the phone down before he could say more. I grinned to think of him standing there, phone in hand, frustrated, wanting to say more.

My life suddenly seemed stunningly simple. I would live near Tom in this transition phase. Of course, it would be a while before we were truly together. I'd have to be patient. I'd get a job, a bedsit . . . any old hole would do for a short time. I wouldn't tell Mama until it was all done. Until there was no going back. Anyway, she was so busy with Ursula she'd hardly care as long as I was out of the way. I shuddered to think of all that old womanish flesh rubbing together.

All I wanted was Tom and I could tell from his voice that he was excited too. Worried, of course. It was a big step, swiftly taken and he was concerned about my future. Of course, he was. He loved me. But *I* was not worried. I had faith that things would work out.

I *do have* a capacity for love. I do miss intimacy. That is a difficulty in here. Since Mama died, I don't even have any visitors. She used to come looking so ashamed, looking really old, and each time a little smaller. Then Ursula died and after a couple of months Mama followed. She came only once between Ursula's death and her own. We held hands across the table and she hardly spoke. Arthritis had crumpled her hands and there was nothing she could do. She couldn't even knit any more. For Christmas she had sent me a pair of gloves with only four fingers on each hand. I don't know if she realized.

'I wonder what the point of it all was,' she said, the last time I saw her. 'I wonder what I did that was so wrong.' 'Nothing,' I said, 'you did nothing wrong.' But she looked around the room at all the other criminals and then at me, and I know she blamed herself for what I'd done. I wanted to take the blame away from her but I didn't know how. All I could do was search for other things to say. I tried to make her smile. 'Do you remember,' I said, 'the time Bob poured methylated spirit on the Christmas pudding and we couldn't put it out?' – but her answering smile was only an imitation.

I was allowed compassionate leave to attend the funeral. It was a chilly November day. I sat between two screws wearing a borrowed black coat and my four-fingered gloves. There were only two more people there, strangers, or so I thought until we were leaving. Then, with a shock like a sharp slap I recognized my old friend Bronwyn's mother. After Bronwyn had disappeared, her mother and Mama had become friends. She liked to see me, encouraged me to visit her, liked to keep up with young people, she said. But I felt awkward to be there while Bronwyn wasn't, awkward and somehow guilty. And now it seemed odd to me that *she* was still here, old and shrivelled, while Bronwyn was gone, was only the memory of a lumpy girl who fancied herself sex-mad. Bronwyn's mother used to like me once, she used to seek me out, look for me outside the school, but now she knew I was bad and averted her eyes.

I was glad to get out of the crematorium. It was all mahogany veneer and taped music and I think the tape was stretched, it sounded so slow and warped. Mama was just a box with a mean spray of Michaelmas daisies on top. A man who didn't know Mama from Adam said some standard things and one of the screws handed me a tissue and squeezed my arm sympathetically but I was hardly moved. It was just a box, and when the curtain lifted and it slid discreetly into a space there was nothing.

Later I cried. Later I howled like a wolf into the mouth of the void that was my life apart from prison. I sobbed for Mama and how hard she tried and how badly she failed to make me good. I sobbed because no one else in the whole wide world loved me. Nobody really cared. And then I got into a fight over a sachet of shampoo and ended up in solitary. That was the first time.

People with children have photographs and hopes. Even husbands sometimes wait. Otherwise the only way to find love of a sort is to turn to the other women. And we are hardly the *crème de la crème* in here. I would, but I am not a lesbian. I don't know what they do. I've never even wanted to find out. But it would not be like that with Debbie. I wouldn't love her because she was a woman, I would love her because she is *Debbie*. I would only like to get close to her. I would only like to smell the fresh air in her hair and rub my grey indoor cheek against her rosy outdoor one. I bet it is cool. I would like to taste her skin which I know would be clean as apples. I would only like to taste, not bite. I would like to put my head between her breasts which are neither big nor small, that are healthy and soft enough to be a comfort. I would like to hear the steady drum of her heart. I would only like to lay my face on the curve of her belly and breathe in the secret smell of her which would be sea-salt, slippery-fish fresh, I just know. And I would like to hear her gasp of pleasure because it would be so surprised. I know. Though I would never dare these things. I am not like that. I loved Tom more than anyone in this world ever loved anyone. But he is not here to love and I am nothing if not realistic.

On Monday morning, I packed my books and my clothes. I took my bank book. I had savings, not a fortune, but enough to put a deposit on a flat and live on until I got a job. I let Mama assume I was returning to university. She gave me the remains of a seed-cake in a tin to take with me. I felt as excited when I stepped out of the door into sunshine that was beginning to smell of spring as if I was stepping off the edge of one life and on to a new one.

I found a basement room near Tom, in Westbourne Grove. It was dim and damp-smelling, but it had a double bed, a sink hidden behind a curtain of bamboo beads threaded on to raffia and a Baby Belling cooker – all I needed. The bathroom was up a flight of treacherous stairs, shared with the tenants on the floor above. The landlord seemed amazed at my enthusiasm when he showed me round. I went straight out and bought tea-bags, candles, joss-sticks and a bottle of wine. On the way back from the shops I tried to telephone Tom but there was no reply so I phoned Jaz instead. I could hear the echoey voices of other students, their feet clattering up the hall of residence stairs, as I waited for her to come to the phone, and I felt superior. I had left all that behind me now, all that paper and learning, for something real.

'I'm not coming back,' I announced. 'I'm moving in with Tom.' I felt this was more of an exaggeration than a lie. I asked her to send the few things I'd left behind. She was aghast and impressed. 'What about his wife?' she asked. 'Gone,' I said breezily and just for a second I believed it myself. Down the phone to Jaz I could be my bright insouciant student self. 'Gone like snow on the water. Good-byeee . . .' 'Don't you feel . . . ?' 'What?' 'Guilty?' I laughed. I did not feel guilty, not in the least. This was not about Moira. It had nothing to do with her.

'When do I get to meet him?' Jaz asked and I said something vague. It made my head hurt to imagine them meeting. They simply couldn't. The idea of it was like trying to force the wrong ends of two magnets together in my head because Tom and Jaz weren't from the same lives, didn't even belong to the same Jenny.

I returned from the phone box and descended the dank stairs to my room. The steps were of cracked stained concrete and rubbish had blown down from the street. I slipped on a discarded condom. I thought I could paint the door bright red and stand pots of plants on the steps. Did I really think that?

I lit a joss-stick as soon as I got in to try and overlay the dirty smell of the fat-stained carpet with sandalwood. It was four o'clock, too late to look for a job, too late to get money out of the bank, too late to do anything much. I pinned some postcards on the wall. There was somebody in the bathroom so I had a shivery wash in the sink with a sliver of dirt-ingrained soap somebody had left behind. The water ran away sluggishly as if there was some unspeakable mess clogging the pipe. I made myself a cup of tea and realized I'd forgotten to buy milk. I drank the tea black, munched a piece of Mama's cake and made a shopping list. I had never had to shop for myself before. The excitement of independence was soon replaced by a feeling of awe at how many things a person needs. I wrote a list on the back of a page of the essay about Prufrock I had started: *milk, sugar, coffee, bread, butter, jam, Marmite, biscuits, fruit*. I started to think of flour and things, but I would not be cooking in here. I would not settle down. It was hardly worth it. I would not paint the door or grow plants in pots. I would not put down roots. *Aspirins, plasters, antiseptic cream, toilet paper, tissues*. But I had to cheer the place up, Tom would be coming here, sleeping here even. *Flowers, sink cleaner, talcum powder, washing-up liquid, washing powder*. The curtains were sad, shiny stuff, salmon pink faded in stripes to distemper in memory of a sunnier room. They were too short for the window. *More wine, fruit juice*. The window-sill was spotted with dead flies and wasps, even a butterfly, a peacock, dead and half desiccated. I picked it up and the dust of its scales rubbed off on my fingers. What was a butterfly doing in a basement? I took it as an omen: a butterfly in a basement, a promise of something bright. I didn't take into account that it was dead.

This was not a promising love-nest, even I could see that, but it *was* only temporary. Tom would not leave me here long. I thought perhaps he'd find me somewhere else quickly, before I moved in with him.

127

It was cold, that was the worst of it. I found that I was shivering, and the shivers drove away my precarious cheerfulness. The walls felt clammy. The wallpaper was coming off in one corner and there were dark mottled stains around the window and above the skirting-board. I tried to imagine Mama's reaction. 'Not fit for a dog,' she'd say, or something like.

I thought about another cup of tea but I didn't like it black. Anyway, the water tasted wrong. I didn't like the crust round the end of the taps. It didn't look healthy. I opened the wine instead and poured it into the only glass I could find, a thick unbreakable glass like the ones we'd had at school. The wine was very cheap, quite unpleasant. I didn't know anything about wine. Tom would never have bought it. It made my tongue feel furry but it cheered me up all the same. Though why I should have needed cheering up, I don't know. I had a new home, all I needed was a job. I would work of course, even when I lived with Tom. I could not quite imagine what sort of work, but it didn't matter. Tom would be sure to know. Tom Wise.

I rang again and again and always there was no reply. I climbed up the steps that I now realized smelled of old urine. *Bleach, scrubbing brush, rubber gloves*. I walked to the telephone box, dialled and waited. I could not believe there was no one there at all. So I kept trying, up and down from the dank and darkening room to the telephone box, a glass of wine in between each trip. It grew so cold in the room that the cold took on a blue and spiteful face. I put money in the slot for the electric fire which, ridiculously, was high up on the wall so it heated a slice of air at the top of the room, and the ceiling and nothing else. I lay on the bed after my fifth glass of wine and covered myself up. The wallpaper had orange and black overlapping circles on it that made my eyes go funny, so I closed them. I didn't know I'd been asleep until I was woken by trampling feet above my head. I heard voices, a radio being switched on. I didn't mind. I looked at my watch. It was seven o'clock. It was nice to have company of a sort, to hear other lives going on – as long as I didn't have to meet them. I woke with a headache. I braced myself to drink some tap water and then I went out to phone. This time Tom answered.

'I'm here,' I said.

'Come again?'

'Just round the corner, Sady Street.'

'Doing?'

'I've got a flat, sort of, like I said. I've done it, left university, left home.'

There was silence for a moment. I could hear music and voices in the background.

'You've done what?' He sounded severe but there was suppressed excitement in his voice.

'I've left everything. For you.'

He was quiet again. 'Can I see you?' I asked.

'Christ almighty,' he said.

'What's up?'

'Moira's just making dinner – we've got friends . . . we're about to sit down.' I heard a burst of laughter, men and women together.

The jealousy that flashed through me, illuminated me bright yellow inside, was a shock. Now I'd been there, I could see it all. The table, candles, flowers, good wine. Moira carefully beautiful, skin glowing, hair piled up or tumbling down, blue-black in the candle-light.

'But I *must* see you.'

'Tomorrow.'

'Tonight.'

'Not possible. Sorry.' His voice took on a formal quality, I guessed someone had tuned in to his conversation. 'Ring me tomorrow,' he said and put the phone down. The click in my ear was like a slap on my cheek.

I wandered around. With my last money I bought a pint of milk and a bar of chocolate. I walked about aimlessly, eating the chocolate. I passed a boy begging. I had not seen anyone begging before. 'I haven't got any money,' I said. I could see he didn't believe me. I considered offering him some of my chocolate but I thought that might be insulting. I walked along the canal, past the *Hunky-Dory* where light and music leaked from behind the curtains. I thought I might suggest to Tom that we bought a barge to live on, one day. It would be so snug, big enough only for the two of us, with little chairs and a little bed. It would be like living in a doll's house.

The night was bitterly cold. Lights glittered on the black water in bright flakes and floated up to dazzle me. My feet were numb. I walked to Tom's house. The curtains were drawn and all the lights were on. It looked warm and secure, almost smug, so safe and cosy. I went up to the front door. I thought of ringing the bell. What could Tom say if I came in? They might even ask me to join them for dinner. That would be fun. Watching Tom's face and watching Moira, so beautiful and unaware. No, it would not be fun. I would look young and scruffy. I would not be able to join in the conversation. Tom would be angry with me. I was suddenly aware that the door-step was rocking beneath my feet and I remembered all the wine I'd already drunk. If I went in I would probably end up disgracing myself and being sick.

I pushed open the letter-box and peered in. I tried to focus my eyes on the bright blur inside and made out a bit of a bicycle, and a child's shoe. I breathed in the smell of curry and a bitter taste rose in my throat. I thought a little warmth came out of the slot with the curry smell – and a sudden laugh. It was Tom laughing and saying something, I could not catch the words but it sounded as if he was teasing someone, Moira perhaps. There was sitar music too. Oh it all sounded so perfect it made my legs go weak. I saw my face reflected in the letter-flap. My features were all squashed up like a pug's and my lips stained blue with cold and the awful wine. I felt very sick. It must have been the chocolate on top of the wine. Or the smell of curry. I let the letter-flap snap shut and then to my horror, I threw up. I had never thrown up like that before, so suddenly and with such an awful retching noise. But there it was, a dark and sticky pool on Tom's doorstep. I thought they *must* have heard me. I did not know what to do so I ran away. I ran all the way back to my basement.

FLAMINGO

I've noticed a crack in the ceiling. I can't believe I haven't seen it before, that there could be something in here that I've never noticed. Maybe it is new. No, it's not. It's simply something I haven't seen before. It's like a river with spidery tributaries or a diagram of the veins in a lung. Around the crack the paint has lifted a bit, loose flakes and underneath the same colour. It is like living in a mushroom with this dim light, this non-colour. No, it is more like being a mushroom. I wouldn't be surprised to feel my face and find it mushroom smooth, the mouth healed up, the nose flattened, the eyes sealed with a fungal skin. Mushrooms, toadstools are so strong, blunt and soft. Their strength is a mystery. I have seen them lift pavements, nose their snub and silent way through tarmac, new laid by tough men and rollered down. Mama used to pick fungi: chanterelle, honey-fungus, beefsteak-fungus, oyster-fungus, horn of plenty, cep. And then she'd fry them for breakfast, horrible slimy platefuls I couldn't believe weren't poisonous, and Bob used to smack his lips and pronounce them delicious. He especially appreciated them because they were free. Once, Mama found puffballs the size of footballs in a field; they were nice, thick slices fried with bacon. Old puffballs went soft and if you kicked them the spores exploded out of them like dust.

There is no dust in here. That is odd. It is actually quite clean although there is the smell of stale distress. And the smell of me.

I hated that basement bedsit but from where I am now, I can't see why I loathed it so utterly. It had a door that opened after all. There was a window through which I could see pigeons hopping, sometimes a pair of legs arriving or departing.

I would love to wash. I'd like a proper wash with hot water and soft towels. Jenks brought me a bowl of lukewarm water with which to wash my hands and some brown soap. What I want is pink soap. Pink soap with a smell like artificial spring that lathers into a million soft and shiny bubbles, that leaves a scent behind it on the skin. The brown soap is coarse and gritty and does not lather, however hard you rub it between your hands you get nothing more than a reluctant slime. What sadist chose this soap? Is it designed and manufactured especially for us, joyless soap for the bad girls and the wicked women to stop us smelling of roses? I would like a bar of Camay. Or a Pears soap with a picture of a pretty girl on the box. I used to dream of being Miss Pears with long shiny ringlets and pink cheeks, my picture on a poster on the chemist's door. I wonder if there is a Miss Pears in here, Miss Pears gone wrong. Even coal-tar soap with its incisive yellow smell would do. Or a fag, or a kiss. Oh Christ.

There were two people kissing on my basement steps when I got back. I waited a moment, coughed and shuffled.

'Excuse me,' I said at last.

'What you looking at?' the man said.

'I want to get in,' I explained.

'You live here?' the woman said. 'Poor cow. Light me a fag, Tez.' They moved out of the way and let me in. They peered through the door with interest when I opened it but I shut it quickly behind me in case they wanted to come in. I wasn't ready for visitors. The chilly air wound itself round me. There was the electric smell of burnt dust from the fire, but no trace of heat left. It was colder indoors than out.

I didn't feel sick now, the run through the cold air had revived me. I went upstairs to the bathroom but I could not go in. The bath was festooned with strange hairs and striped with rings of scum – but it was the smell of urine-soaked floor-boards that drove me out. I made myself a cup of tea and, suddenly ravenously hungry, finished off Mama's seed-cake. A caraway seed caught between my teeth and its friendly wholesome taste made me want to cry. It made me want to run straight back home. I felt foolish. Tom and Moira would be in bed together now, if their guests had gone. Mama and Ursula would be tucked up too, tangled together in Ursula's hair. I could be in my neat narrow bed in the hall of residence where it was warm and safe. But I was not. I had chosen. I was freezing cold. I picked the seed out from between my teeth, balanced on a chair to pee in the sink, and climbed into bed, still dressed. I spread my coat on top of the blankets.

As I lay waiting for sleep, I listened to the tenants upstairs. They were moving about, getting ready for bed. I could hear the amiable to-and-froing of a conversation, running water – and from behind its beaded curtain, my sink gurgled. As the days passed I grew familiar with this idiosyncrasy of the plumbing – whenever they let water out of their sink, it rose up in mine.

I went out and phoned Tom in the morning. I was half afraid he'd accuse me of vomiting on his doorstep, but he didn't mention it. He said only that he was busy and we arranged to meet in a pub in the evening. I used the day well. I put my name down at an employment agency, I found a bank, I did my shopping. I felt cheerful and positive, all my night-time heeby-jeebies had vanished. It was a bright, hard, sunny day and I was a bright, hard, sunny woman. Though I had slept only by pretending I was at home, not now, not now that Ursula was there but when I was a little girl. I knew it was pathetic, but it worked. I made the strangers' voices upstairs be Mama and Bob's downstairs, I made the wide saggy bed my own narrow one and I kept my eyes screwed up against the contrary evidence until I slept. And in the morning I was all right and glad I was not there but here. As long as there was Tom I was all right. I was a balloon and as long as he had hold of the string I would be fine.

I told Bronwyn to go to the church where Johnny, the mad tramp, was. I knew he was dangerous. I had seen the sharpness of his nails, the silver blade in his suitcase, the blankness in his eyes. I had heard his crazy stories and I let Bronwyn go there. I encouraged her to go. And then she disappeared. Sometimes I wake in the morning with a sickly taste in my mouth. Bronwyn used to smell of sweat and bacon. She had a cloud of red-brown hair. I suppose it was beautiful hair. She had no friends, she was worse off even than me for friends. She thought I was her friend, but I was not. I get a hopeless feeling when I wake from dreaming about Bronwyn, because there is nothing I can do. Because I did nothing wrong, nothing *really* wrong. I let her take her chance, that's all. But I did wish she would disappear, and she did. I didn't mean it. And I get a hopeless feeling because there is no end to that story. Nothing neat about it. I don't know what became of her and will never know.

I have five lozenges on my arm. The first is faded to green. I would love to have some paints. I haven't ever painted, except splotchy things at school. But perhaps that is something I can do. Perhaps you can make meaning out of paints without words, another language. I put a tiny thing in the empty box that is my freedom: the plan to learn to paint. I would appreciate the colours like no one else. Pillar-box red and yellow. I can hardly believe in yellow. Colour deprivation is what I am suffering. If only they would bring me an egg with a round yellow yolk. I would break the skin and see the thick yellow running over the white, hardening into paler trickles on the plate. The only eggs I've seen lately are scrambled – and scrambled, what is more, until they're grey. Egg-yolk, sunset, holly-berry, daffodil, tangerine. Water melon! How I could feast my eyes on a slice of water melon, on the mottled green rind, the wet shocking pink flesh and the smooth white pips. No they are yellow. No, black. Oh God, I

am forgetting. Salmon pink, flamingo pink. To think that somewhere in this same world that I inhabit there is a bird with pink
feathers, a free wild bird with spindly legs and feathers the colour
of water melon. Flocks of them blotting out the yellow sun, a
pink cloud of feathers in the blue sky. Bob told me it is only
because they eat pink food that they are pink. Can that be true?
Otherwise they are grey. It is only what I am fed that makes me
grey. One day I will be free and pink again. Could I ever bear
another lover to plumb the pinkest depths of me?

Memory is terrible. I think I should stop remembering. But
memory is insidious, like damp or a draught. It will find its way
in. I bolster my mind with other things, safe things, like sandbags
round the edges. Grant is kind. I asked her about Debbie –
whether she has gone. I'm not supposed to ask questions. She's
not supposed to answer. Someone else was standing outside
when she came in for my bucket, of course, in case I was to go
berserk, fly at her neck with my teeth and claws, so she could not
say much. But she did say 'Bollocks', and she did *smile*. It was
like a slice of fruit, her smile, as refreshing as that. And, what is
more, I smiled back. Preposterous! Five days in solitary and I am
smiling at a screw. A triumph of human nature I would call it. It
was a fascinating sensation, the tightening of my cheek muscles,
the opening of my lips, the upward stretching of the corners of
my eyes. It almost hurt. I felt a sort of fizzing in my face and then
she went. She looked sorry and a little afraid. Perhaps she thinks
I'm going mad. Madder. She is beautiful in her own way. I would
like to clean her up, brush all the dandruff from her shoulders,
clean her glasses, shine her shoes. The way she said 'Bollocks'
was wonderful. I have smiled at them sarcastically, curved up my
mouth in a parody of a smile. But this one was real. Unfortunately it left me open. I don't blame Grant. I believe her sympathy
– even liking – is genuine. I don't blame *her*, but when the smile
slipped off I found it had left a gap for emotion to get in, flood in
and I found my mouth contorted the other way, bent down, hard
as an iron bar. I felt a searing knot in my throat, a pain behind my

nose and tears welled in my eyes. They ran like rain, from both corners of both eyes and from my nose. I sobbed. My shoulders bunched and shook. I was like a puppet. I let myself go into the contortions of it. The strings jerked crazily – the puppet master in a fit. The tears ran into my mouth and they tasted like sea water. I sobbed and wailed. The slot opened and snapped shut and I didn't even look.

In the boiling turmoil of the sinking ship, Hester took charge of Peggy. As the prisoners and the crew fought and joined forces against the command, kegs of rum were split open and the fight became a drunken brawl, the sails blazed, the decks ran with blood and rum, men fell or jumped or were flung overboard into the glittering orange waves. It was as if someone had stirred a sunset with an angry spoon and thrown in a thunderbolt for good measure. Spears and blades of orange light leapt all around, flames roared their ravenous way through the ship devouring wood and canvas rope and flesh. Peggy would have burned, there is no doubt she would have burned and gone down with the ship, but Hester found her. There were lifeboats and there were murderous scrambles for them. Women and children first was part of civilization and civilization was forgotten in the chaos that was like a bible picture of hell.

Hester found a small craft, a one-or-two-man boat, used for rowing to shore. The fiddle man was by it. He had stopped playing but did not fight. He held his fiddle in one hand, his bow in the other and he just stood and looked at the madness. He leant against the small tarpaulin-covered boat. Hester got him moving, they were beyond the bulkhead out of sight of the roaring fray. Hester found Peggy and led her across the slithery deck, over bodies that rocked with the motion of the ship, across bodies that were really dead and bodies that groaned their last. Hester and Peggy and Saul – the musician – cast themselves adrift in the small boat. The waves rose and threatened at first to dash them against the towering hull of the ship. The water's surface sizzled with bits of flaming wood and cloth and the hot reflection of the flames. As the current drew them away from the great ship there was a whoof and the flames leapt – as if blown by a giant mouth – leapt and enveloped the ship so that it seemed a black silhouette in an orange globe. The heat was like the heat of the sun on Peggy's face and she closed her eyes against the thrilling destruction, the horror that was so beautiful, beautiful enough to die in. But Hester had not let her die, Hester was like another part of her, she thought as the cold sea lifted the little craft up and down, as the flames baked the flesh of her face. Hester was the clever part, the part that would guard her against herself. If Hester and I were one, she thought, we would be a woman entire.

The boat drifted away. The sky sighed and the storm passed across them trailing its ticklish electric hairs far beyond them into the south. From across the glistening ebony water they watched and felt the *Cunning Maid* go down. Flames lit the black lid of the sky, quenched the starlight, smoked away the moon. When the ship slipped under the water the roar was terrific, a gargantuan cracking and crackling, a sizzling steam and a rising gulp as the sea opened its lips and swallowed the burning wreck. The surface heaved and flakes of hot ash like midnight snow flew hot and soft in Peggy's face. Sparks danced in the air, red dazzles rising to the moon, drifting up until Peggy's eyes were too weary to follow any more.

Saul had not spoken more than a word or two. He held his fiddle against his chest as if it was a baby and just stared with great wide eyes, and Peggy saw that he was young, not much more than a boy. Hester lay with her head in Peggy's lap, sleeping. Peggy stroked her hair, coarse and damp from weeks of filth and the sweaty terror of the night. The ship had gone. That giant thing, just gone. The air was thick with the smell of burning, of charred wood and cloth and meat. From here and there small bits of wreckage carried the voices of survivors, convicts, officers, crew. It hardly mattered which, they were all equal in the immense waste of the ocean. All as helpless.

Peggy was overcome with a drowsiness that allowed no further movement and hardly even thought. It was not quite sleep, it was the weight of her loaded mind at rest. Here, rocking dangerously adrift somewhere in the southern seas, in a small boat with Hester and a stranger who might have been Satan himself for all she knew of him, she felt safe, safer than she had felt from the moment the peacock struck her with its beak. Her hand was too heavy to lift and feel the raised, dart-shaped scar as this sluggish realization dawned. For now she was free.

Saul put his fiddle to his shoulder and began to play a slow and tearful air. The dragging notes were like phosphorescent snakes winding behind Peggy's eyelids as she slipped below her mind and into sleep.

He was late. I'd been sitting in the pub for ages. I'd arrived early with a book, to make me look occupied. I sat in the corner near the door where I could not possibly miss him and where I could also clearly see the clock over the bar. I could not read the book, every time the door opened my eyes jumped and my heart bundled in my chest. He was twenty-five minutes late. The pub was filling with stupid raucous people who stood in my line of vision. The angle of the black clock hands widened and gaped with his lateness. The minutes were made of elastic and as they stretched my pleasure and anticipation thinned. When he came through the door, I started and grinned stupidly and almost spilled my drink. It was only days since I had seen him but it felt like months. He seemed different, smaller, tenser, more concentrated. In the pub among the other people I saw with surprise that he was quite small man. And so good looking. I felt proud.

He nodded and went to the bar, came back with a half of bitter for me – though I had been drinking wine. He kissed me as he sat down, his beard brushing my cheek. He took off his leather jacket. I saw that he had on the red silk shirt and black waistcoat he'd been wearing at Christmas and I thought it was a sign that he was mine.

'So . . .' he said, raising one eyebrow. 'What *is* all this?' He ran his hand through his hair and I noticed his wedding ring. He had not worn it before, I was sure. The little black hairs on his fingers overlapped the gold band.

'I told you.'

'Let me get it straight. You've left university, you've left home. Well, we can soon get that sorted.'

'What?'

'You can bloody well go back.'

'Tom!'

He sipped his Guinness. 'Look, kid . . .' He had never called me kid before. 'I can't let you do this. It's mad. Christ almighty!'

'But I can't concentrate anyway. It's so stupid.'

'You must. Have a bit of discipline.'

'Discipline!' I would have laughed if I hadn't been so frightened. Tom twisted the wedding ring on his finger. Discipline was not a Tom sort of word.

'You've never worn a ring before,' I said.

He looked at it. 'Moira found it in the bathroom. Pointed out I hadn't been wearing it. Don't like them much, rings. But, if it makes her happy. Anyway. What have you done about leaving university?'

'Just left.'

'Not done it officially?'

'No.'

He smiled for the first time. 'Thank Christ for that. Well you can turn round and go straight back.'

'I *can't*. I couldn't concentrate.'

'Look, sweetheart. I care about you, you know I do. But I'm married, well and truly. And you're so young.' He paused. I could see him softening. He touched his finger to my lips. 'So young and sweet.'

'I thought things . . . I mean things between you and Moira weren't great.' I sipped my bitter beer to keep my mouth from turning down.

'They aren't great, but they're OK. One advantage of my years of experience – you realize that OK will do. You search and search for true love, fireworks, the lot. And then you settle for OK.'

'Tom! Don't you want more?'

'Of course, but more doesn't exist. Not in the long run. Say I left Moira, say *we* got married . . .' My heart leapt as he said this. 'How long would it be before we became dull, run-of-the-mill? OK, if we were lucky. OK's not so common you know, not in the long run. You shouldn't knock OK.' He paused and looked at my bewildered face. This was not what he'd said before, he'd never spoken in such a defeated middle-aged way before. 'One day you'll understand what I'm saying,' he added.

Patronizing shit, I thought. I wanted to chuck my beer at him. He had a rim of Guinness froth clinging to his moustache. I clenched my fists but the anger sank as quickly as it had risen and my face contorted as tears welled behind my eyes and spilled over.

'So you don't want me,' I said, and my voice was a child's.

He sighed and gave me his handkerchief. He looked round the bar before putting his arm round my shoulder. 'Don't, sweetie. Of course I want you. Come on, drink up. You can show me your place.' His handkerchief was dark blue with red spots, crumpled and warm from his pocket. I wiped my eyes and blew my nose and breathed in the smell of him that clung to the cotton. I held his left hand and twisted the ring on his finger. It was smooth gold, warm and worn with tiny scratches.

'Have you eaten?' he asked. 'We must look after you.'

I relaxed a bit. Already he was relenting. Of course he was because now he was with me he was remembering that what we had was real, not just OK. It was marvellous.

He rolled a joint while I cut up the pizza and opened the wine. 'What a dump,' he'd said when I opened the door, and I'd felt hurt and pleased. Hurt because I had bought flowers, cleaned, burned joss-sticks until they made me sneeze and spent pounds

141

on the useless heater. Pleased because, of course, I couldn't stay in a dump. He couldn't let me stay there.

'I used to have a place a bit like this,' he said. 'Makes me feel quite nostalgic. Forget about that . . .' He gestured at the electric fire on the wall. 'Best thing is to put the oven on with the door open.' He searched through his pockets and piled some silver coins on top of the cooker. 'Can't have you freezing to death, can we?'

I sat beside him on the bed. 'My grandmother, it turns out, is a lesbian,' I said as he lit the joint. He snorted and choked on the smoke. I patted his back, let my hand linger and slide on the silky back of his waistcoat against his silk shirt.

'Come again?'

'Mama and Ursula are lesbians. I caught them in bed.'

'Christ,' he said meditatively letting the smoke roll out of his smile in a smooth stream. 'Well, well. You live and learn.'

'And they've chucked me out, as good as.'

'No . . .'

'As good as. There's not room for me any more. Not room for Ursula and me in the same house. Not with all their sculptures. Anyway, she doesn't like me.'

'And the feeling's mutual?'

'You know it is.'

'Hmm.' He took a bite of pizza. 'But you haven't *actually* been turfed out?'

'No. But . . .' He held up his hand and I was quiet. The wine was clean and white. It went perfectly with the soft grey smoke, my mind was softened and sharpened at the same time. I believed then, for that minute, that Tom was really mine. I thought I could see it in his eyes, the loving curiosity, the greediness of them on me, travelling over my body so that I could feel their path, soft and probing as a tongue. We made love more gently and slowly than ever before. It wasn't a snatched moment. Now I lived near by and I was a real part of his life. I was only half-an-hour's walk away. We could see each other every day and it wouldn't be long before he stopped resisting the inevitable, that he accepted that I was right, that he couldn't live apart from me, that I would give him more, understand him better than Moira.

'Caught them in bed doing what?' Tom asked. 'Christ it's cold in here. Come here little one.' He held me against his chest. I was uncomfortable. His beard tickled my nose, my arm was going numb but I did not want to move. Ever.

'Watching "Little House on the Prairie",' I said. He laughed so hard that he coughed and I did move then, shiveringly from the bed to get him some water, feed a coin into the meter and switch on the cooker.

' "Little House on the Prairie", eh?' he said.

'That's not the point. The point is, they were in bed watching it. Naked.'

Tom shrugged off his grin. 'Live and let live,' he said. 'Had Ursula down for a dyke from the first – but not your granny.'

I curled up to him again. I ran my hand over his chest and his soft belly and cradled his penis in my hand. It was as small and soft as a sleeping mouse.

Sometimes I make love to myself – though I try to resist it. But I don't know who to hold in my mind. Sometimes I imagine Tom is with me while I touch myself, while my fingers rub and slip and sometimes that works and I imagine him touching me, opening me, pushing into the aching space. Sometimes that works but often it stops being me. Sometimes it becomes Moira or another lover, for surely he had droves of them – none quite so naïve as me. None quite so angry. And the anger stops the pleasure and then I am charged up with energy, *sexual* energy but too angry to release it and that is the most frightening sensation, here in this box with nothing, nothing, nothing. And I pace though there is not room for more than three paces either way and I drum my fists on the walls and sometimes kick them, knee them which is futile and painful. But pain is a physical sensation, at least. It is dangerous to get so charged up so I exercise, exercise, exercise.

143

Down and up and down and twist oh christ oh christ oh christ oh christ. I get so turned on I don't know what to do, try to stuff my head with something else, with Peggy, but then it is Neptune I see with his fishy skin and his trident filling her filling her filling me with all the water from the sea. Sometimes I cannot stop myself reaching for Debbie and thinking how it would be to be touched by a woman who knew me like she knew herself, who would unfurl me with her woman's tongue. But that is no good so I bend and stretch and bend and stretch and then I fall down and I cannot stop, I do not know what to do and my fingers are not big enough or long enough to reach inside myself, and if I come at all it is a sad spasm and I shout out as a protest, not out of any sort of joy, as a protest that the spasm is so puny, the pleasure is hardly greater than a sneeze but sadder. Oooh so lonely. And the slot opens, some cow watching, smirking, I don't care. And then I regret it, how I regret it, for I am left open then to desolation and despair. And I shiver and memory floods into the gap. I wish I would not do it because afterwards I cannot remember why. I am sickened by myself. I am like some chimpanzee in a cage, like a randy dog rubbing itself against a chair and I am left in a shivery heap of self-disgust.

I must not feel. I have told myself, taught myself that I must not feel. It is not necessary. I have a mind that will stretch and belly with imagination like the sail of a great ship. I need not be tethered to my body and its responses, to my puny, sordid memory. I need not.

Peggy woke to a white gaping hole in the sky through which light and heat poured in a heavy smothering stream. 'Peggy,' Saul said. His face was dark against the brilliance of the sky, his hair a messy halo. 'It's us now. Just the three of us. See how we've drifted.'

But all Peggy could see was water all around and dazzling bouncing sizzles of heat, no marker to show how they had moved.

'It is calm,' Hester kissed Peggy. 'We will live,' she said, as if she had peeped into Peggy's mind and read the hopelessness there.

'Live?' Peggy said. 'Hester, to live we must first eat and drink.'

'Have faith,' Hester said.

'Faith! Faith in what Hester?'

'In God,' Saul said.

'In the God that brought us here?' Peggy gestured at the sea. 'I have more faith in Neptune.' Saul and Hester were silenced. Peggy looked away, screwed her eyes up against the dancing diamonds on the water, but she knew that they looked at each other, her companions, she knew that they were shocked. And she was shocked herself. Such a thought would never have entered her head on dry land, or in society, but here among all the nothing of sea and sky, her mind opened freshly. She could see they were alone. And she did not care what she said.

There was quiet. The gentle lapping of water round the boat and otherwise quiet. And then Hester laughed. 'Look!' A fish rose from the water in a shimmering arc. 'See, a jumping fish!' Another followed and then another until there was a shimmering exultation of them all around, soaring from the water, trailing silver scribbles and vanishing beneath the water again with scarcely a splash or ripple.

'Breakfast,' Saul said. He grinned at Peggy. 'The Lord has provided.' He took off his shirt and caught one, two, three of the fish. They fairly begged to be caught, leaping into the shirt he held out like a net and from the shirt hurling themselves on to the floor of the boat, flapping and gasping and battering themselves till Peggy feared they would upset the boat and tip them all into the ocean. And then a fourth fish rose and flipped itself into the boat, landed on Peggy's lap so that she laughed at the nonsense of it, these great fish rising from the ocean as if on command. As if God was calling her a fool. Or as if Neptune flung her a love-gift. The wet heavy thing wagged on her lap, a great frantic muscle and she had an urge to lift it and tip it back in the sea but it flipped off and landed on the floor beating its body against the planks. Peggy, Hester and Saul looked down at all the struggling silver treasure round their feet.

Hester picked one up, forced her finger and thumb into the gaping gills and smashed its head sharply against the side of the boat. She dropped it and picked up another. The fish that Hester killed still twitched and squirmed. Wonderingly, Peggy picked up one herself, marvelling at the iridescence of its skin. The gills gaped and fluttered in the heat, wide muscular spaces meant for the wet, drying in the sizzling light. She held the wet weighty creature in her hands, studying the overlapping silver of its scales, the fluted bluish fan of its tail. She held it until the bright button discs of its eyes filmed over and it went limp. She felt its life slip between her fingers and evaporate.

TRUE ROMANCE

I could have worked in an office. I could even have joined the Civil Service but that was not the sort of life I had in mind. Instead, I took a job as an office cleaner. I worked from 6 a.m. to 9 a.m. and from 6 p.m. to 9 p.m. The hours suited me well. It meant I was free to see Tom for lunch or in the afternoon, and at night. The hours suited me when I did see Tom, especially the nights. I would get home from work, wash, switch on the cooker to warm the flat, light candles and joss-sticks and put on the silky robe I'd bought from the Oxfam shop. He'd arrive at ten o'clock, or sometimes later, with a bottle of wine and some food – bread and cheese or cold chicken, picnic food, and we'd sit cross-legged on the bed eating and drinking, and then make love. He'd leave me in the early hours and I would bathe. I had bought strongly scented bath oil – Lily of the Valley – to perfume my skin and disguise the stink of the bathroom, and rubber gloves and Vim to scour the bath. I discovered that there was plenty of hot water at 3 or 4 a.m. and that was also the best time to have an uninterrupted soak. Then I'd go to work, come home, and sleep the cold and dreary day away.

I liked the work. At first I did, when I was happy and hopeful. I was on the fifth floor in the mornings, and the seventh in the evenings. I had to empty the bins and ashtrays, polish the desks, sterilize the telephones and vacuum the floors. It was strange working in the dim rabbit warren of a building, almost alone but for the sound of distant vacuum cleaners. It all smelled of nylon and stale cigarette smoke. The carpet was pale blue and crackled sometimes under my shoes. I was full of static, reaching out to touch a desk or shelf would sometimes send a sparkly shock down my arm to my funny-bone. It was undemanding work and I did it well. Tom was hardly available in the daytime, some new recording contract kept him busy, so day turned to night and night to day for me. As I pushed the vacuum cleaner to and fro over floors that were already clean, to occupy my mind I fantasized about sneaking Tom into the building, making love to him in the cigar-scented executive suite on the squashy leather sofa.

It was always dawn dark or dusk dark when I started. Sometimes I forgot which it was, morning or evening, which floor I was on, the fifth or the seventh. But there were differences, in the morning the city came alive while I was there, the sky lightened, the traffic yawned outside. Sometimes the sun even shone which surprised me, the sight of the sun and even the suggestion of warmth some mornings because I had become a nocturnal creature. My basement did not entertain daylight, and nor did I.

I hardly spoke to the other cleaners. I felt we were an army of moles. Many of them were friends, shouting cheerily to each other from landing to landing, even singing, some of them. The woman on the floor beneath mine, a West Indian, liked to sing choruses, loud and clear, her voice soaring above the sound of her vacuuming: *The foolish man built his house upon the sand, the foolish man built his house upon the sand. The foolish man built his house upon the sand, and the rain came tumbling down.* I remembered that from school, and as I pushed my own vacuum cleaner under desks and between chairs it came back to me and I too began to sing. *The rain came down and the floods came up, the rain came down and the floods came up. The rain came down and the floods came up and the house on the sand fell flat.* But I sang quietly, my voice drowned by the monotonous electric whine. I don't know why I didn't talk to the others. They were fun, they laughed together, but I did not want to be one of them. I felt very precarious. I was holding my life together with all my will-power. I was balanced on a tightrope and I could not be distracted.

When Tom did not come, the night became an impossible tunnel. I tried to read. I even had another go at T. S. Eliot, for old times' sake. I started to write poetry but the search for true words hurt me too much. There was too much danger of slippage. I could not let myself really think or really feel; like looking down from a tightrope, I knew what I saw, if I really looked, would make me wobble, wobble and most likely fall. I was afraid of introspection. I thought that if I looked too closely at words it would force sharp points of meaning through the mist that was my mind and that might drive me mad. I am almost frightened of poetry. It is the most pure expression, it is almost naked. There is no armour, no shell. So I read magazines instead. At first I bought them, then I stole them from the desks at work.

When Tom didn't come for days at a time I became lax at work. I decided it was a waste of time to vacuum every office every day, so I just emptied the bins, picked a few specks up with my finger-nails then went through the drawers of all the desks. At first I only borrowed magazines but then I stopped putting them back. I could never remember where I'd got them from. The worst ones were the best, the true love story or confession magazines, full of stories about jealousy, revenge, divorce and death, abortion, lies, betrayal. And then I began to steal other things: sweets, money – though unfortunately there was never much of that. I made myself tea and ate the office biscuits. I lounged on the executive leather sofa, sipping brandy filched from the cocktail cabinet and reading my magazines. I rang Tom, rang Mama and pretended I was at university, rang Jaz and invented elaborate lies about my new life, listening with surprising pangs of regret to her university gossip.

I took the magazines home to read on the nights when Tom
didn't come. The language was safe and woolly and repetitive, all
the characters ordinary, selfish – quite nasty. All grasping and
grabbing, wanting and expecting nothing more than true and
faithful love for ever and ever. I found them a comfort.

Sometimes I knew Tom was coming, sometimes I merely
waited and hoped. One night I waited and I felt the hope grow
cold around me, begin to stale to hopelessness. I had not
spoken to him for several days, I could get no answer when
I phoned, only Moira sounding strained. I had started putting
the phone down when she answered, when time after time it
was her and she only lied to me and said he was away. I waited
for Tom and willed him to come. I worried that he might be ill,
angry that I had no right to see him. The flat smelled of
sandalwood and flickered with candles. I wrapped myself in a
blanket and read magazines. In the flat upstairs Bob Marley
was wailing and people were talking, sometimes there was a
shout of laughter. I felt so left out of the world I could hardly
stand it. I closed my eyes and clenched my fists and sent all my
thought energy to Tom. I resolved that if he didn't come
tonight I would go out. I'd go to his house and try to see
him there; knock at the door and confront him and Moira – if
he didn't come soon.

Then there was a knock on the door and my heart leapt, silly
flapping thing, into my mouth. I loved him so much. Relief was
like a hot wave travelling through my body, despite the chill. But
when I opened the door I saw that it was Moira.

She wore a black trench coat and black shiny boots and she did
not smile.

'May I come in?' she said. I stood back. She walked into the
basement and looked round.

'Sit down,' I said. I did not know what else to say. There was
nowhere to sit but the bed. It was so cold she did not even take
her gloves off. They were fine leather gloves, grey. *True Love*,
one of my magazines, lay by her feet and I saw her look at it and

smile wryly. I did not know what to do. Her hair was piled high and pinned with an elaborate silver hair-slide. She wore red lipstick and her skin was beautiful in the candle-light. While I had been waiting I had brushed my hair until it shone and outlined my eyes with black kohl and I had felt beautiful. But beside her that illusion fled away. I was a red-nosed, childish, scruffy fright.

'Does Tom know you're here?' I asked. I sat down too, smoothed my crumpled flowery skirt over my knees.

'This is a terrible place,' she said. 'It can't be good for you. Look . . . you can see our breath.' And it was true, little clouds of it hung in the air and ran down the window-pane between the open curtains. 'I'm sorry, I didn't mean to be rude,' she added.

'Does he?' I insisted.

I could see the bulge of rings on her wedding finger through the fine leather of her gloves, at least two rings, maybe three.

'No, he doesn't, but . . .'

'Then how did you know I was here?'

'He told me.'

'He told you my address?' For a moment I didn't believe her and then I did. I thought with a firework soar of hope that they had had a show-down, he had told her everything.

'Look, is there any coffee?' she asked. 'Or I could take you out for a drink. I would like to talk to you.'

'I'll make some tea.' The kettle was already hot. I kept boiling it and letting it go off the boil when I hoped Tom would come, in case he wanted tea when he arrived, not to waste time. I made tea in the cups with tea-bags and powdered milk.

'Thank you.' She held both hands round the cup to warm them.

'So?' I said. I sat beside her again, noticing how shiny and pointed her boots were on the old carpet, what tiny feet she had.

She took a deep breath. 'Poor Tom is at his wits' end.' The

steam rose from her tea and clouded her face as if she was a blurred reflection in a glass. I said nothing. I felt sorry for her. Such a lie. He had never given her my address. How had she got it? Grubbily, that was the only way, she had grubbed through his pockets, through his drawers, his private things. How else? Or she might have followed him on a previous visit like someone in a true romance. So she was not so perfect, after all.

'Oh yes?'

'He . . . oh dear. This isn't easy,' she said, looking at me as if for sympathy. Her eyes were very black, I saw the points of candle-flame reflected in them. I didn't help her. 'He's got in too deep. Yes, he told me about you. I knew there was someone. There usually is.' I stiffened, guarding against the pain of this, but of course, that is what she would say, that is what any wife would say to her rival, her successor. 'That's Tom,' she continued. 'He's so transparent, it's really quite endearing. It's why his first wife left, of course. But I won't. I thought I could change him . . .' She tailed off thoughtfully and then smiled. 'I was young – like you. When he first, when *I* first found out about his unfaithfulness I was going to leave . . . but, oh I didn't want to hurt Beth and over the years I've got used to him. Somehow I don't even mind too much any more. I've got a life of *my* own, you know.' She smiled significantly but I couldn't believe what she was implying. 'But this time he's got in too deep.'

'He's in love with me,' I said.

She opened her mouth and closed it again. When she spoke her voice was careful. 'He falls in love with almost every pretty girl he meets. He's like a little boy in a sweetshop. He can't resist.'

'He's in love with me and he wants to leave you,' I said.

'Jenny.' I flinched at her use of my name. 'He wants to stop seeing you but he's afraid.'

'Afraid? Of hurting *you*, yes.'

'No, afraid of you. You've given everything up for him – is that right? He's afraid of your . . . intensity. You shouldn't have given up your degree when for him it was just a . . .'

'Just a what?'

'A sort of whim. A peccadillo.'

'Peccadillo!' I stood up, but as soon as I rose I knew that I must stay calm. Of course, she would say that. She was fighting for her man. It was the stuff in all the magazines. All's fair in love and war.

'Sorry, that was cruel. He doesn't know how to end it. He thinks you're . . .'

'I'm what?'

'Well I don't know . . . a bit unstable.'

'What! Did he say that? That I'm unstable? Mad does he mean?' I did stand up then and stalked round the room.

'He didn't say that. Not in so many words. But he wants out, he doesn't know how to end it.'

'Does he think I'll murder him then? Or you?'

'Don't be silly,' she spoke sharply. 'Sit down.'

'Did he ask for your help?'

'No. Look, Jenny, you mustn't let him do this to you. Ruin your life. He'll never leave me. And even if he did, do you really think you could handle him?'

'Of course.'

'He's fifteen years older than me and that's too much – but there's thirty years between you!'

'I know that.'

'He's pathologically unfaithful.'

I snorted. He might be unfaithful to her but he never would to me. He wouldn't need to be.

She sighed. 'I can see I should have let Tom do his own dirty work.'

'Ha!'

'But you see, there's one more thing. A reason why this is of more than usual concern to me.'

'Oh yes.' I had sat down again. I affected boredom, stretching out my hand to look at my bitten nails, but my fingers trembled. Somehow I knew what she was going to say.

'I'm pregnant.'

'Oh yes.' I didn't believe her. It was what women did, wives and lovers at moments of desperation, tell this lie, it was their trump card but I was not trumped.

'Funny Tom didn't mention it.'

She almost laughed. 'Anyway, he doesn't know. I don't want to tell him over the phone. I'll wait till he gets back. He'll be delighted. We've been trying you know.'

Then I knew for sure it was a lie. Tom and Moira hardly made love any more. There was no passion left between them, no plans for a future of any sort. 'Get back?' I asked.

'From the States. Didn't he say? He'll be back next week.'

I felt the cold then, suddenly. Hanging clouds of breath and half-evaporated words wrapped round my shoulders like a chilly shawl.

'At least *you're* not,' she said.

'Not what?'

'Not pregnant. That would have been a mess. At least you're sensible.' She smiled properly then, a dazzling magazine-cover smile. 'I was almost afraid you'd tell me you were.'

She put her cup down on the floor. She had hardly touched the tea. Little yellow globules of half-dissolved powdered milk stuck round the rim. Her profile was very clean and clear. I recognized the smell of her perfume, the perfume I had worn in her house. I wanted to hurt her.

'I came to your house, you know. We made love on your bed.' She froze for a moment and then she carried on as if I hadn't spoken.

'I *am* sorry,' she said. 'I've made a mistake . . . coming here. I thought I could be your . . . well, perhaps not friend . . . I thought I could help. I do feel responsible somehow.'

'You!'

'I should have stopped him.'

I did not get up. I raised my eyebrows at her. Friend!

'Good-bye,' she said. I did not look at her any more. I kept my eyes on the magazine. *I Stole My Sister's Husband*, it said, and *The Man with Thirteen Wives*. The door banged shut and I heard the elegant click-click of her heels on the steps. The night was a dark tunnel ahead of me. I picked up the magazine and curled under the blanket. No. I was not pregnant but I was not sensible either. I had taken no precautions. Tom never asked. Perhaps he thought I'd taken care of all that, but I hadn't. But neither had I conceived. I don't know why.

Next morning, when I arrived at work I found I'd got the sack. No explanation, just my cards in an envelope. Just a filthy look from the supervisor who had always smiled before. I didn't know I'd been depending on that smile. I walked back out into the chilliness. I felt terribly, ridiculously upset. It was only a cleaning job. But it was the only safe thing I had had. The only thing that gave my days a structure. Now I was all loose and with Tom away there was no sort of control and no one to care. Why had he not told me he was going away? I even thought about going home to Mama but I could not do that. I had to wait for Tom.

I walked by the canal, watching a wispy mist rise off the water as the darkness began to thin. The *Hunky-Dory* was asleep, its curtains drawn. I fancied I could hear it snoring. A cat stalked the path, a swaggering male shadow, with startling lantern eyes. I started to write a poem in my head but the loneliness of it was too much to bear. I tried to make a plan for my life now that there were no edges. I thought I would be a writer. Not a poet, but I could write about what I know. I could write true romances and true confessions. I could spin out that fluff with feeling. But not too much. I could squirt pain and jealousy out of my pen, I could fill pages with betrayal. I knew about love and older men and jealous wives.

I walked fast. I walked to Tom's house and stood outside. I watched the milkman leave three bottles on the step. I saw a frozen paper-girl force a *Guardian* through the slot. I saw a light come on behind the curtains in Tom and Moira's room. I walked past the house several times that day, monitoring the changes, the curtains opening, the cat dozing on the window-sill, the lights switched on or off.

I scratched the shiny green side of Moira's Renault with a nail-file. I can't say it was a spur-of-the-moment thing because I bought the nail-file on purpose for the task. I did it quite openly. It is surprising what you can do in the light of day and no one will stop you. I kept watching the house, day after day, walking past and so I knew when Tom got back. I saw his profile through the front window. I went straight to the telephone box and dialled his number. Moira answered.

'I want to speak to Tom,' I said.

'Tom is away,' she replied. She knew it was me, I could tell by the sigh in her voice.

'He is not away,' I said and put the phone down. I tried again and again. She answered every time.

'You're not doing yourself any good, you know,' she said.

I knew he would come that night if he could. And when he did not come, I knew it was her fault. Feelings gnawed like animals at my ribs. I don't know what feelings, a savage pack of them is all I know. I bought some wine with the last of my cash and got drunk. I had to get another job. I took out my pen and chewed the end of it thinking about stories, trying to think of stories that were not real.

I could hardly believe that he did not come. I kept going out and ringing but in the end she took the phone off the hook. I thought he would be dying for me, pacing the floor. I longed for him. I wanted to tell him that I'd lost my job, that I planned to be a writer. I thought he would laugh but would be proud, encouraging. What was she saying to him that night? Was she seducing him? I wondered whether she had told him her lie, or told him she'd told me; whether she'd told him what she had done, put her shiny little, pointy little boots over the line between her life and mine.

I went and stood outside their house but I did not dare to ring the bell. Sid came and wound his body round my legs and butted his head against me, purring like a motor. I picked him up and buried my face in his warm fur. He smelled faintly of Chanel no. 5 and I put him down. They knew I was outside. The upstairs curtain moved aside just after midnight, and though the bedroom light was off I could see the outline of a figure. It was Tom, not her. Tom was looking out at me and I smiled up although I don't think he could see my face properly. I smiled to let him know I knew how he was feeling, what a trap he was in. He didn't even dare to wave.

I was so cold I stopped shivering when the curtain was drawn again. I tried to ring but the phone was still off the hook. The smug sound of the tone – beep-beep-beep-beep – taunted me. It was like something childish. *Na-na-na-na-na, you a-re ou-t.* It made me feel left out, like a girl in a cold playground. A girl with no friends. I crept back to my hole.

When I did see him he said, 'Moira is pregnant.' There was an odd sound in his voice, a sort of excitement and pride as if a current of champagne bubbled through his words. He did not say it at once but waited until after we'd made love. We were still in bed, he was still inside me, curled round my back, one hand cupping my breasts. I did not move. I thought the way he had responded so quickly to me, loved me with so much passion had meant it was all rubbish, the pregnancy, Moira's ploy. Emotions washed over me like colours. Anger flashed red, jealousy green, betrayal yellow and I was left blue, curled just the same within the frame of his body like a creature in a shell, but blue and suddenly cold.

'Yours?' I said, my voice stiff and crisp as a little wafer.

'Of course, mine.' He sounded slightly scandalized at my implied suggestion but there was a warmth in his voice that was not for me.

'Of course,' I mimicked but he chose not to hear the edge in my voice. I felt his penis shrinking and slipping out. It stuck against my thigh, a warm, wet slug sticking just as it must stick against Moira's elegant thigh.

'You didn't get it, did you?' he said.

'What? Didn't get what?' But he didn't answer, just let out a long groaning breath. All I could see was the pillow crumpled, dappled with the dirty yellow and grey of electric light and shade. It was early afternoon. Voices drifted down from upstairs, water rose and gurgled in my sink. 'I thought you didn't do it much, with Moira.'

'I never said that.'

'But you said there was no passion!'

'Well, be realistic, sweetheart, we've been married ten years.'

I moved his hand away from my chest where he might feel the frantic beating of my heart. I groped in my memory but it was true. He had never said that he and Moira were no longer lovers. He had implied it. When he came to me wanting sex so desperately isn't that what he meant? When he complained about Moira's perfection, her even temper – she never raised her voice, God damn it, she never *shouted* – surely he was telling me that she lacked passion? I had tried to prevent myself thinking of them together in their bed at night while I lay alone in mine. He had fucked me on her bed in her dressing-gown and it had not felt like me at all. How could I love a man like that?

'I haven't lied,' he said, moving away, hardly physically, but still somehow a space widened between us on the bed, grew into a chasm I had to call across to reach him. I felt that if I rolled towards him I would fall down. Perhaps he hadn't lied but he *had* deceived. Everything he'd done and everything he'd said had implied an untruth. That he wanted me and not Moira.

'Moira told me she was pregnant. She came here. I knew before you.' I was growing steadily colder. A car roared past. A shadow, like the shadow of a bird, darted across the ceiling.

'You must go back,' he said. 'You must go back and pick up the threads of your life.'

'Perhaps I should.' I felt that I was balanced on a narrow ledge of reality. The curtain rustled like a captive creature.

'Shall I make some tea?' he asked. When he got off the bed the mattress shifted and I had to hold on with both hands to stop myself falling off. The tap water made a hollow sound in the kettle. Through the bead curtain I watched him. He moved the plates out, stood on tiptoe and peed into the sink. Then he ran the hot tap, picked up a bar of soap, lathered it between his hands and washed his penis very carefully, very tenderly as if it was a baby. Thoroughly he cleansed himself of me. 'I'm sure it goes without saying that I feel different about this now,' he said.

'Oh yes?'

'All this deception.'

'So?' He pushed through the curtain and stood in front of me. I saw the middle-agedness of his body, the leathery nipples among the grizzled hair. I sat up and had to hold my head in my hands because of the trampoline bounce of the mattress. Inside my heart bounced too, and the skin of my brain against the bone of my skull. I felt seasick, I couldn't find a point of stillness. My voice was normal. I think it was normal. It had a far away sound, each word like a separate pellet. A fly was in the room. It buzzed a wiry trail of sound. I could not stop listening to the fly as if it was as important as Tom, as what Tom was going to say, as what he needn't say because I already knew. But which I had to let him say all the same to launch me off the edge. A deception was all it was to him, this thing that was the purpose of my life, *was* my life, just a deception. Is that *all*? It is my life, I wanted to say. Is that all my life is then? Somebody else's deception, somebody else's lie. As soon as I thought it I knew that it was true. I am nothing but somebody else's lie. A dirty hairy sound was that fly's buzz.

The kettle whistled. He made me a cup of tea, didn't even stay for one himself. It was too weak. He didn't even have time to let it brew properly. Of course not. He wanted to wipe up this mess and disappear.

'So?' I said. I looked at his balls hanging low in their pink sack, heavy blue-veined fruits, one slightly larger, drooping lower, and at his penis hung above, a shrivelled thing like a dead flower. Altogether his genitals looked like something from the hothouse at Kew, something luscious and absurd.

'Must be funny to be a man,' I said.

'What?'

I put my tea down on the shelf by the bed and some of it spilled in a pale pool. He scratched his balls and put on his pants. My feelings were changing, I sat perfectly still and felt them change, like a weather front moving across me. I had hated Moira for her hold over him. I had attempted to ignore her, more, *negate* her. She was too beautiful to take seriously, too perfect, not a real woman at all. I had scoffed at her beauty and niceness as if they were faults, as if they placed her beneath me in some crazy hierarchy. Then I had supposed her sneaky, snide, weak and clinging, needy. Now, as I closed my eyes against the sight of Tom buttoning away his chest, I perceived her differently. She was beautiful and her beauty was valuable currency. And she was not only beautiful, but good and wise. Wiser than Tom, wiser than me. She wanted Tom and she knew how to keep him. I had wanted to see Tom as the victim before, entrapped by her terrible beauty, her placidity, her love for his brat. Now he emerged as villain, his sheep's clothing tumbled to the floor and I saw the dark hair on his hands and the faithless glint in his brown eyes. I saw the sharpness of his teeth. And I believed what Moira had said, that he had whined about me to her, that he had called me unstable, a burden. He was a liar through and through. He probably believed himself.

He did up his belt. I noticed he had a new ring in place of the old scratched one. It was wide, yellow and white gold twisted together. I did not say that I had noticed it, reflecting that he had not taken it off when we made love. He dressed quickly and clumsily. My breasts were naked but he did not look at them. He darted uneasy looks at my face. I could have helped him. I could have said, 'Well, perhaps we should call it a day,' something like that, something breezy. But I did not want to help him. I was interested in what he would say. My heart was a cold fist clenching and unclenching but I was calmer now, balanced. I could see him very clearly, this middle-aged man. Too old to be a father again. He'd be in a geriatric ward before the child left school. Poor kid. It made me remember Bob, how I used to believe he was my father although he was too old. Did I ever believe it? Which one of my selves was so credulous? I grow through myself like skins.

'See you on Thursday?' I asked at last. I couldn't bear the waiting. I had to get to the worst.

'Not Thursday,' he said. He pulled his head through his sweater and looked at me. His hair was ruffled and slightly greasy.

'Friday then?'

He sat down on the bed beside me. The mattress rocked dangerously and tilted, but I was all right. I had found a point of balance somewhere on the tightrope between love and hate. A temporary point of balance. 'Jenny,' he sighed. He took my cold, small hand in his hot and hairy one. His hand enclosed mine as his body had enclosed my body in bed. 'Don't you hear what I'm saying?'

'You haven't said much.' I tried to inject humour into my voice. I clung to a fading wisp of hope. 'Do you have to go straight away? Shall I get up? We could go for a drink, a walk. At least I could walk you home.'

'I'm not going home.'

'Where then? I'll walk you wherever.'

'I'll find a cab.'

'I'll come with you then. Where?'

'No, sweetheart. I'm meeting Moira. I'm taking Moira out to dinner.'

'Celebrating?'

'Well. Yes.'

'OK, so Friday then? Saturday?'

I was like a child picking at a scab, picking and picking. I could not leave it alone. I had to flick the top off, see the blood rise. I had to extract the most pain, make him feel it too, feel the responsibility for my pain. He had said it, to Moira, that I was a responsibility. What else? A millstone, no doubt, that's how he saw me. All right then, let him feel the weight.

'Not Saturday,' he said. His hand was too hot and tight. My own escaped like a hermit crab from its shell and scuttled across my sheet, found my other hand. Two small cold hands clasped and I felt my own nails. 'Jenny, I'm trying to tell you. Now that Moira's pregnant . . .'

'What? What difference does it make?'

'What difference? Don't pretend to be so naïve.'

'I'm not pretending.'

'We've been longing for this to happen, for her to conceive, for us to have our own child. I can't carry on now. We've been trying.'

'Trying?'

'She's been trying to conceive. She's been so brilliant with Beth, but . . .'

I stopped listening. Conceive, naïve. A rhyme. Funny how rhymes jump out at you like that.

'Well. Congratulations,' I said.

He looked at me warily. 'I told Moira I'd see you this afternoon. She guessed about you, that we'd had a scene . . .'

'You are a liar,' I said. 'You *told* Moira. She came and told me what a responsibility I've become, how unstable.'

He reached for his shoes and tied the laces. One of the laces snapped and he had to tie it together. I didn't offer to help, I just watched how he fumbled, how his fingers trembled almost as if he was scared. He made little noises of exertion like an old man. Then he sat up and shrugged. 'Whatever. Anyway, I told Moira I'd see you this afternoon, but that it would be the last time.'

'Did you tell her it would be the last fuck?'

'Of course not.'

'Why not?'

'Don't be wearisome, Jenny. Come on, you're a big girl. What difference does it make? One fuck more or less. You wanted it. The thing is, it's over.'

'Would Moira go along with that?'

'What?'

'One fuck more or less – what's the difference?'

He looked at me as if I was a tiresome child. His eyes were quite cold.

'You think it's that easy?' I said.

'What?' He sounded really exasperated now.

'To get rid of me. You think you can just walk out and get away with it? That I'll just disappear?' He took a comb from his pocket and combed his hair back from his forehead so I could see the parallel lines stamped there. His shirt was buttoned up wrong at the neck but I didn't say. Let Moira spot it.

'I *am* sorry,' he said before he left. He bent to kiss me and I let him. His lips were human lips kissing stone. Because I let him kiss me he thought he was half forgiven. 'I should never have let it go on . . . beyond Christmas. But that was something, wasn't it? That summer house . . . whoosh!' he laughed and stopped abruptly when he saw I didn't. 'I didn't mean . . .' he flailed his hands, 'all this. But Christ almighty you were so sweet and willing. I can't take all the responsibility for that. I'm only flesh and blood, for Christ's sake. I can't take responsibility for your life.'

'It's not your business, my life,' I said. I meant to hurt him but he only looked relieved.

'No. It's not. And I didn't force you to do any of the things you did, did I? They were your choices.' He put on his jacket, jingled his money and keys in his pocket. 'Well.' He stood awkwardly by the door shrugging his shoulders. 'Well, be seeing you then.' I did not reply. I watched the door shut. The fly, which had been fizzing dirtily round the ceiling, landed on my pool of spilled tea and stopped.

JAMMY DODGERS

I do hear breathing and I don't think it is my own. I hear it at night particularly, though there is hardly a difference between night and day. Night means I have a mattress to lie on. I cover my face in my blanket – grey, needless to say – and listen for it. My mind travels away. I can send myself anywhere. It is pathetic for a woman of my age – nearly thirty, for God's sake – to imagine herself in her childhood home. I return to myself at eleven or twelve. Home was safe. I return to the room with the pink candlewick and the view of the garden and the radiator, creaking and clinking out its friendly warmth. I imagine I am lying in that bed and that I can hear the muffled voices of Mama and Bob downstairs; the sound of one of them in the kitchen, the clink of cups, a tap running. And I hear the breathing, it intrudes. It sounds like Tom, asleep. I am almost sure it is not me, that it is the breathing of a man, but when I stop breathing myself and listen it is harder to hear. It's when I'm not paying proper attention, lost in my imaginings, just drifting off to sleep that the sound is the loudest. I used to be scared. It seemed like a haunting thing, but now I don't mind. I like the illusion of company. I listen for the gentle shushing in and out like waves on a far-away beach, dragging the shingle backwards and forwards, backwards and forwards. It is quite distinct until I hold my own breath and focus my ears, then it stops.

I do sleep in here which is a miracle. I wonder if they put

tranquillizers in the food because I should not sleep. It is endlessly twilight in here, neither night nor day, and there is nothing to tire me except my exercises and the awful whirring of my brain. I am glad though that they don't turn off the light at night, for then it would be pitch black, utter dark and then how would I know myself? There would only be the feel of my skin, but it would only be my self feeling it and where would my self be in the dark, that rubbery thing that I live inside? If it was dark and I could not see there would be nothing. I have lost my face anyway. Oh yes I feel it, the contours, the greasiness of my skin, the damp holes, the hairs that are brows and lashes – but I cannot see it. I have my limbs still, my legs that are strong with their long brown hairs, the knobs of my ankle bones, rough yellow skin on my heels. Between my toes are little worms of dirt. My arms are downy and on the insides the flesh is dense and white, blotched with the love-bites that mark the time. The veins on my thin wrist skin are blue and green and there are little soft knobs of white cartilage or something. My wrists are braceleted with lines, the hands traced with them. I have these things but I have lost my face. I dread the blunt mushroom head that invades my dreams now. All it would take to restore my face would be a mirror.

Last night I had a terrifying dream. Now that I know I am awake, I'm not so sure it was a dream. I woke. I sleep on my back in here usually, neat as a corpse. I don't like to bury my face in this mattress so I lie on my back with the grey blanket covering my face to shut out the light, my arms folded on my chest. I woke and was confused by a gentle pressure against my face. I opened my eyes and there was a wall straight ahead, the blanket was not over my face and I was pressing against a wall. I saw a crack, a crack like a river delta, or the veins in a lung. Then my heart did a porpoise flip as I saw that it was not the wall but the ceiling of this cell that I was pressed against. Levitation, I thought in the dream which may not have been a dream at all. But then I looked down. Don't ask me how, eyes upward, I looked down. There is no sense in this. I looked down and saw myself on the mattress, a still figure, face covered in a grey blanket. I looked – no, it was less directed than looking, there was nothing muscular about it, rather it was like soaking in. I soaked myself in, a blank-faced figure in a grey shroud, a sort of effigy. Then I snapped back, ravelled back with a thin sharp shock like a fisherwoman reeling in her line too fast for breath and there was the blanket, itchy on my face again. I did not dare to move or look about me then. I stayed stuck on the mattress on the floor like a helpless creature on its back. I could not remember the name for that experience then, if it was an experience and not a dream but I have heard of it before. It was my astral self that floated up. My star self. If there had been no ceiling, where would it have stopped?

After Tom had gone there were days and days with no punctuation between them. I stayed in bed for a long time. In that room the light was soupy, it flickered when a person passed. The traffic was a steady grey noise. Once I heard two dogs fighting, a savage snarling and snapping and the shouts of a woman and man as they dragged them apart. That was the most interesting thing that happened in that time. I listened to the rhythm of the lives upstairs. Sometimes I got up to pee. I drank tea occasionally and ate the end of a loaf but I wasn't hungry. Tom's semen leaked out of me for the last time, sluggish and sticky. The fly dropped from the lampshade on to my bed and died.

Eventually I made myself get up. I put on my coat and went out. It was the middle of the night. I had put my clothes on in bed because it was so cold and now they were dirty and crumpled with a stale wash-bag smell. My hair was tangled and greasy but I hardly cared. I bought a hot-dog and a polystyrene cup of coffee from a van. The man in the van had a rubbery red face, lips like the frankfurters he was selling. Red ketchup congealed in black clots down the side of the squeezy bottle.

A boy stopped beside the van and smiled at me. He had a cardboard sign propped against his legs while he bought a hot-dog. The sign said: *Homeless. Penniless. Please help*. He smiled at me as if I was a fellow being and I realized how I must look to him, with my hair all wild and my dirty clothes.

'New round here?' he asked.

'Newish,' I said. He was about seventeen with a shrewd face, eyes jumping bright as a monkey's.

'Fucking freezing last night. Were you out?' He shivered and looked at the sky. 'Going to be another bleeder.'

'I wasn't out.'

'Lucky bitch.' I noticed that his tennis shoes were worn into holes where his big toe rubbed. 'Got a place then?'

'Yes.' I sipped the last of my coffee and started to go.

'Wait. You couldn't spare?' He held out his hand. I stopped and looked at him again.

'I've seen you,' I said. 'I saw you begging one night. I didn't have anything to give you.'

'Got anything now?'

'No. Not to spare. Sorry.' He was a nice boy. I was touched by his bright brown eyes like Tom's but not cynical. Tom's eyes were louche, I thought, lounge lizard's eyes. Where did that come from? The sort of thing Mama might say, lounge lizard, but it suited him. I could just see him arranged on a *chaise longue*, in a paisley smoking jacket, a cigarette in a long holder between his finger and thumb, his old eyes melting their charm like sticky chocolate on any fresh young thing, his tongue flicking out lizard-quick and greedy.

'Oi!' The boy waved his hand in front of my eyes and laughed. 'Anyone home?'

'Sorry . . . miles away.' I put my hand in my pocket. 'Honestly, I haven't got enough cash to share – but you could come back with me and have a cup of tea.'

He grinned.

'I'll buy some milk then.'

'Fan-fucking-tastic,' he said and stuffed the end of his hot-dog into his mouth.

The sole of his shoe had come unstuck and made a slapping sound every time he took a step. 'What's your name?' I asked.

'Davy.'

'How old?'

'Seventeen,' he said, then looking at me sideways, 'well, sixteen – nearly.'

'What're you doing living rough?'

'What's it to you?'

'It's nothing to me.'

He grinned. 'That's all right then. Big bust-up at home on Christmas Day. Fucked off out of it. Did a runner. Didn't mean to, like, *leave*.'

'No?'

'Can't go back though, tail between my fucking legs. They don't give a toss, anyway.'

We went into a shop and I bought a bottle of milk. 'Garibaldi or Rich Tea?' I asked, stopping by the biscuits, looking for the cheapest.

'How about these?' he said, picking up the Jammy Dodgers. 'Bleeding hell, I haven't had a Jammy Dodger for years.'

'No, nor have I.'

We reached the basement and I led him down the steps. I opened the door to the coldness, the smell of old sex and candle-wax stained the air.

'Bleeding dive,' he said with approval.

I filled the kettle.

'Who doesn't give a toss? Your mum?' I asked.

'What are you, a frigging social worker?' He looked round again and grinned. 'No, I can see you're not.' The tip of his nose tilted up when he grinned and I could see what a boy he was, cheeky-faced, not long graduated from his Lego.

The bed was crumpled, the sheets filthy. I pulled the blanket over them so he could sit down.

'She's an actress,' he said. He dropped his bag and sat on the bed. 'Good at it. Pretty too, young looking, you know? Likes to make out she's about twenty-seven – but what does that make me? A figment of her fucking imagination?'

I gave him a mug of tea and he cupped his hands round it gratefully, bent his head so that the steam rose and warmed his face. His hands were rough and red, swollen from the cold and his nails were black and broken.

'She was doing panto,' he said. 'Cinderella. She *was* Cinderella. Good, see?' He sounded proud. 'She used to sing us all these songs, really stupid songs to make us laugh. What was it? *You're a pink toothbrush, I'm a blue toothbrush, Have we met somewhere before?*' He sang in a cracked and husky voice, paused to think, then held up his finger. 'I've got it. *I'm a pink toothbrush, you're a blue toothbrush. Yes, we met by the bathroom door.*' Then he stopped, looked down, sipped his tea.

'Have a biscuit,' I said. He took the top one from the packet and put the whole thing in his mouth so that his cheeks bulged and then sipped his tea, closed his eyes and sucked. 'Look,' he said eventually and opened his mouth to show me the red circle of jam that was left on his tongue. 'We used to do that as kids,' he said. 'Me and my brother. If you suck it, all the biscuit melts away and you're left with the jam. Sticky little buggers we were.'

'Where's your brother now?'

'Still there, far as I know.'

'What happened?'

He shrugged.

'I bet your mum's worried. Have you phoned?'

He shook his head. 'Sent a postcard. Said don't worry, I'm fine. That sort of stuff.'

'Take your shoes off and get under the blanket,' I said. He looked frozen, as I was too. I couldn't afford to put the money in the cooker any more, Tom's pile of silver had long gone. 'I'll get in too. Just for warmth.'

We leant against the pillows and covered ourselves in the blanket and sat there like two children playing at something, I don't know, playing at life. It was a relief to think about someone else. I cannot say I really cared about him. I wish I could. It was as if Davy and his problems were behind a sheet of cellophane, I could see them, and I could see how I should respond but they didn't touch me.

'What did happen?' I asked.

He let out a long sigh. 'She was tired, see. Up all hours with her panto and there was me and my brother – he's twelve and the baby, Leila. She's two. Her fella, Leila's dad, he's a fucking bastard, thinks we're a pain in the arse, Jonny and me. It's all Leila, Leila, Leila. She's a nice little kid though. Really funny, you know?' He sipped his tea and wriggled his finger in his ear. 'Looks just like our mum.'

I was afraid he was going to cry. I didn't think I could bear that, I had no resources for it. I dipped a biscuit into my tea and looked away.

'And we had a bust-up. He called me a fucking pervert. He hit me.' His voice lost its rough edge as he said this. He was sounding more and more like a little boy.

'Why did he?'

'I was playing horses with her. I like little kids. I like her. She is my fucking sister. She was riding on my back. She'd pissed herself. Taken her pants off. Mum was cooking Christmas dinner. I was keeping her out from under her feet. I didn't know she had no fucking pants on, did I? *He* came in, took one look and swiped me round the head. Christmas dinner time it was, *him* drunk already, rolling in from the pub expecting his dinner. Crackers on the table, Mum roasting the turkey. Chucked me out didn't he?' He scrubbed the back of his hand angrily against his eyes.

'Didn't your mum try and stop him?'

'Yeah. She said, "He leaves, I leave," but how could she with Jonny and Leila?' His voice grew stronger, I could see his head sitting more cockily on his neck. 'And I'm not a fucking pervert, I'm fucking not. Nothing funny never entered my head. I was playing with her that's all. Keeping her out of Mum's way. She is my fucking sister.'

'I know,' I said. Of course I did not know. I felt I could believe anything of anybody at that time, but I did think he was telling the truth. Why tell me otherwise? 'You should go home. Your Mum'll be going spare.'

'Probably glad I'm gone. Now she can pretend to be twenty-seven.'

'Oh, Davy.' I could see through the cellophane that I should put my arms round him, but I didn't have the energy. He was a hurt boy. He needed someone to make him go home, needed someone to comfort him. But I was not the one. There was not enough of me. I sat beside him knowing what he needed, seeing it as clearly as if he had instructions printed on his forehead. And seeing just as certainly the sensible thing for me to do, to go home, to go back. And knowing that I wouldn't do it either. Not yet.

'Have another biscuit,' I said. He stuck it in his mouth and started sucking noisily. He stuck out his tongue with its circle of jam.

'Do you make a living, then, begging?' I asked.

'Depends what you call a living.'

'Couldn't you claim benefit or something?'

'Too young, no address. Anyway, can't be bothered with all that stuff, form filling, interviews . . .' He shuddered. '*You* on Social?'

'No.'

'Working?'

'No.'

'I could earn,' he said. 'Streets crawling with fucking ponces. "Pretty boys are in great demand." ' He mimicked someone, a high-pitched high-class accent and pulled a face. 'Tried it once. Bum boy, you know?' I didn't, quite, but I nodded. 'Never again, never a-fucking-gain. You ever thought of that?'

'Prostitution?'

He nodded.

'No, of course not!'

'Only asking. Have you tried begging?'

'I never could.'

'Course you could. Look . . .' His eyes brightened again, he was like a little boy coming up with a plan, his face was impish, triangular and grubby. He smelled of jam. 'Let me stay here. Go halves on the rent . . . what is it?' I told him and he grimaced. 'Still, I reckon I could pay half. Both of us out there, I reckon we'd do it.'

'But I *couldn't*.'

'Go on, I dare you. What else are you going to do?'

'Write,' I said. 'I'm going to be a writer.'

'Well then. Just till you make your first million. Where do you get your money from anyway? The rent for this shit-hole?'

'Savings, a bit of grant – I left university. I'll have to get a job soon.'

'Try it then. Go on. There's nothing to it. You just ask nicely,' he said. 'Be polite. Don't ask for too much – the price of a cup of tea or a bus-fare. Go on . . .'

I looked into his eyes and right through them into the empty days ahead of me.

'I suppose I could try it,' I said.

Saul gazed at Hester. She had taken his knife and was gutting the fish, casting the bloody entrails into the sea where they were swooped up by great grey sea-birds that had materialized round the boat. Peggy watched Saul watching Hester and she saw the admiration in his eyes. She, too, was impressed by Hester's competence. She saw what Saul saw, a muted beauty that needed time and good luck to blossom, she saw the quick and clever fingers shiny with blood opening the fish as if they were purses and throwing out the jewels to the birds. Unlike Peggy, Hester did not quail. She was quick and matter of fact. She was, after all, a fisherman's daughter.

Peggy watched Saul's eyes and she was glad for Hester. Saul was a gentle man. He had been a music tutor, he said, to a pair of rich children and he had stolen some silver plate. It was stuff that was never used, stored dustily in a cupboard. He didn't think it would be missed, but it was and he had to confess when the blame was attached to some harmless serving girl. He was not bitter. He had known the risk he was taking. Hester told him her story that curiously was the mirror image of his. '*He* let me take the blame,' she said bitterly. 'Never spoke up for me.' Saul's eyes opened wide with amazement at such wickedness. He shook his head, and Peggy saw that his fist clenched as if he would like to fight the man who had so wrecked Hester's life.

Saul was falling in love with Hester, Peggy realized, and she was both glad and sorry. They would have made a handsome pair, he was fine-featured like Hester but darker, his eyes deep and long-lashed. She was sorry that they had to meet like this, perching on the very brink of death.

As if reading her mind, Saul said, 'We have food. We might yet meet another craft. We might drift to land.'

Peggy looked around and there was nothing, nothing but the hard sun glinting on the empty sea, nothing but sea stretching and sloping away to the horizon. 'Do you see land?' she asked. 'Do you see another ship?'

Saul shook his head and they both looked away from the sea that was too bright for their eyes, looked at Hester and the slithery scarlet and silver on her lap.

'Do you not burn with thirst?' Peggy asked. 'We won't live long without water.'

'You sound as if you wish us to die,' Hester said impatiently, wiping her hand on her skirt.

'Could we not drink the sea?' Peggy asked, knowing the answer but tempted by the delicious lapping of water against the boat.

'Peggy! It's full of salt,' Hester said.

'But still, it is better than thirsting. I *am* parched.'

'It would make you thirst more. It would make you mad,' said Saul. 'It pickles the brain. We must not drink the sea.'

Hester hacked the fish into ragged pieces. 'Eat,' she said. Saul took a piece and put it in his mouth. Peggy accepted a bit of the dense grey meat. It was freckled with blood. Hester's hands were silver with the creature's scales and they glistened like sequins on her dress. Peggy put the fish in her mouth but could not bear to embed her teeth in the raw flesh. She swallowed it straight down, the mass stuck in her throat and lodged, she had to swallow and swallow to force it down her dry throat. It tasted almost of nothing.

'There is moisture in the flesh,' Saul said.

'I'll lay it out and it will dry in the sun,' Hester said, arranging it along the edge of the boat, 'then it will not turn bad.'

'You think we'll live long enough for the fish to rot?' Peggy asked.

Hester smiled. 'Of course we will,' she said, but the gulls swooped down screaming, beating the air with their wings and snatching away the morsels of fish in their claws and beaks.

'I could catch a bird,' Saul said, but he said it as the last scrap of fish was taken and all that was left was a skin of blood dried like red enamel and flecked with scaly silver. The birds rose high until they were only a fidget of flapping lines in the sky.

'There will be more fish,' Saul said.

'If there are gulls, land cannot be far away,' Hester added and they all squinted round at the empty horizon.

Grey feathers had fallen in the bottom of the boat. Peggy picked one up and stroked its spiky filaments with her fingers until it was as smooth as silk.

'Excuse me, could you lend . . .' but the woman had gone, brushed past me as if I was a mere object, her eyes snatched away as soon as she saw my outstretched hand. Davy had told me not to recoil, not to retreat when this happened or I would lose my nerve. I wanted to, I wanted to shrink into nothing and disappear but I held out my hand again to a man emerging from the tube station steps and opening his umbrella. 'Excuse me . . .'

He stopped, vaguely interested. 'Could you spare . . .' and he was gone, the beginnings of a flirtatious look sliding from the sudden ice of his face. I thought, *I cannot do this. I cannot humiliate myself like this.* 'Excuse me,' I said. 'Excuse me.' But nobody would stop. 'Get a job,' somebody said, 'bleeding beggar.' 'What is she, a gypsy or what?' someone asked their companion. The time passed and I did begin to shrink, every rebuttal whittling me away a little bit more.

'Excuse me . . .' I was almost at the end of my patience now, I could not do this. 'Excuse me . . .' I was hardly able to look the people in the face any more, let alone the eye, when a woman stopped. 'Yes?' She was a white, white woman with silver hair. I couldn't tell whether she was young or old. Her skin was fine and soft as white poppy petals. I felt ashamed. 'Could you spare some change for a cup of tea?' I said. She wore dark glasses so I could not see her eyes.

'Let's see,' she said, and took a purse from her bag. Her fingers were white and thin as bone and each one was decorated with many silver rings. She took out a five-pound note. 'This do you?'

'Thank you,' I said. I was so grateful that my heart drummed and a fuzzy tide rose up behind my eyes. I took the money and felt myself grow a little, a scrap of dignity restored. It was not the begging itself that diminished me, I saw now. When someone saw me as a human being with a right to what I requested, I felt all right. It was being looked at like dirt, or worse, not being looked at at all that damaged me. The woman smiled and her smile was startlingly red in her white face as if all her blood lived in her mouth.

'Will you be all right?' she asked.

'Yes, yes thank you,' I said.

'Good luck and be careful.' She walked away trailing a silvery Indian scarf and a scent of jasmine oil behind her.

She changed my luck, the silver woman. I began to look people in the eye and some of them gave me money and some of them didn't but if they didn't it was they who were diminished not me.

And some people didn't only give me money, but stopped and talked to me as if I was a person.

'Why are you doing this?' a girl said, fishing some money out of her tight jeans.

'Because I'm broke.'

'I'll buy you a coffee.' As we drank it she explained she was killing time before meeting her boyfriend. She kept sneaking glances at herself in the café's mirrored door and pushing her hair away from her face in a way that exaggerated its length.

'Are you going out with anyone?' she asked.

'Sort of.'

'My boyfriend's in a band,' she said, 'plays bass guitar.'

'Mine plays sax,' I replied.

She looked deflated. 'Does he know you're begging? John'd flip if it was me.'

'Oh, we live our own lives,' I said airily.

'What's his name?'

But I could not say his name, even the thought of him stung, came rearing painfully up, ripping through the padding around my heart.

'Are you seeing him tonight?'

'We're playing it cool for a bit,' I said and I sounded normal though sadness and anger were burning like acid in my veins. 'Anyway, must go. Thanks.' I escaped, hurried out where I could pace the streets until I had my emotions safely numbed again.

I met Davy just as it was getting dark. I had made five pounds more than him – the five pounds from the silver woman. I described her to him.

He grinned. 'Oh yeah, the patron saint of down-and-outs.'

'What?'

'She's a total nutter. An albino, some sort of heiress. She's always around giving hand-outs.'

'I don't think she's a nutter.'

'No? Is that what you'd do if you had a fortune?'

'I don't know, I might.'

He looked disbelievingly at me. 'Come on.' We went in a café and ate chip butties and warmed our hands round mugs of tea.

'It's not so bad,' I reflected. The chips were warm and fat and the vinegar soaked warmly into the thick white bread. 'This sort of life, I mean.' I picked at a crispy golden bit that had fallen off my plate.

'Don't get carried away, Jen. You've still got a roof, you've had one day of it. Beginner's luck.'

The days passed and I felt I was in some sort of vacuum. Davy and I fell into an easy companionship. We begged, separately, all day and bought bottles of cider at night and walked or sat in the flat wrapped in blankets. He bought some grass once and we sat at home for three nights, smoking big inexpert joints and giggling at stupid things. I let him touch me, once. We were quite drunk and he began to fumble at my clothes and I didn't care. He was a virgin, he said, didn't know where to start. So he fumbled at me, all shivery and breathless and cider-drunk. But it never came to anything and it never happened again. There was no passion on either side, he was more like a younger brother than anything else, or what I imagine a younger brother to be. After that we shared my bed amicably, grateful for each other's warmth, affectionate but chaste. He should have been a comfort. His presence, his warmth, his smiles, should have been a comfort but they did not penetrate the chill that enveloped me. I kept my mind caged in that time. I managed hardly to think about anything except living from minute to minute. My mind learned to shrink from the very idea of Tom, or of any alternative way of life. I kept it numb with cider and swaddled my heart again.

But sometimes, in the evening I tried to write stories. I thought up plots and invented characters. I gave them names and strained my mind to find them faces. But the names were always false, the faces always masks and as soon as I warmed to my story and the words began to flow, everything warped and the male character, whoever he was supposed to be, would become Tom, suddenly that name would leak from the end of my pen, his mask would slip off and smash like a plate on the floor and there would be Tom – and Moira not far behind. I could not invent someone more beautiful than Moira though out of spite I tried and tried. And always there was a girl, sensible as I tried to make her, who hurled herself at their marriage like a frail craft at rocks and smashed herself to pieces. Whenever the people became those people and the story their story, I screwed up the paper, lit it with a match and let it burn in the sink into soft wet ashes.

Sometimes I wrote while Davy was there. I almost succeeded in shutting him out in order to concentrate, but I was always dimly aware of his presence hovering at the edge of my vision. When I finished, when, inevitably, I leapt up to destroy my evening's work, he would stare at me, puzzled. 'Why do you do that?' he would say. 'Why do you always burn what you write?'

'Because it's shit,' I would say, and would say no more, diving under the blankets and hiding my eyes from the light.

And one day, when I was begging in the street, I saw Tom. I had just approached a fur-hatted, lipsticked woman, I was holding out my hand, 'Excuse me,' I was saying. I looked her in the eye but then my treacherous eyes skipped off her and, just over her shoulder, they found Tom. He saw me too. I saw his own eyes darting, judging whether he could slip past and escape, but he could not.

'Yes?' the woman said impatiently.

'Could you spare . . .' I began but her eyes flicked off me. I saw myself become nothing to her, worse than nothing. I had lost my power. It was him. Even the sight of him weakened me and I saw myself as a beggar and I was ashamed.

'Jenny,' he said. 'What are you doing?'

'Do you care?'

'Of course I care.' He stared at me as if appalled. 'You look awful . . . awfully pale, I mean. You weren't . . . you weren't *begging* were you?' He emphasized the word as if it was ridiculous.

'Begging?' I said.

'No, no of course you weren't,' he comforted himself. 'Look, sweetheart,' he glanced at his watch, 'I have to dash.'

'Nice to see you.' I gave my voice a glittering edge.

'See you soon,' he lied and then he almost ran away, scuff-lingly, a little ratty man. If I had not loved him so much I would have despised him but as it was he merely took my strength away. I had been in control. I think the people who gave me money could see that I was in control, that I had a natural authority. Of course they would give me money. Why wouldn't they? But as he left I felt my strength drain away like sawdust leaking from a doll. I stood and watched him go. He didn't even look over his shoulder, his head was jammed so far down it looked as if he had no neck. He vanished among the people on the pavement and I stood and looked after him. I became an obstacle and people had to push round me. 'Excuse me . . .' I said. 'Excuse me . . .' but it did not work. The spell was broken. I didn't believe in myself any more. It was rush hour, nearly going home time. It was very cold. 'Too cold for snow,' people had been saying all day, but between the tall buildings the sky had threatened it, great clenched fistfuls of the stuff had blotted out the sun and now the fingers opened and flakes fluttered down, big flakes that landed like cold licks on my face. The snow excused the people that I approached. Heads down, hands in pockets, they did not even hear me.

I went back to the flat and lay on the bed. After a long time, Davy arrived with a bottle of cider, a loaf of bread and some sausages. There were snowflakes like a crocheted cap on his hair and his face was raw and red. 'Fucking feet are fucking frozen,' he said. He sat on the bed and peeled off the sopping rags of his shoes and socks. Then he turned and grinned. 'You all right?' he asked, but I could not answer. 'Cat got it?'

'What?'

'Your tongue.' He stuck his out and when I did not react pulled a sad clown's face and turned away. He sat and rubbed his feet with the blanket for a minute, then he poured cider into two mugs and put the sausages in the pan. 'Watch these for us,' he said, 'I'm going to the bog.' He went upstairs.

I forced myself to stand up and look at the pink glistening things. I never liked to look at sausages, even as a child I found they made me think of penises. Maybe it was having a naturist for a grandfather, I don't know. I used to avert my eyes from Bob's penis, I could not understand how he and Mama could sit and eat sausages, slicing them up and stuffing their mouths with them, as if they couldn't see what they were like. Now these pale pink sausages flinched in the pan as they warmed up, warped and wriggled. They made me think about Tom and the way his penis had twitched when he played the saxophone, how insistently it had twitched inside me. Now six penises began to sizzle in the pan, clear fat seeping from their ends. I stared sick and fascinated at them as they stiffened and crusted, as they blackened.

'For Christ's sake, Jen!' Davy said, pushing past me. 'Wake up. You've burned the fuckers.'

The next morning we woke to grey light and a stuttering world. Cars coughed to life and grumbled along. When I forced myself to climb out of the warm blanket cocoon that Davy and I had made and open the curtains I saw that the snow had blown down the stairwell and clogged the spaces between the iron palings. I could hear tentative footsteps on the path. It was early and slithery cold out there. I put the kettle on and got back into bed.

'Wish we had a sledge,' Davy said. 'My dad made us a sledge, me and my brother. Our real dad. Red and white wood. He gave it to us for Christmas before he left. It was a good sledge though. Had our names on. David and Jonathan.'

'Like the bible story.'

'Yeah.'

'I can't go on like this,' I said.

'No,' he agreed. I looked at him, he was such a child. He held out his arms. He had taken his shirt off in the night and he held me against his chest. It was smooth and bare and bony. His

181

nipples were flat and babyish. I thought of the furry softness of Tom's chest, the flesh I could hide my face in, the man smell of him. Incredible to think that Davy and Tom were both men, in some ways both the same.

He put his face in my hair and mumbled, 'Go home, Jen.'

'I can't.'

'You're not well.'

'What do you mean?' I pulled away. 'I'm fine.'

He shrugged. 'All right, you're fine.' The kettle began to whistle and he got out of bed to make some tea.

I went out early leaving Davy in bed.

'Stay in,' he said. 'Stay in and help me keep warm. I can't go out in this with no proper shoes.' But I could not, there was too much going on in me and I had to move about. 'The cold makes people mean,' he warned. 'You'll get fuck all.'

When I got out, squeaked up the steps through the thick snow that was almost clean, only a faint speckling of blackness yet, I found that the world was entirely numb. There was a humming noise in my ears like the dialling tone of a telephone. The snow had stopped falling. It had made fur hats on the doorstep milk-bottles and fairy trees out of even the meanest shrubs and weeds. But in the gutters at the road edges it had mixed with sand and salt into a brown fudge. It leaked through my shoes and froze my toes. My fingers first hurt then disappeared. I looked around for the silver woman, I thought she would be there to bring me luck again, but she was not. I held out my vanishing fingers. I could not believe that people could be so cold, colder even than the day. Again I was diminished, every pair of eyes slicing past took with it a shaving of my self. I begged for an hour or two receiving hardly enough for a cup of tea. Davy was right. 'Fucking mean bastard,' I said to someone. My voice was frosty as a harpsichord in the air, it came from somewhere else.

Then a man approached me. He gave me a friendly smile. 'Down on your uppers, my sweetheart,' he said.

He called me sweetheart, like Tom. He was about Tom's age

and he smiled at me as if I was a person. I almost believed him. Some idiot bit of me responded like one of Pavlov's dogs.

'That's one way of putting it.' Again my voice came from far away. I watched myself and the man as if we were characters in a play.

He held out a five-pound note and I thought maybe he had something to do with the silver woman, but when I reached out to take it he whisked it away. 'There's plenty more where this comes from,' he said. 'Come on, sweetheart. We'll find something to warm you up.'

Do not ask me why I went. There was no decision involved. I was not a whole person any more, just a series of responses. Just a grinning watcher, egging myself on. How much worse could it get? I had no fingers, no toes and something had happened to my soul.

He took me to his flat to get his cheque book, he said. I knew that was a lie, of course. And when we were inside he locked the door and tried to rape me. He did not. I fought too hard. I don't know where the strength came from. My arms and legs were metal things, heavy and mechanical and I watched with interest the way they fought.

'Come on,' he kept saying, holding me down, his knee between my legs as he struggled to undo my jeans. 'That's what you want, isn't it?' He was heavy and his breath, even so early, reeked of whisky. 'That's what you were asking for, isn't it? Come on,' he said. His face was red and beads of sweat stood on his forehead. 'Come on darling.'

He'd pushed me down on to a deep white leather sofa. It was a flat full of expensive things. A woman lived here, I could see her coat hanging by the door in the hall. There were framed pictures of children on the walls. Somebody graduating. The smell of the sofa reminded me of Tom's jacket. Oh Tom was no rapist. He got what he wanted, only his method was more subtle. He not only got what he wanted, he got me begging for it until he bestowed it as a gift. The man was hardly there, my mind streamed on above him and my limbs flailed and crashed below him. I wanted to cheer myself on. I fought valiantly. I was not even afraid. He tried to force the wetness of his mouth on mine. The flesh on his face fell forward from his bones. I almost wanted to laugh at this grotesque struggle, at his grunts and his fervent concentration. Was what he wanted really worth the struggle? I wasn't frightened. I knew he would not get inside me.

'Come on, darling,' he said. 'We both know what we're here for.'

He moved his weight in order to have a fresh assault at the zip of my jeans and I lifted my knee sharply and got him in the balls. He jerked away with a groan, scissored over on his knees, his head on the floor. I got up and went to the door.

'You whore,' he gasped. 'You filthy cunt.'

With my hand on the doorknob I smiled at him, my most brilliant smile. My anger was in cold storage. I knew I wanted to hurt him, to kill him, but the anger bubbled under a crust of ice. I watched my exit from the flat. 'Filthy teasing cunt,' he shouted and as the door closed behind me I snapped into myself again. I thought that I must go home. The only way I was going to be safe from the violence inside me that clawed up at the ice like a drowning cat was to go home to Mama. Home where I know myself, at least.

I walked back to the basement wrapped in the cloud of my breath, sliding on the slush. The sound of melting snow dripping from gutters was almost deafening.

Davy was still asleep. He didn't wake when I came in, just stirred and wriggled luxuriously as if unwilling to let go of some dream. And who was I to snatch it from him? I stood and looked at him for a moment testing my feelings, but there were none. His face was softened and blurred in sleep. He was a pretty boy. There were soft blond whiskers on his chin. He was good but would come to no good in the cold wild world unless he found someone to love him. I listened to his sleepy breath and then quietly and swiftly I stuffed all my grubby clothes in my bag. I left everything else to him, tea-bags, books, even my piece of fire-warped glass and the little bundle of Tom's hair that I had collected from the pillow every time we'd made love. I wrote a note: *Stay here till you're chucked out. I'm going home. Why don't you . . .* I began but crossed it out. It wasn't my business to tell him what to do.

THE DAILY DOZEN

'So you're back,' Ursula said. 'The prodigal returns.'

Mama hugged me. 'Oh, Jenny. Where have you been all these weeks? We've had your tutor on the phone . . .'

'Give the girl a moment,' Ursula said. 'I'm sure she has an explanation.'

I said nothing.

Mama shook her head. 'You look . . .'

'She looks like something the cat's dragged in,' Ursula interrupted.

'There's been a girl ringing too . . . Jess, is it?'

'Jaz,' I said.

'That's it, otherwise I'd have rung the police. She said something about a man . . .'

'I want to go upstairs,' I said. 'I'm sorry. I can't talk just now. I have to be alone.'

'Marlene Dietrich now, is it?' Ursula threw at me as I pushed past them. Mama and Ursula both looked too big for the hallway as if they were giant puppets of themselves. Through the open sitting room door I could see sharp twigs poking. The light bulb throbbed inside its shade.

'Jenny,' Mama began reaching out her hand but Ursula restrained her.

'Let the girl be,' she said. I stared at Mama. Like everyone else she looked back at me through glass and all the feelings there

186

were – I don't know what, guilt, sorrow, fear – were on her side of the glass and they did not touch me.

I went up to my room. On the bed was a pile of letters: a bank statement; a letter from the university; a library book reminder; a dental appointment. And one other letter – from Tom. He had the most precise writing, thin lines like hairs, written hard enough to dent the paper. 'You didn't get it,' he'd said. I hadn't understood him. I thought he'd meant I failed to get the point somehow, as if our affair had been some sort of joke and I'd missed the punch line. But he was not that clever or metaphorical. All he'd meant was that I hadn't got his letter. But I didn't need the letter now to tell me it was over and that he was a middle-aged shit, a liar and a hypocrite.

I took off my shoes and sat on the bed. I considered throwing the letter away just as once, when I was a girl, I had considered throwing away another letter that told me a truth I needed to know, that told me that Mama and Bob weren't my parents, that the girl I'd thought was my sister was my mother. It had shocked me to the very core, set my whole world askew. As I clutched Tom's letter in my hands and closed my eyes I felt that tilt again, as if the earth lurched. When I had read the first letter I had been sitting on a swing, now sitting on the bed in my safe room something inside me moved like that swing.

I did not throw the letter away. I thought it would be amusing to see what he'd said, how graceful his assassination of our love affair, how carefully chosen each neat and spindly word. Inside the envelope addressed to Mama's home was another. *I came to put this under your door. Guess you're not there. Guess you've gone home. Good girl. I'll post this there.*

I was confused. When in that time was I not there waiting, hoping, willing him to come back again? I strained my mind to the time before his last visit. I was confused. There had been no edges to my life in London once I'd lost my job. No calendared divisions, no shifts of rhythm between work and not work. But before I'd met Davy there had been an occasion when he'd called at the flat and I was not there. That seemed incredible to me. Was it even true? I did remember a banging that might have been the door one soupy time when the light bulb hung dull as a rotting pear from the ceiling and I, fuzzy with wine and no food and hovering on the edge of a dream, had ignored it. It may have been Tom at the door then, but I'd thought it was probably upstairs that I could hear. There were always people moving about up there, living ostentatiously busy lives.

DARLING JENNY,

I'm off to the States in the morning and I thought this would be the best time to break things off with you. I'm sure you sense this has been coming, clever girl that you are. How sweet you were last time we met. I meant to tell you then, but how could I hurt you when you were so pleased to see me? And how could I resist you?

This has been all wrong. I can't bear to see you in that dump. I can't bear to think that you have wrecked your life for me. Please go back and pick up the threads. Nothing is irravocable.

You are the dearest girl, the sweetest thing that has ever happened to me. When I first saw you looking so dewy with those big bright eyes, how could I resist? Randy old goat that I am, I know. There is no excuse but I can forgive myself that attraction, even the snatched and sneaky consammation of it since you were so eager too. It was hardly a difficult seduction after all, was it?

What I cannot forgive myself for is letting it carry on. It was that fire. So bloody meladramatic, so somehow glorious and romantic and so frustrating having to break off like that, midfuck.

But I should have known better. You think you are in love

with me, perhaps you are a little, as I am with you, a little. But if we stop now those feelings will fade, I promise you. And I know.

As you know I am well and truly married, even quite happily married. Moira is the only woman in the world who would put up with me. She really loves and understands me and she loves Beth. I have no intention of leaving Moira. I'm sorry if you misunderstood.

So please, forget about me, go back to university, pick up your old life. It's not too late. Find a boy your own age – lucky swine he'll be, you're a wonderful fuck. One day you'll be a stunning woman. I know you'll be hurt by this, but believe me, hurt is the last thing I ever intended.

WITH LOVE,
TOM

I read the letter twice. Once silently and once aloud, speaking it in Tom's voice. I gloried in the spelling mistakes. Once I might have found them endearing – all that sophistication and he couldn't even spell. *'You're a wonderful fuck.'* I looked at myself in the mirror and said this and I was frightened by the way my mouth, my cheeks and chin moved but my eyes held still. How could he say that, reduce it to that, reduce me to that? The more I read his words, the more my anger grew. I felt the ice crack against its rearing force. Not my anger. It was just anger, not mine because there was hardly a me left. I was just a wonderful fuck, just a collection of parts. The only sure things were my eyes, the points of them were like wire threads holding me to the mirror, anchoring me in the midst of the anger that moved around like blowing curtains and masqueraded as the roar of distant traffic and a creaking floor.

I went to bed holding a hand-mirror with my name in cross-stitch on the back that Mama had made me. I lay on my side looking into the mirror so I did not lose my eyes.

There was a scrabbling at the door. 'Jenny . . .' Mama's voice was a pipsqueak voice, I could hardly hear it.

'Let her alone,' boomed Ursula.

'Do you think I should get the doctor?' Mama fretted. 'She's not right . . . she doesn't look right . . . her eyes. You don't think she's taking . . . ?'

I stared at my eyes and my eyes stared back and they were the only right thing about me.

'See how she is later,' Ursula said and she moved away, I could hear the creaking of her joints or of the floor-boards. I heard Mama whimper and the sad creak of her old bones. She would have come in if Ursula hadn't spoken. She would have sat on my bed like she used to, making it dip, trying to make everything safe for me and for herself. They went to bed and I slept. I lost my eyes as I fell asleep, I do not remember falling. I dreamt sweet childish dreams in fluorescent colours. A round sun with yellow spikes, swings and see-saws and balloons with strings floating all gaudy free in the blue sky.

When I woke it was to a familiar sound, so familiar it took a few moments to realize its strangeness. It was a lumping thumping sound, regular and rhythmic. It was one of the sounds of my childhood. It was Mama and Bob doing their 'daily dozen'. I jerked upright when I realized it could not be. The mirror edge had been digging into my face. I saw myself in it, flushed, misted, a red diagonal line across my cheek. My eyes still there. I put the mirror down. I was all right, I thought. I stood up and I was enormous in the tiny room. I opened the door and crept downstairs. I was as quiet as I could be. 'Come and join us,' Mama might say if she saw me and I didn't want that. I just wanted to see. The sitting room door was ajar. I saw Mama's naked back bending and then I saw Bob and I screamed. 'Bend and bend and bend,' he was saying but he broke off when I screamed and Mama turned and her mouth gaped appalled. I looked again at Bob and I saw he had long iron hair that hid his chest but did not cover his large male genitals.

'Well,' he said, but it was not Bob's voice, it was Ursula's, and then I understood and my face split into a sort of grin, split anyway into some sort of stretch that I could not control. I went back upstairs and into my room. I lay face down on my candlewick bedspread and traced the fuzzy caterpillars with my finger. My laughter came then, little squirts of it soaking into the bed. I screwed up my eyes against the fuzzy pink. The world, reality, the whole lot topsy-turvied and twisted around me. Ursula was a man! Was that better for Mama, was it worse? Only a bit of my face was in the mirror, a little scoop of cheek. On the floor lay Tom's letter with its furious hairy writing like the hairs on his chest.

I got up and got ready to go out. I did not see Ursula or Mama, only heard their voices burrowing behind their bedroom door. I went downstairs, made a marmalade sandwich to eat on my way, took ten pounds from Ursula's purse and left.

It was easy to get a train back to London and the scenery flowed past the windows like a roll of film repeating, the same strip of gardens, the same field with horses, the same scrap heap, round and round until we were there. I rang Tom's number from a phone box and he answered warily, as if there was someone he was afraid of. I nearly spoke. I opened my mouth but what was there to say? Until I heard his voice, until that moment I don't think I had any plan, but then I knew what it was that I would do. It was obvious, pleasing, a pattern, a poetic justice. Our affair had begun with flames – a chrysanthemum blooming in the Scottish winter sky – and so it would end.

I think there was a smile on my face. It was a sort of joke and it was a joke that he would get, like it or not. I bought white spirit, matches and a box of man-sized tissues. I thought that was funny – that the tissues were man-sized. It made me giggle in the shop and giggle in the street. On the tube I smiled at people and some of them smiled back and some of them looked away which made me laugh all the more. I walked to Tom's house. The snow had nearly all gone from the road edges. The air hung heavy and wet. Some crocuses like gone-out fireworks flopped yellow and purple in their front garden. Moira's car was not there. That was good. I had nothing against her, the beautiful, patient fool. She would be out with the child. That was fortunate.

There was a light on upstairs. Tom would be up there, doing what? Skulking? Screwing his next little girl? I was not surreptitious about my actions. If anyone had been looking they could have stopped me. I felt quite justified. Hurt had been done to me and I wanted to hurt back. I wanted him to learn that you cannot do that, you cannot rob a person of themselves and say good-bye, tell them they're a good fuck as if that is a comfort and a compliment. As if they should be grateful. I say 'they', I mean 'I'. I did not want to kill, only to hurt. Only to brand my message home. Quite openly I stood in front of Tom's house – he could have seen me himself if he had looked out – soaked a wad of tissues in white spirit and posted them through the letter-box. Then I struck a match and dropped it in. Nothing seemed to happen. I could not tell if it was lit. I thought it might have gone out as it fell. I peered through the letterbox but couldn't see much, just the child's bicycle parked in the hall. I dropped another match in and then another. Finally I lit a piece of paper from my pocket. I saw with surprise that it was Tom's letter. I had not thought I had it with me. I lit it and posted it through quickly before it scorched my fingers. And then I heard, like a gasp, the tissues ignite. A man with a dog walked by as I posted the flaming letter. He saw me. Why did he not stop me? I think I wanted to be stopped. It is amazing what you can get away with in the light of day.

I went round the back of the house. Sid sat on the back window-sill licking a paw and cleaning his whiskers. He purred when he saw me and I stroked him. I repeated the process at the back more easily, dropping tissues and matches through the cat-flap. I clapped my hands and tried to shoo Sid away but he only wound himself round my legs purring more loudly.

I walked away. I did not really think the fire would take hold. Two small blazes. Tom would smell the smoke, dial 999. He might get hurt a little, his fingers burnt. I didn't care what exactly as long as there was something. At the very least it would be a nuisance, some of their things would be ruined. The house would stink of smoke and even saintly Moira would lose her patience with him if his philandering led to that.

I walked to the canal. The *Hunky-Dory* had gone, leaving no sign that it had ever been there. I stood in the place I thought it had been, staring at the blank water. I went into a café on the waterfront and drank expensive frothy coffee. The windows were steamy with the warmth inside for it was a cold afternoon. I squinted back down the tunnel of the day, my waking shock, my leaving, my train journey, the tube ride, the walk to Tom's house, a string of events which were my initiative, in which I was the main character, but seemed to have little to do with me. I sat and watched the froth on my coffee shrink and darken as the tiny bubbles burst. The white-aproned man behind the counter kept looking at me but I did not look back. When the coffee was almost cold I stirred the froth in and drank it. The steamy windows cut me off from the outside, the dirty water, the damp and the grey. I heard a siren, two sirens but they didn't register. The steam was a fine warm insulation between my thoughts and me. The sirens approached, their sound-waves tangling and bending, distorting as they passed. Only then did a thrill of horror pass through me. I closed my eyes and gripped the edge of the table.

'All right?' the man asked. 'You finished?'

I got up to go. I shivered. I had no gloves or scarf, only a thin jacket. I had not noticed the cold before. I was still wearing the filthy jeans I'd been wearing for days. I don't know why I hadn't put on something fresh. An ambulance passed me, blue light flashing like a bright idea. I wanted to shout after it that it was a mistake, they didn't need to come, the emergency people, the fire-brigade, the ambulance, the police because it was not real, not something meant. It was only something in my head. It was not supposed to be real. I pushed through a sort of resistance in the air in time to see the transformation I had occasioned. Tom's street was a chaos of flashing and shouting and red fire-engines. Men were running importantly about, preparing to put out this fire which wasn't even supposed to be real. I saw the scene through rosy cellophane but with the heat the cellophane began to melt and I saw that it was real. I felt the blast of heat come through, the black smoke, saw the flames dancing against the windows like sexy women and then the sudden smash of exploding glass and the hot daggers flying out. I watched the firemen attaching their pipe to the water-main, so organized, so co-ordinated and I was impressed. I looked for Tom among the people on the road, people like woodlice crawled out of nowhere, gawping children and the man with the dog who looked at me oddly and then looked away. I couldn't see Tom. I wanted to be able to meet his eyes, to grin shamefaced at him because, of course, he would know it was me and would be angry. He would also see the joke, though, see how I had completed the pattern. I thought he'd smile wryly, unwillingly, the way he sometimes did when he disapproved. I thought he'd know I didn't mean any harm, not *such* harm.

I heard a scream. It was a thin, white wire among the bushy black crackling and smoke and the sinuous flap of the long flames, flame tongues stuck rudely through windows and through the doors. I walked away then. As the masked firemen fought their way into the blaze I walked away. It felt as if the soles of my shoes had melted, that I was stuck to the pavement. I walked round the block listening to the commotion that continued in my ears, to the thin cheese-wire of a scream that was not a man's voice, could not have been Tom. I stood by the canal looking at the brown water on which things floated, crisp-bags, fag-ends, a yogurt pot. I stood for a long time. I thought my heart might stop. It struggled like a bird, beating its wings against my ribs until I was breathless. People passed behind me. A man with a dog. I heard the pitter of its claws on the tow-path and its eager breath. I heard the man's heavy footsteps that seemed to ring on the concrete as if he had metal boots, ring and send shivering vibrations through the water. I did not turn to see if it was the same man and the same dog. I thought perhaps he would push me in as he passed and I don't think I would have stopped him. But he passed by.

I did something for hours. I think perhaps I had another cup of coffee in another café. I've got memory of a warm place and a cup of coffee on a table, brown sugar crystals scattered on a white surface. I went to a toilet somewhere and looked at a square on the wall which I thought was a mirror, but it did not reflect me back so it couldn't have been. I did walk for miles along the canal until it was quite dark and it became a dangerous place to be. And then I walked back.

I passed the house. The street was quiet now although two police cars still stood outside. The front door had been boarded up and the downstairs windows. Sid sat on a wall across the road and I stroked him. His fur was cool. He recognized me and purred frantically, arching his back up against my hand. There was a sickening smell of old smoke, cold smoke, wet charred wood. Cold smoke still rose. I saw that the flames had even reached the roof. It was grotesque, an exaggeration. I did not mean it. It was only an idea, a fantasy. It was not what I meant at all.

I walked to the tube station. *Inferno. One dead one critical*, flapped a news-stand, big black enthusiastic letters. I bought a paper. Tom and the child had been there. Tom had saved the child. He had died in the ambulance. A hero, the paper said, Tom

Wise, fifty-two, talented backing musician. I put the paper on the seat beside me. There was black on my hands. I thought it was just the newsprint but then I lifted my fingers to my nose and smelled the smoke.

TWO WHITE FISH

Peggy stared at the little pool of water on the tarpaulin for a long time before she realized what it was. 'Look!' She dipped her finger into it to taste and found it was not brackish. 'It's water,' she said.

'The Lord has provided,' Saul said, with a sideways smile. There was not much water, scarcely enough for one, but the three of them shared it, sipping and dipping their faces into its warm and rubbery taste.

'Hail,' Peggy decided. 'It must be a gathering of last night's hail, melted.' It cheered them for a moment, that little sip.

'We will burn,' Saul declared, for the sun's heat was strengthening, crashing down, bouncing from the sea, blinding. 'We should shelter under the tarpaulin, but one of us must keep watch. There *may* be a craft, or another shoal of jumping fish.'

Hester and Peggy rested under the tarpaulin first. It was hot as an oven beneath it, hotter than their convict's quarters had been but after a while they ceased to sweat because they had nothing left to lose.

Hester whispered to Peggy, 'We will not die.'

'If we do,' Peggy said, 'at least we die free.' Her finger touched the peacock scar.

'I do not want to die,' Hester said sadly, and then, 'I like Saul.'

'I know,' answered Peggy, 'and he likes you.'

They slept for a little, more like baking than sleeping, a slow drying out and weakening. Saul woke Peggy, lifted the tarpaulin so that the sun scoured her face with its whiteness.

'Your turn to watch,' he said. 'There is cloud on the horizon. While you watch, Peggy, pray for rain.' His voice was hoarse and there were blisters on his lips. 'Peggy,' he whispered. 'Is she sleeping?' He gestured to the slight hump under the tarpaulin. 'If we were not so sure to die, I would make love to her, to your friend. I think, though it seems so bold and soon, that I would ask her to be my wife.'

Peggy smiled at his burning face. 'You should ask her,' she said. 'If we die it makes no difference. It might give you, her, a little pleasure.'

Peggy shaded her eyes with her hand and stared at the grey smear on the distant horizon. If it would rain they could collect the rain, fashion the tarpaulin into a great dish so that they could sip water and cleanse their dry faces, the crusts round their eyes and noses, wet their lips. They could live for a few more days then, long enough perhaps to drift into the path of another vessel, or perhaps even to some island shore. She did not believe this would happen and instead of hurting herself with fruitless hope she let the memory of Sam visit her, his apple cheeks, his round solemn eyes and the folds of silken fat on his thighs. She heard the muffled murmur of Saul and Hester's voices and she tried to close her ears. She saw movement and she knew that they were kissing, touching, though how they could bear to in such heat she didn't know. She swallowed dryly, her head throbbed, a regular pulsing rhythm like the tolling of a bell.

She closed her eyes and saw Sam staggering through the long wet orchard grass where the apples hung like green and rosy moons. She saw him pick up a windfall, examine it seriously and then bite it. The sound of his crunching teeth woke her with a start.

Hester touched her arm. 'Peggy,' she whispered. 'Look.' Before them, a long way off, was a small ship. Her eyes still full of cool and green, Peggy blinked at the craft as if it was an apparition. It was painted black and gold, a small, smart, single-masted ship, but displayed no sail or flags. It swelled and shrunk in time with the throbbing in Peggy's head.

'Ahoy!' shouted Saul waving his arm, but his voice was dry. 'If we had oars,' he said despairingly. 'Oh Jesus, this is our chance of life.'

Hester grasped his hand and Peggy's. 'What shall we do?' she implored. 'We cannot die, Peggy. Look at us, we are not meant to die.'

'I'll swim,' Saul said. Hester grasped him with both hands.

'It is too far, you cannot.'

'But, Hester, it is our only chance,' Peggy said.

'*I* will swim then,' Hester declared. 'If anyone is to swim it must be me.'

'No, I cannot let you,' said Saul. 'I am a strong swimmer.' They held each other's hands, looked at each other, eyes pure with love.

'I am half-mermaid,' Hester said, 'that is what my father used to say. I am easy in the water as a fish.'

Peggy, who had never swum, gazed at them dumbly, wondering at the flowering of love and spirit between them. If one perished in the water the end would be unbearable for the other, such a promise of happiness snatched so quickly away. All the time they argued the little ship seemed to be drifting further away.

'We shall swim together,' Hester decided. 'We shall see who swims the most strongly. And when you tire, Saul, I will haul you up.'

'We cannot leave Peggy,' Saul objected. 'If we both perish, she will be alone. We cannot leave Peggy. It is terrible to be alone in this . . .' He gestured at the sea whose surface was turned oily green in the heat.

'Can you swim, Peggy?'

'Not a stroke,' Peggy said quietly, 'but both of you go. If someone does not go we will certainly die. If one of you goes and dies it will break the other's heart and there is no earthly use in that. So go, the two of you, and do not die. Swim to the ship and bring rescue to me.' She almost wanted them gone for her head pained her beyond endurance. It hurt to see the love growing between them like a wild green weed, tendrils unfurling. It was not just that hope for *them* was so scanty, *she* longed for tenderness too, and though she tried not to, she resented Saul snatching Hester's love from between her two hands, resented Hester's so swiftly shifted allegiance. She was jealous. She wanted to be alone.

They looked at each other, the three of them. There was suppressed excitement in Hester, Peggy could see it in the jumping lines of her face.

'It is our only chance,' Hester said.

'Yes.'

'God bless you,' said Saul. He handed Peggy his fiddle. 'I would never go anywhere without this,' he said, 'if I did not believe I would return.' He stripped off his shirt. 'Do not look,' he said and took off his trousers. Through lashes which sparkled peacock feathers in the sun, Peggy saw his thin green-white legs and buttocks before he jumped into the water making the boat rock wildly. Hester pulled off her dress. Her ribs were a frail ridged cage and her breasts were tiny and childish. She bent and kissed Peggy with dry lips and then she turned. Peggy saw the tracery of blue veins like ink lines on her back and knobs of her spine before she dived into the ocean. Peggy hung on as the boat bobbed, light as the sun's own dazzle on the surface, now that she was alone.

Hester disappeared below the surface for a moment too long and Peggy opened her mouth to shout just as Hester rose, her head shining silver-wet. She smiled and waved her arm to Peggy, then she turned and side by side Hester and Saul swam away like a pair of pale forked fish. They swam towards the boat which seemed impossibly far away, a mile or more, who can tell in all that smoothness how far distant it was? They made a small splashing but it quietened as the distance grew until there was no sound but the lap and creak of Peggy's own lonely craft. She closed her eyes again. She could not bear to watch one of them recede from her, she could not bear to watch one of the two heads disappear. They would die, she was sure of that, but they would die quickly before their hope was extinguished. They would die in the cool and the deep, clinging together. They would not die alone.

Peggy lay back down under the tarpaulin. She stroked the hot varnished surface of Saul's fiddle and plucked a string with her finger. It gave a numb, tuneless twang. The hot cloth pressed down on her, smothering the breath from her body, but even that was preferable to the hard glaring burn of the sun and the bounce of heat from the sea that was not empty any more, but carried two tiny dots towards a third and receding dot, away and away and away.

She was glad to be alone. She preferred to be alone. She was happy for Hester and Saul, but ashamed of the sour nag of her jealous self. She had remembered Percy with pleasure all this time, clung to the scraps of tenderness rescued from their love play, patched them together over and over until they were quite threadbare. But next to the love that had grown so rampant between Hester and Saul she saw that it had not been love at all. She had not loved Percy. She had never been in love, and never would be now. There was only Sam. Behind her eyes she saw him splashing in a little stream, diamonds of delicious water standing on his round tummy and brown arms. She saw him drinking sweet milk from a little cup and grinning his dribbly grin, a cool white moustache on his baby lip.

Ursula and Mama were in the kitchen when I arrived home. I paused outside the back door watching their blurred shapes through the frosted glass panels. My breath made frosty ferns lit yellow by the kitchen light. When I opened the door the warm air and light embraced me as if I belonged. I saw that they were about to eat their dinner.

'Back again,' said Ursula dryly.

'Jenny,' said Mama and got up from the table to greet me. She smelled so familiar it made me want to cry. We stood holding each other stiffly. 'Are you feeling better?' she asked, tentatively. I didn't know what to reply, I didn't know. I wasn't sure what she meant.

'I suppose you expect some dinner,' Ursula said, getting me a plate, grudgingly pouring me some wine and sliding a little of the elaborate glistening salads they had heaped on their plates on to mine. Ursula lit the tall blue candles that were wedged into a twisted branch of driftwood and switched off the kitchen light. The candle-flames wavered and jumped, tiny pet flames. In my ears was the roar of the fire and I reeked of smoke. I could not believe that Mama, who was loath to let go of me, left her hand like a bur on my sleeve, could not smell it on me. I felt as if my hands were black although I had washed them on the train. I had locked myself into the toilet cubicle, swaying and jerking sickeningly across Essex and Suffolk, and lathered my hands over and over until the liquid soap dispenser was empty and the roller towel exhausted. I knew I had washed away the smoke but when I stopped looking at my hands they felt black again. There was still the tiny scar where I had touched the burnt embers of the summer house. I rubbed it with my thumb.

'We really can't be doing with all this coming and going. All this mystery,' Ursula said.

'Eat up, Jenny.' Mama gestured towards a small brown brick on the table. 'Have some bread.'

We were silent but for the sawing of bread, the sound of Ursula chewing, the clinking of forks on plates. I could not bring myself to meet their eyes. Especially Ursula's. I did not know how to talk to this man in woman's clothes.

'Where did you go?' Mama said. 'We didn't realize you'd gone . . . we thought you were in your room.'

'Leave her be,' Ursula snapped and Mama looked down. I

thought she looked as if she would cry, but it could have been just the wavery candle-light that made her features blur.

'We've been baking,' Mama said.

'What *we've* been doing is hardly the point in question.' Ursula speared a kidney bean.

I put down my fork. I could not eat. I sipped some wine which was warm and sweet, wine that Tom would scorn. I forced myself to look at Ursula. I imagined the penis concealed beneath the kaftan, the seashell kaftan that had fascinated Mama at Christmas. I tried to see a man in Ursula's features. The snaky coils of hair were confusing. I saw now the bigness of the jaw though there was no stubble or sign of shaving, the skin was soft and withered like an old woman's, not a man's. I could not understand why Ursula did not seem more abashed that I had discovered so suddenly, the secret. I did not know how to think about, how to talk to a woman with a penis, a woman who had grown up as a boy, a lesbian man.

Ursula wore a necklace of huge glowing beads over the kaftan, dangling almost to the waist. I stared at them. 'Amber,' Ursula said, pulling the beads off and passing them to me. 'A present from Lilian. Look closely.' It was an attempt at a friendly gesture. The amber beads felt warm in my hands. 'In one of them there is a fly. Prehistoric. Preserved for eternity.' I found the black speck, that looked like a flake of ash or fleck of soot.

'Aren't they beautiful, Jenny?' said Mama.

I nodded and handed them back.

'Birthday present.' They fell back round Ursula's neck with a dry rattle, catching on a sea-horse and snapping off its tail.

'Ursula is a Piscean,' Mama said. 'Water sign.'

'Oh.'

Ursula ate noisily. I could hear the squelching of beans and cucumber between the teeth that looked as brown as the beads. I could not eat my own salad, it looked too shiny and alive. I picked up my heavy slice of bread.

'Unleavened?' I asked.

'Just unsuccessful,' Ursula laughed and it was a man's laugh. I had never heard that sound before or I'm sure I would have guessed.

I took a bite of the bread. It was dense with a dried yeast taste. I washed it down with a swallow of wine. Ursula sighed and filled my glass again. I wiped my mouth on a hand-woven oatmeal napkin. It looked more edible than the bread.

'Jenny, I don't want to go on,' Mama said, ignoring Ursula's look. 'I won't ask you another thing. But just tell me. *Will* you go back and finish your degree?'

How can I, I thought and the roar of the flames filled my ears again and I heard the cheese-wire scream. I gritted my teeth and held on to the edge of the table. I forced my voice to answer, forced it through the roaring in my head.

'I might,' I said. 'Honestly, Mama, at this moment in time I don't know.'

'Tautology,' Ursula snapped. Mama flinched.

'Sorry?'

'What else can a moment be but in time? How I abhor these nonsensical idioms.'

'Oh, Urse,' Mama said, sounding suddenly terribly tired.

'Well thank you for pointing out my error,' I said and smiled full into the man/woman face until Ursula looked down, discomfited.

'We're thinking of taking up taxidermy,' Mama said. 'Evening class at your old school.'

'Oh really, do you *have* to be so grotesque!' I shouted and got up. How good it was to shout. I opened my mouth and the roar of flames came out with my voice. My chair grated on the floor then fell back with a crash. The roaring stopped and I felt my breath come out like smoke, but of course, that is impossible. It was only the smoke in my clothes and hair that I smelled. I looked at my hands again and again they were black. The candle-flames were like pet birds on perches, hopping and fluttering.

'There's no need for that,' Ursula said.

'Oh sod off, you pervert,' I said and I felt a huge grin spread over my face. I dragged my eyes through the air which was watery, the light making ripples, to look at Mama but her face was appalled, she did not look at me or Ursula or anything. As I moved I moved the air so that the candle-flames wobbled and I felt seasick in the wash of light.

'That's it, I should go up,' Mama said. 'A good night's sleep . . .' Her voice travelled to me in silly little ineffectual bubbles. Ursula sat rigid, staring at the table, the moving shadows accentuating the manly jaw.

In my room I looked in my mirror where the girl me had drowned so many times and now a gaunt woman rose to the surface which was tarnished, I saw, with flecks like trapped flies. The face I saw was a white triangle. Flames still danced in the black circles of my pupils. I could hardly believe my face was so white. It should have been covered in black smudges and smuts. I knew that inside I was black, the lining of my nose and trachea and lungs coated with a soft sticky soot. My hair was choked with it, cold smoke between every strand. I picked a tail of it and put it in my mouth to suck. It tasted of cinders.

I bathed and shampooed my hair, rubbing the lather in and rinsing it three times, rinsing until the water ran cold. I scraped under my nails with a metal nail-file. I cut my finger- and toe-nails. I shaved under my arms. I scrubbed all over with a loofah until my skin looked pink and boiled. I washed until the soap bubbles stabbed and stung my eyes with prickly light.

I sat in front of the mirror again drying my hair and looking for the girl, watching the strands of hair separate and lift and lighten. The girl had had very long hair, long enough to sit on until she was thirteen. Now she was growing it again. It reached her shoulders. It smelled of shampoo. Her skin smelled of soap and talcum powder. She had left all her smoky clothes in the bathroom, but still there was a smell of smoke. She thought it was her breath.

*　　*　　*

Peggy was drying like a leaf, her tongue curled, parched inside her mouth, her fingers splayed. She could feel her heart beating, sluggish and heavy, driving the thick blood through her veins, beating in time with the throbbing of her head.

She felt the boat buck under her. *This is dying*, she thought. She did not know how long she had been under the tarpaulin that pressed down on her like a hot fish skin, that stank of rubber or tar.

Scenes lit up behind her closed eyelids, flashed to life and splintered as if stars exploded in her head.

The luminous red iron curls her father beat into horse-shoes, the searing smell of scorched hoof, hard shavings picked up and treasured in her pinafore pocket. The sweet blow of a horse's breath, patient. Her father, leather aproned, bent over his task. Her own voice murmuring into a warm velvet neck. The bang-bang-bang of the hammer on iron danced in her skull till the sparks leapt.

Percy, teasing and bossing until they were undressed, and how he changed then, tender, unsure, amazed and tentative as he weighed her breasts in his hands, traced his finger right down her body slowly, right down between her legs. How he marvelled at her. She, grown up in a cottage among brothers, was not amazed at the rising of his cock but at the milkiness of his skin, the blond hair on his belly, his smooth chest and the baby way he gasped and clung to her, filled his mouth with her breast.

Circular waves of bone crashing against bone, the decision to let her body go, give way, the feel of her bones stretching open to the head of her son. Her flesh splitting like fruit and the sudden hot, wet, steamy slither of the baby on her belly, the incredible separate heaviness, the streaky white wax and blood, the smell that was strange and familiar as the smell of her own soul. The moment that he opened his mouth and gasped in his first dry air. How she felt for him, felt how it must have seared his new lungs, forced them dry and stretched like moth wings expanding in the sun and how he wailed with the pain of it, his voice rising like a bright thread in the air, his voice come to join all the voices of the world.

The peacock's fan that had entranced her with its hundred eyes, taunting her for what she could not have, could not give her son. How it maddened her. Sam shouting 'Duck', Sam stretching out his chubby hand, wanting only to touch that brightness. The greed that rose in her chest for him: why should he not have that brightness? The feel of the feathers in her hand, cool and stiff and soft. The peacock's cry that raked her ears, the jab of its beak on her cheek and the blood running down hot as tears as the man twisted her arm behind her back.

A woman called Sarah folded in upon herself, upon her misery and burning, burning until the flame went out.

A scoop stolen from the moon. Neptune rising from the sea, as the ship slipped across an invisible line. Neptune's trident ripping the sky with its triple points until the lightning poured through. A fish-wet fullness in her belly and sea water trickling down.

The insignificant splash of two new white fish in the ocean. Their glossy heads, their legs scissoring away. Two swimmers entwined now, going down, tumbling over and over, Hester's hair winding around them, bubbles rising like spray, like silver dust. Would they kiss as they fell, drown into each other's mouths, hearts stilling together?

The canvas itself throbbed with the heat. There was no breeze, no swell. The boat hardly shifted. It was so still it hung on the water's surface like an object suspended in air.

Peggy could not swallow. The panic of not swallowing rose in her throat and her tongue fluttered and scraped against the dry roof of her mouth. Her eyes hardened behind their lids. The pain in her head lessened, it softened to a wa-wa-wa sound that may have been the sea or the sky or something inside Peggy's own ear. Somebody gave her a seashell when she was a little girl, an inland girl who never even thought she'd see the sea. It was a dry white spiral, pearly pink inside with a taste of salt when she licked it. Someone had told her the magic, how if you put the shell to your ear you can hear the secret whisper of the sea. And now her ears were shells themselves full of the self-same whisper.

The urge to swallow came again and her throat contracted. She forced open her dry eyes. She did not know how long she had been asleep. Asleep or not she did not know. She looked to see if the ship was nearer, if Hester and Saul had reached it but she could see nothing, only dancing dazzle and sun-spots in her eyes. The sea rose like a sudden sigh, lifted the boat and let it fall. There was nothing to see but dazzle so she closed her eyes again.

The girl wound up her musical trinket box, lifted the lid and lay on the bed, propped on one elbow, watching the little doll pirouette on her pointed pink foot, listening to the tinny music, the *Nutcracker Suite*. The ballerina had a white tutu, stiff as a frill of icing round the tops of her thighs.

But when she closed her eyes there was the blasting smash of windows, a howl of flame and the thin white wire that was the child's scream. She had not known the child was there. It was Tom she wanted to kill, no not kill, just to hurt, just to *show* him something. What? She did not know. She had meant the child no harm. She had meant no harm.

She fell through a gap in time. She fell through herself like a sieve. She heard the voices of Mama and Bob downstairs, just the rhythm of their talking, no words, just a to-and-froing, footfalls, a tap running, the sound of dishes being washed. She was old Jenny again, child Jenny, safe at home and her life was a sampler neatly done. Mama's sampler with the sun a yellow circle for ever in the sky, a red roof, everlasting candy-coloured flowers round the door. And she was stitched there too, a girl with a smiling cotton mouth and bright blue cross-stitch eyes; a girl stitched to the canvas like a butterfly. A butterfly with a pin through its centre, frail and dead but there for ever and ever. She fell through time into that place and the ballerina winked as she twirled on one stiff foot, turned slower and slower as the plinky-plink music stretched and warped towards its end.

A doorbell rang and she heard voices but she did not move. She had forgotten what she had done though the smoke leaked from her pores and stained the candlewick. She thought it odd, the doorbell ringing like that in the evening because Mama and Bob never had company, never in the evening, hardly ever at all.

And when Mama came up, new Mama, old in a new way, the music stopped and the ballerina froze and Jenny saw the terror on her tiny face at the sight of this old woman who had leapt through the years as if through a hedge backwards so that the hair stood up round her scalp in wisps and the lines on her face were black and she was all pulled down, all the structure of her face collapsed.

'Jenny,' she said and her eyes sought Jenny's eyes but they had gone. She had lost her eyes. She had fallen through herself. 'There's someone to see you,' Mama said and her voice was desolation.

Seven love-bites on my arm and the first faded to a memory. All those hours and minutes and seconds passed. Time done. Today I will be out of here and I will learn what comes next. I am frightened of what comes next. They will give me work. I expect the laundry, the steam and bleach and starch, dermatitis and lanky hair. I do not care. I will have a smoke, catch my own eye in the mirror.

Oh, I think I will co-operate this time. They will not recognize this woman. I am not all bad. If they let me work in the garden I would be in paradise. Imagine, fresh moving air, vehicles flowing free behind the fence, birds and sky. Sun and rain, cobwebs caught with dew-drops, Michaelmas daisies drenched mauve to bury my face in, spiders and pink worms. Green and blue and the wet brown of earth, red of berries and buses, the buzz of an aeroplane high in the sky and a finger-nail scratch in the blue. Frost on puddles. My heart jumps like a child's on Christmas morning. I am terrifyingly excited.

And I am terrified. Terrified of what? Of freedom.

'Are you deliberately sabotaging your life?' the shrink asked. She has got over her fascination with me. I snorted. But perhaps she is right. It is safe to long for freedom when it is far away but when it creeps near, freedom is fear.

Freedom to do what?

I am overwhelmed by the idea of all that freedom washing around formless as water but laced with invisible traps and snares. I have never got it right, life. I have never known how to be with people.

I quite like it in here, alone, if only they would leave me alone and not interrupt. I can live in my head. I can expand to fill the room, the walls awash with the images of my mind. It is edges I cannot deal with, I cannot stay the proper size. Either I am huge so that people barge into me, right in, beneath my skin, or else I am tiny as a nut. Negligible. Something to crack underfoot.

When I am out I will be a good and co-operative prisoner. That is my intention. I will see Debbie and smile. Perhaps I will speak to her, make her my friend. I will join in with life in number five without a murmur. One day I will be free . . . again the gasp of fear as if my heart opens its mouth to scream. But I will be, *will be*, free. I am naked in here, stripped of my selves, this cell is strewn with the skins and shells of all the selves I have shed. There has been no face to face and when I touch my own face I am comforted that the features are not gone, they have not been eroded. There is the nose, the eyes, the mouth. I can pinch my ears between my fingers like leaves. I have a voice. I have something to express. When I am free I will buy paints to express the joy of colour. I will choose words to express the joy and pain of life. For there is joy.

Mama used to say, if we got off on the wrong foot – another thing she used to say – 'Let's start again,' as if you could do that, rub something out and replace it. Well now I am naked to the gasping heart and ready to begin again.

*　　*　　*

And Peggy is left drifting on the sea. She is lying on top of the canvas which was too hot to stay under, pressing and reeking as it did. Now the sun slants low across the sea and it is cooler. Her eyes are closed so she does not see the beauty winding round her, water snakes coiling on the water's surface, shimmering blue and silver and iridescent green.

I wonder, will she die like that, pressed flat and dry by the weight of all that sky? Perhaps, driven mad by her thirst she might drink the sea water, reach over to dip her hands among the oily snakes and see the peacock colours there. With the salt madness she might laugh a high shrill laugh against the memory of a hundred teasing eyes. And she might tumble in, splash through the greens and blues and roll over and over, hair rising like a peacock fan, eyes open in the salt-wet, mouth opening and bubbles rising like streams of winking eyes.

Or there is just a chance of rescue. There is always the possibility that it might rain and the boat drift towards a shore. Or that Hester and Saul reached the ship and are on their way to rescue Peggy, hand in hand at the prow, straining their eyes to spot her.

There is always a chance. And Peggy is left drifting on the wide and glittering sea.

ABOUT THE AUTHOR

Lesley Glaister was born in Wellingborough in 1956.
She teaches a Masters Degree in Writing at Sheffield
Hallam University, and writes regular book reviews for
the Spectator and The Times. She is the author of *Honour
Thy Father*, which won the Somerset Maugham and a
Betty Trask award, *Trick or Treat, Digging to Australia,
Limestone and Clay, Partial Eclipse, The Private Parts
of Women*, and most recently *Easy Peasy*.
She lives in Sheffield.